Praise for Debbie Howells

'A terrific new talent'
Peter James, author of the Roy Grace series

'Dazzling'
Daily Mail

'Sharply written . . . holds you tight and then drops you
like a stone'
Liz Nugent, author of *Our Little Cruelties*

'Haunting'
Good Housekeeping

'A sinister, twisty tale you won't want to put down'
Sam Carrington, author of *The Open House*

'I was completely immersed . . . a superb thriller'
B P Walter, author of *Hold Your Breath*

'Brilliantly twisty'
Tammy Cohen, author of *When She Was Bad*

'Utterly compelling and addictive'
Samantha Hayes, author of *Until You're Mine*

Debbie Howells is the bestselling author of *The Bones of You* (Macmillan), a Richard & Judy Book Club pick. It was followed by *The Beauty of the End*, *The Death of Her* and *Her Sister's Lie* (Macmillan).

The Secret is her second book with HarperCollins, following *The Vow*, which was a #1 eBook bestseller.

www.debbiehowells.co.uk

You can follow @_debbiehowells on Instagram or @debbie__howells on Twitter.

Also by Debbie Howells

THE
SECRET

DEBBIE HOWELLS

avon.

Published by AVON
A division of HarperCollins*Publishers*
1 London Bridge Street
London SE1 9GF

www.harpercollins.co.uk

HarperCollins*Publishers*
1st Floor, Watermarque Building, Ringsend Road
Dublin 4, Ireland

A Paperback Original 2022

1

First published in Great Britain by HarperCollins*Publishers* 2022

Typeset in Bembo by Palimpsest Book Production Limited,
Falkirk, Stirlingshire

Printed and Bound in the UK using 100% Renewable Electricity
at CPI Group (UK) Ltd

For my sisters
Sarah, Anna and Freddie

Niamh

It began with Dylan and the way he captivated people, drawing you into another world where anything was possible. Once you glimpsed those glittering horizons of his, you couldn't go back. Not ever.

Hollie didn't have a chance. She was too fragile, looking for a love she needed but had never had. Not even from the people closest to her: the mother she adored who screwed her up, then killed herself; the father who didn't have time for her; the stepmother who tried to love her, but couldn't give her the mother's love she craved.

It seemed inevitable that Hollie and Dylan would fall in love. And, for a while, it was glorious. In a village where we were the only teenagers, they were a common sight – hand in hand, his dark head towering above hers, Hollie in ripped jeans and an oversized coat that only accentuated her ethereal beauty. When love consumed you the way theirs did, everything else was irrelevant.

Until the day of yellow sky and wild winds, when it all stopped.

Chapter One

Elise

I'm strapped into my crew seat. As the aircraft accelerates down the runway and takes off for London, I watch the woman sitting in the first row opposite me. Her blond hair is shoulder length, her eye makeup minimal, her lips red. I'm envying the biker jacket and green dress she's wearing, when I'm drawn to a headline on the cover of the magazine she's reading: *'Only Ten Per Cent of People are Good'*.

Ten per cent . . . It seems a small number. I frown, trying to work out if I'm one of them. As the ground falls away I glance through the window, watching the world shrink, snow-capped mountains suddenly dominating the view. There's a chime as the seat belt sign goes off and I get up, glancing for a moment down the length of the aircraft. One hundred and twenty-three faces that can see my neatly pinned-back hair, my mask of immaculate makeup, my navy uniform dress and smart shoes. One hundred and twenty-three lives I know nothing about, just as they know nothing about mine.

As I set up the drinks trolley, the statistic on the magazine cover stays with me, and I think about how many people who, for all kinds of reasons, cause suffering to others. I used to believe that even the worst behaviour could be explained by abusive childhoods or desperation. But that was before I realised people have choices; make decisions. Before I realised that brutality can be intentional.

The passengers are mostly students in big coats and trainers, blank-faced business travellers, and wealthy Italians in designer wear. As I serve cups of tea, I usually imagine them to be parents, families, friends, vacationers. But none of us knows what lies behind appearances, or what we're capable of in extreme circumstances. As I look at them I'm wondering which of them are in the ten per cent – out of one hundred and twenty-three, that's only twelve or thirteen – but it's impossible to tell.

Now and then, I catch a glimpse through a window of the bird's eye view of which I never tire – a view of a world that's endlessly beautiful. At thirty-five thousand feet, you see the landscape in large scale: stretches of sea, jagged mountain ranges, hundreds of miles of patchwork farmland. Today, beneath a pale blue sky, the mountains have given way to a sea of snow fields, broken here and there by a circular town or a spider's web of serpentine roads; by monolithic chimneys from which vertical smoke rises, scored into the whiteness. Over northern France, the snow reduces to an icing-sugar dusting. Then, as we start our approach into London and I go through the cabin checking seat belts, the clouds thicken and the reality of my life on the ground comes flooding back.

*

The passengers disembark and I make my way on the bus to the crew room, then onto another bus that takes me to the staff car park, my face impassive for the journey. Only when

I'm alone in my car do I let my feelings show. As I leave the airport perimeter road, I open the window and breathe in the cold air, suspending my reality for as long as I can: of the neighbours who think they know me, my cheating husband, Andrew, whose patients think he's God, my changeling daughter who lives in her own world . . . How tenuously our family life is held together.

Abingworth is a thirty-minute drive from the airport and as I turn off the main road, my eyes narrow when I think of Andrew, wondering who *she* is this time. As far as I know, this is his fourth, though I've no reason to believe there haven't been more. This latest one's been discreet so far and I'm grateful for that small mercy. The humiliation of not being enough for your husband is multiplied a hundredfold when everyone else knows.

Reaching the village, I slow down as I pass the sign reading 'Abingworth'. We moved here seventeen years ago, after I discovered Andrew was having an affair for the first time. Wanting to believe his assurances that it was over and that he'd made a terrible mistake, I'd let him persuade me to view a large country house here, with a tacit agreement that this was a chance for a new start. After moving in, naïvely, I'd believed it possible. But not for long. My husband is a serial adulterer, our home no longer somewhere I want to be. The only reason I stay is for our daughter.

Now, as I drive, I try to remember how I had felt back then. My hope for a new life tainted with mistrust; my jaded anger with Andrew. My overriding need to protect my family – that took precedence over anything else.

I turn into our lane, then again a little further on, through the tall gateposts flanking our driveway, my tension easing slightly when I notice the empty space where Andrew normally parks. The garden is surrounded by flint walls, the cedar trees in front of the house giving it seclusion, privacy. My relief that I'm alone is instantly squashed by the thought that's never far from my mind. *He could be with her.*

Once, I would have phoned his practice to confirm my suspicions, desperately cobbling together an excuse for calling when I didn't need to, but I no longer care enough. Today, I park by the back door and take my crew bag inside, thinking about the three days off that lie ahead, imagining tidying the house and going for a run, or catching up with one or two friends before next week's flight schedule starts. Maybe I'll take Niamh shopping and get her a new pair of those awful velour leggings she lives in. *Maybe Andrew will dump his lover. Actually see me properly again. See Niamh. See anyone but that fucking bitch he's sleeping with.* But even if he did, I'm not sure I'd want him. Swallowing hard, I blink away the hot tears filling my eyes, hating how the thought of him makes me feel.

In the kitchen, my heart skips a beat as I see the light flashing on the house phone. I leave it until I've showered and changed, until I've made myself a cup of coffee. Putting it off until I can't any longer. When I play the message, there are no distinguishable words, just a faint crackle before the caller hangs up. After it plays through, I delete it, then retrieve the caller's number, my blood suddenly like ice in my veins. I write it down with shaking hands, knowing it's *her*, even though there's no need for her to call here. But then, I know it's one of Andrew's games – telling her to call him here, in our home. It's a way for him to twist the knife, undermine me. It's what always happens when he starts seeing someone new. It's just a question of when.

There is no escape from my husband's betrayal. Even in my home I'm surrounded by the ghosts of his lovers, their silent

6

messages of possession. Most women would have left. And I would, if it was possible. But I can't. Not yet. So the only way through is to play the part of loving wife, hide the truth from Niamh, and let Andrew do what he wants to do, knowing the day will come – one way or another – when it ends for good.

I pick up my mug and sip my coffee, finding it cold, bitter. My hands still trembling, I hurl it at the wall.

★

The latest message on the house phone has unsettled me. With an hour or so before Niamh's bus gets back, I pull on running clothes and shoes, needing to shift my sense of unease before seeing my daughter.

The sky threatens rain as I slip the back door key into a zip pocket, pulling up my collar and walking briskly down the drive onto the lane. Breaking into a run as I reach the main road, I feel the cold clinging to my hands, my cheeks; it's only as I run harder that the slow spread of heat through my body begins thawing them.

I see no-one through the village. Windows are closed and dark, drives are empty, gardens damp. Only as I pass Ida Jones's house are there signs of life: the warm glow of light from her downstairs windows, wood smoke spiralling from her chimney. A thought comes to me suddenly: Ida's lived in the heart of this village most of her life. She knows everyone and I wouldn't mind betting she knows what goes on. Maybe she even knows who *she* is.

I could ask her, but I'd rather not admit to what's going on under my nose. I carry on past the last houses without stopping, taking a footpath that slopes down through woods and across a stream. Under the trees, the path is dark and muddy, fallen leaves making it slippery underfoot, and I pick my way carefully over the narrow bridge, then up the other side before coming out of the trees into the churchyard.

Here, among the dead, I stop, looking at the graves that have become familiar to me. My eyes pass over their inscriptions as I walk between them, always pausing in the same place to read words I know by heart about a life that ended too soon. *Never forgotten.*

Most days, I find a quiet sense of peace here, but today I'm thinking of the magazine statistic again. Only ten per cent of people are good. The rest are like Andrew. They charm, captivate and seduce, but eventually you see the truth about them – that they do what they want, whatever it takes to sate blind ambition, perpetuate arrogance, slake lust.

As I stand there, a desperate sense of hopelessness washes over me, as instead of fighting my tears, I let them stream down my cheeks. The woman I was when I married Andrew had hopes and dreams. But nothing has worked out as I'd imagined it would. Instead, I was foolish enough to be taken in by the charming doctor, a man who consistently cheats, while the only thing keeping me going is my daughter. In my pointless world, Niamh is the only person who's important to me.

Niamh

I live on a road to nowhere in a village of tall trees and stone walls; a place of cold hearts and secrets. As I get off the school bus, cold air rustles the leaves and I feel the first spots of rain. My stop is the last and I'm the only teenager from my village who goes to my private school. No-one gets off with me.

While I walk up the lane, no traffic passes by. 'Hey, Cat,' I say to the cat that often sits waiting for me. A motionless sentry perched on the wall at the side of the road, his yellow eyes are unblinking, his black head battle-scarred. I know that his presence is an honour, rather than a given. A cat belongs to no-one but himself.

By the time I turn into our drive, he's already vanished. Gravel crunches under my feet as I walk towards the house, its grey, stark façade softened in spring by lilac wisteria.

I walk around the side to the back door, where music from the radio drifts outside. As I go into the kitchen, I find my mother wearing jeans and a wide-necked sweater that slides off one of her tanned shoulders.

'I need some money for the science trip,' I tell her, putting down my school bag and getting juice from the fridge before going to the larder for a bag of crisps. Opening it, I take a handful, watching her leaf through today's mail. Her hand pauses on a letter, her intake of breath audible, coupled with the perceptible paling of her skin.

'It'll have to wait, Niamh. I don't have any cash.' She adds, 'Don't eat all of those.'

Taking another handful, I ignore her. 'Whatever. You can pay online. Probably easier.' I shrug as her phone buzzes, her face closing over as she picks it up and glances at the screen.

'Remind me later, honey. I have to get this.'

Noticing a catch in her voice, I stare at her. 'Who is it?'

In the time it takes her to respond, the hairs on the back of my neck prickle. 'A friend. No-one you know.' As she glances in my direction, I notice the semitone rise in sharpness in her voice, the five seconds of fake brightness in her smile. She turns her back and leaves the kitchen, and it's only when she knows she's out of earshot that she starts talking.

That's when I know it's another of her lies. She'll tell herself I haven't noticed anything wrong, then forget all about it. Taking the bag of crisps, I go outside, shaking off my uneasiness as I wander down to the end of the garden where it borders the road, wondering if all families lie to each other.

Pulling myself up onto the same flint wall where the cat was waiting for me just minutes ago, I envy the simplicity of his life; his past forgotten, his future uncontemplated, his only concern the eternal present.

I like to sit here and watch our neighbours, all of them hiding who they really are – just like my father in his doctor's office, my mother in her airline uniform – putting on the faces they want the world to see when, underneath, they could be someone else entirely.

★

It's dark when Hollie appears in my bedroom doorway later that evening. Her long hair is windswept, her cheeks tinged with pink, as though she's run here. I can tell from her eyes she's been crying. Staring at her face, I'm already guessing what she's upset about.

'Your dad?' I ask. He's the only person Hollie cares about. She nods as words, tears, and snot begin pouring out of her. I've never seen anyone cry as messily as Hollie does.

'He was talking to someone on his phone.' Her hair gets in the way as she breaks off to wipe her face on her sleeve. 'Whoever it was, they're a bastard.' Her voice is filled with hatred.

Not wanting my mother to overhear, I glance towards the open door, then lean towards Hollie, curious, asking quietly, 'What were they talking about?'

Her lip wobbles. 'I can't tell anyone.' Then her shoulders start to shake. 'Do you know how that feels?'

I've no idea what she's talking about. 'You can tell me, Hollie.'

She shakes her head. 'I can't. You're too young.'

I wonder what she means. She's only two years older than me.

But then she comes towards me, awkwardly stroking my hair before perching on the end of my bed as she tries to get control of herself. When she turns to look at me, her face is tear-stained, her distress obvious. 'I wish I could tell you, Niamh. But I can't.'

Chapter Two

Elise

'I hope you haven't forgotten about tonight.' Without offering a greeting or explaining why he's late, Andrew walks into the kitchen and puts the kettle on. He never justifies anything. Even off duty, he behaves with the same air of authority he has at work.

My heart sinks as I remember. He's talking about drinks in the pub – a village tradition – meant to celebrate the end of January and a month off alcohol, which no-one ever actually achieves. I *had* forgotten. If I hadn't, I'd have invented an excuse, but it's too late for that now. 'I had, actually.' I pause, wanting to say I'm too tired as it's not untrue – I had an early start this morning. Instead, I glance at the clock and give in to the inevitable. It's seven thirty. 'What time is everyone meeting?'

'Eight.' Evidently changing his mind, Andrew switches off the kettle and uncorks a bottle of red wine.

'Fine.' My mind is restless. If *she* lives locally, as I suspect, the population of the village is so small that she'll almost certainly be there. The probability is I'll know instantly – I usually do. 'I'll go and change.'

Upstairs, I pull a black tunic on over my jeans, knotting a pale scarf over it, then brush my hair and touch up my makeup. The spritz of perfume is defiant, reflecting my mood – it's one I know Andrew doesn't like. As I go downstairs, I hear there's music coming from the sitting room. I push the door open wide enough to see Niamh slumped on the sofa and Hollie sprawled on the rug in front of the fire. Neither of them looks up.

'We're just going out, girls. We won't be late.' My voice is intentionally light, painting the picture that Andrew and I are off on a cosy evening out, but I suspect it doesn't fool anyone.

Niamh turns briefly, hair the colour of flax falling across her face. 'OK, Mum.' Her face is expressionless, her eyes blank, mirroring mine. Not for the first time I berate myself for not being the kind of mother who can make everything right in her world with a hug, a laugh, a joke . . .

I look at Hollie. 'Are you staying, Hollie?'

Hollie Hampton lives at the other end of the village from us. At sixteen, she's two years older than Niamh, but they're kindred spirits. Riveted to the television, Hollie nods imperceptibly, pulling her long dark hair over one of her thin shoulders. Elfin-faced, with pale skin, in the frayed jeans under the silver dress she's wearing, she's diaphanous.

'There are snacks in the cupboard if you're hungry,' I remind them. 'See you later, girls.'

Pushing the door closed behind me, I go to find Andrew. Already wearing his coat, he barely glances at me as I pull on a jacket and knitted hat.

'Ready?' His tone is brusque, but unless there's anyone around to notice, Andrew is never affectionate towards me.

★

14

We walk to the pub in silence, the air damp, the drops of rain from earlier yet to turn into anything more.

For some reason, Hollie is on my mind. Her father, James, is a writer, her stepmother, Stephanie, a hairdresser – I've been to her salon in the next village once or twice. Over the last couple of years, Hollie's seemed increasingly troubled. I've seen it when she appears at the door, uninvited, looking as though she has nowhere else to go; sometimes it's as if her mind is far away, while other days emotions race across her face like storm clouds scudding across the sky.

Hands in my pockets, I hurry through the darkness, trying to keep up with Andrew's brisk, staccato steps. Like everything about him, they're deliberate, purposeful. I wonder if he's thinking of *her*. Fighting the urge to turn around and go home, I remind myself, this could be my opportunity to find out who *she* is.

When Andrew speaks, he takes me by surprise. 'We should plan a holiday, Elise.'

For the second time today, I'm hit by shock. I should be delighted, but instead I'm outraged, upset, cynical, smothering the urge to flail my fists into the softness of his overcoat, to scream at him: *Why this pretence, when we both know you want to be with her?* But outrage is pointless and the feelings are quickly replaced by numbness.

'Richard's going to Dubai next month. He was talking about it today.'

As he speaks, the penny drops. Richard is a colleague of Andrew's and Andrew simply wants to be able to brag about where we're going to sound impressive, to outdo everyone else's holidays, while at the same time perpetuating the myth that we're a close family when the reality is we're anything but.

I put my hands in my pockets. 'Let's see, shall we?' I know my cool response won't be what he's expecting.

'You're always saying you want me to make more effort,' he says through gritted teeth. 'But the trouble with you, Elise, is that it's only ever one bloody way – your way.'

Angst rises inside me. It's the opposite of the truth. There's only ever Andrew's way, but there is no mileage in pointing this out. Instead, as the pub comes into view, I steel myself for his metamorphosis into the charming village doctor everyone believes him to be. Andrew's practice is four miles away and most of the villagers are his patients. In public, he never puts a foot wrong.

Niamh

When I first met Hollie, I'd already seen her enough times in the distance to know she was different. She was in the church-yard that day, standing with her back to me, her long dark hair reaching halfway down her back. She turned quickly when a twig cracked under my foot.

I stared at her for a moment, taking in her wide eyes and pale skin. In her thin white dress she looked delicate, as though the wind could blow her away. 'I'm Niamh.'

Her eyes darted around before settling on mine. 'I'm Hollie.'

'I know.' I shivered. It was as though Hollie was a ghost surrounded by the silent graves between us. I was about to walk away, but curiosity got the better of me. 'Are you OK?'

She nodded, but I saw loneliness in her eyes. The first rain-drop fell on my skin then, and as more started to fall, I glanced up at the sky just as the heavens opened.

Hollie nodded towards the church. 'Maybe we should go in.'

I followed her towards the wooden door, which creaked open once she lifted the heavy latch. Standing in the doorway, watching the deluge, neither of us spoke for a few seconds.

'I like your dress.' My words were almost drowned out by the noise of the downpour on the tiled roof as I gazed at her, her dress translucent where the rain had caught it.

She didn't reply. Instead, I watched her eyes drift across the churchyard. 'You can feel them, can't you?' she asked, her arms tightly hugging herself. I could tell from the way she spoke she was talking about the souls of the dead.

I nodded, imagining the heartbreak of their families lingering in the air, wondering if after enough time had passed, the rain washed it away.

'I always think about all the people who've come here . . . The christenings, weddings, funerals . . .' Her words echoed through the church as she fell silent. 'My mum died when I was eight. I wasn't allowed to go to hers.' Her voice was small, choked with tears.

I thought of my father, spending another Sunday in a fug of red wine and temper, how my mother was never happy, how nothing changed. The crash of thunder overhead startled me, and without thinking, my hand reached for hers.

'They say she killed herself.' Her eyes were blank as she stared outside at the rain, becoming defiant as she turned her head and looked at me. 'They're wrong. I know they are.' There was anger, frustration, sadness in her voice. As a streak of lightning lit the church, I saw the emotion in her eyes.

'I told them she wouldn't have done that. But no-one listens to me.'

Chapter Three

Elise

When we reach the pub, I hover outside, thinking of the charade that lies behind the door.

'What's wrong with you?' Andrew is typically unsympathetic.

'Absolutely nothing,' I tell him. 'I was just remembering something.' I've long stopped caring about lying to him because Andrew's entire life is a lie. People think he's the amiable doctor, the caring father, the solicitous husband, the solid neighbour, when in truth he's none of those. He's a cruel, manipulative liar.

'For God's sake, go in, Elise. It's far too cold to stand around outside.' He sounds impatient.

'Then don't,' I say tersely, pushing past him. Opening the door, I latch on to the first familiar face I see, feeling my heart sink. 'Julian!' Unbuttoning my jacket, I pin on a smile. 'How lovely to see you! Is Della with you? How was Goa?'

'Very good.' As he kisses my cheek, the smell of his after-shave is cloying. 'And very hot. She's over there,' he says, pointing across the pub to Della, who raises her hand, looking slightly anxious. Craning my neck, I see why – she's been snared by Christian, who can talk about himself forever. I pull a sympathetic face at her before turning back to Julian.

'Drink, Elise?' Andrew's voice comes from behind me.

'Vodka and tonic. I've never been.' I'm referring to Goa.

'Julian . . . good to see you. Can I get you another?' Andrew's display of bonhomie is typical of him.

'Thank you. Yes. Scotch.' Julian knocks back what's left in his glass before passing it to Andrew. 'Good way to end such a ludicrous month, don't you think?'

'You mean dry January?' I doubt Julian and Della stuck to it in Goa. 'I can't say I take much notice of it.'

'You? The good doctor's wife?' Clearly finding himself funny, he winks at me.

'Oh, I think you'll find Andrew isn't a shining example, either.' It certainly doesn't stop him driving, but Julian's probably the same.

'That'll be our little secret!' Seeing the gleam in Julian's eye, bile rises in my throat. Then I see Andrew coming back with our drinks.

'Here you are, darling.' The endearment – for Julian's benefit only – makes me cringe.

Taking my glass, I make my excuses and leave them together, drifting in the direction of Della, who's the only person I'm remotely interested in talking to. Waiting while she extricates herself from Christian's lengthy and no doubt mind-numbing monologue, I glance around the pub.

Most of the village are here. On the other side of the bar, James and Stephanie Hampton are talking to a couple of other villagers. As I catch Stephanie's eye, a brief smile flickers across her face. It occurs to me to bring up my concerns about Hollie, but the thought is pushed to the back of my mind as Della joins me.

'Bloody circus, isn't it?' She kisses me on both cheeks. 'I swear Christian's the most boring man on the planet. I honestly don't know why we put ourselves through this.'

'So that we can gloat over our successes and crow over each other's failures. You look great, Della.' The Calders are often away somewhere exotic and Della's skin is freshly sun-kissed, her hair lightened. It reminds me that my own hair needs highlighting and I glance at Stephanie again, seeing she's still deep in conversation.

'I ought to have a tan after two weeks in Goa! Sadly, it won't last around here in this god-awful weather. Luckily we're off to Barbados for a fortnight soon. Are you going anywhere in the next little while?'

'Andrew mentioned going away, but we don't have firm plans yet.' My words are expressionless. There's no way I can face a holiday with Andrew, but I won't tell him until I have to, knowing it'll cause another fight I don't have the energy for.

She frowns at me. 'Are you all right?'

'Fine.' I sip my drink, unable to taste the vodka. I put it down then close my eyes for a moment. 'Actually, I'm not. My vision's gone blurry.' Della knows about my migraines. I search my bag for my pills. 'I can't believe it. They're in my other bag.' I glance around, noticing Andrew on the other side of the room talking to someone I don't know. 'Do me a favour and tell him, would you? I should go home before it gets any worse. Can we catch up another time? I want to hear about Goa.'

Della's concern is genuine. 'He should take you home. I'll get him.'

I'm shaking my head. 'Please, don't. We've only just got here. I'll be fine on my own.' And I'd rather be on my own than with Andrew.

'You're sure? Would you like me to walk with you?'

Shaking my head, I suddenly feel claustrophobic. 'If you could just tell Andrew . . .'

Slipping outside unnoticed, I take a deep breath. I have no migraine, just an aching weariness at having to pretend, even to Della, that everything's fine in my marriage. I walk home knowing Andrew won't come after me, or even call to check if I'm all right.

Thinking of Della, I frown as it creeps into my mind that given the limited pool of suspects, she could be his latest. But she's been in Goa, I remember, relieved.

So, if not her, who?

Through the darkness, the sound of an owl reaches me. Since moving here, I'd hoped to grow to love the countryside and the changes of the seasons, but I haven't. Instead, the emptiness and the silence suffocate me. In a small village, there is no privacy. I wonder how much longer I can keep up the pretence that Andrew and I have a functioning marriage, just as I wonder how many people already know we don't.

As I reach our drive, I hear the unmistakable sound of footsteps running on gravel, just before Hollie springs through the open gate, her hair caught in the dim glow from the lamps on top of the gateposts. She carries on up the lane without looking round, as the sound of sobbing reaches me. Hollie's always been melodramatic, but there seems to be something different about her lately . . . I shake my head. The trouble with Hollie is her hype. Nothing small ever happens to her.

Inside, I linger in the kitchen, aware of Niamh moving around upstairs but she soon comes down, no doubt wondering why I'm back so soon. If she's surprised to see me, I can't tell.

'I have one of my migraines,' I explain. 'Have you eaten?'

Niamh's face is blank as she looks at me. 'We had pizza.'

Out of the corner of my eye I see the empty box on the side. 'Is Hollie OK?'

'She's fine.' But Niamh's answer is too quick and Hollie clearly wasn't fine.

'I passed her just now.' I wonder if something happened between them in the hour I was out. 'She came running out just as I got back. She seemed upset.'

As Niamh shrugs, I realise she isn't going to tell me anything. She wanders out of the kitchen and then I hear her light footsteps on the stairs. Fetching a glass, I make myself another vodka and tonic – full-strength this time, rather than the insipid version the pub serves, then go over to the sofa at the far end of the kitchen, flicking the TV on.

The kitchen is my favourite room – calm, light, cosy. Looking around, I imagine Andrew in the pub, no doubt smugly holding forth to anyone who'll listen, knowing there'll be plenty who will. Self-pity washes over me, but it's fleeting. I take a sip of my drink. I chose this life, just as I choose to stay with him. Not because I love this lifestyle or this house – they've long since lost their appeal. The only reason I'm here is because of Niamh.

★

By the time Andrew gets home, I'm in a vodka–induced slumber, which absolves me from having to talk to him. When I awake late the following morning, I find the bed beside me empty. As I lie there, the sound of Andrew crashing around the kitchen reaches my ears, then the quieter sound of Niamh's bedroom door opening, her footsteps growing fainter as she goes downstairs.

Closing my eyes, I think about staying in bed – I'm often on an early flight so the two of them are used to mornings without me – but I force myself to get up, propelled by a sense of maternal duty.

'Are you better?' Andrew barely looks at me as I walk into the kitchen. He misses my nod as he grabs his keys. 'I'll be late,' he says abruptly. 'I have a meeting.'

I look at Niamh, her face implacable as she watches him. 'I hope it goes well.' For Niamh's sake, I try to sound caring to counteract the fact that he is anything but.

'See you tonight.' As he grabs his jacket and marches outside, Niamh glances at the clock, then pulls on her coat.

I watch her pick up her school bag. 'Have a good day, Niamh.'

'Bye.'

She looks small as she walks outside, pulling the door closed behind her. Her face is paler than usual this morning, bleached by the negativity between me and Andrew that she can't escape. I wait for the sound of his car starting, but instead I hear him swear loudly.

Flinging the door open, he marches back inside. 'Some little shit's been at my car.'

'What?' I'm incredulous. Nothing like that happens around here. 'What's happened to it?'

'The fucking tyres have been slashed.' Andrew's face is white with fury. 'I'll have to take yours.'

I frown, wondering when it happened, how none of us heard anything. 'You should tell the police.' As his eyes search the kitchen, I reach for my keys before he sees them. 'You're not helping yourself to my car, Andrew. I have plans.'

'You can change your so-called plans,' he says nastily. 'You have a day off, don't you? Whereas I don't. I have a job to go to, patients waiting to see me. I'd say that's far more important than anything you might be doing today.'

His arrogance renders me speechless. He has absolutely no

24

idea what I'm doing. And I wouldn't mind betting it isn't his patients on his mind, more the so-called meeting he has after work, probably with *her*.

'No.' My fingers close around my keys.

'For Christ's sake, Elise.'

As he glares at me, I realise I wouldn't put it past him not to grab my arm and twist the keys from my fingers. 'Call a taxi, Andrew.' Slipping them into the pocket of my pyjamas, I try to ignore the churning in the pit of my stomach as I turn around and go upstairs.

Chapter Four

Elise

I could have offered to run Andrew into work, or arranged for someone to come here and fit new tyres, so as to save him the trouble, but I don't. Nor do I give in to his demands. In a marriage based on infidelity and lies, there is no kindness. Instead, as I change into running clothes, I hear a taxi arrive to take him to his medical practice.

It's another chilly February morning as I set off down the drive, pausing beside clumps of pinprick green shoots pushing up through the grass. They're the first snowdrops, their subtle green and white a prelude to the soft yellow of the wild daffodils that have colonised under the oldest trees. A sudden desire to fill the house with flowers grips me. I want beauty, colour, and fragrance to neutralise the odour of my marriage. Breaking into a jog, I think of the small florist shop in the next village.

As my body loosens up, I run harder, heading along the narrow strip of pavement remaining where the grass verge has yet to encroach, passing the first of the footpaths to the church before turning up Furze Lane. Half a mile along, I take a path that leads into an area of woodland and for several minutes I run hard, my feet cushioned by fallen leaves, slowing down to take the rough downhill steps hewn into the earth before the path slopes uphill again and the woods open out on the furthest side of the churchyard.

I rarely see anyone at this time of day, but this morning, as I slow down, I see a slight figure leaning against one of the tallest oaks. It's Hollie. When she sees me looking at her, she seems to shrink.

'Hey.' Slowing to a walk, I stop in front of her. 'Are you OK?'

Standing among the oldest gravestones and clutching her hands, her white knuckles protruding from bunched-up, too-long sleeves, it's clear she's agitated. At first, she doesn't speak, just continues to stare at her hands.

I feel myself frown. 'Shouldn't you be at school, Hollie?'

'Does it matter?' At last she speaks, her eyes darting around, looking anywhere other than at me.

'Well, yes.' I'm trying to sound reasonable. 'You have exams to think about. You don't want to miss too many lessons.' Then I frown, realising that she seems irritated with me.

'I can't think about school,' she mumbles. 'Not now. There's too much going on.'

The look on her face worries me. 'Such as what?'

This time, tears blur her eyes as she stares right at me. 'I can't tell you.' She turns away. 'That's the problem. I can't tell anyone . . .'

'I'm sure that isn't true.' Knowing she's prone to overdramatising things, I try to sound conciliatory. 'Why don't you talk to your dad? You have a good relationship, don't you?' But as I mention him, her face takes on a stricken look.

She shakes her head quickly. 'It won't do any good. It'll make it worse.'

Frowning again, I take a step closer. 'Has something happened, Hollie? If it has, if you want to talk to—'

But she interrupts. 'Please don't.' Her eyes blaze but her voice is desperate. 'You have no idea. You can't do anything. No-one can.'

It isn't my place to interfere, but whatever's going on, she should be at school. 'Fine. It's your life, but you need to think about the consequences, Hollie. You can't just take days off whenever you feel like it.' It comes out more sharply than I intended.

She stares at me. 'What difference does it make? If you had any idea what people around here are doing . . .'

I frown at her, puzzled. *What does she know?* 'What do you mean?'

Before Hollie can reply, Ida Jones appears from under the trees across the churchyard. As she walks towards us in a tweed skirt and quilted jacket that swamp her, a look of panic crosses Hollie's face. 'Don't say anything to her. *Please . . .*'

Before I can ask her what she doesn't want me to say, I hear Ida's gentle voice. 'How are you, my dears?' Then her eyes linger on Hollie. 'I didn't know it was the holidays.'

I'm acutely aware of Hollie's discomfort. 'No. Hollie wasn't feeling so well this morning.' The lie just slips out. I've no idea where the need to justify Hollie missing school comes from.

'Oh dear . . .' Ida scrutinises Hollie's face. 'You do look pale, dear.'

'You're better for a walk, aren't you, Hollie?' I change the subject. 'How's your little granddaughter, Ida? Is she over her chickenpox now?'

'She's all better. I've missed her though.' A wistful smile spreads across her face. 'But I'll be seeing them all this weekend.' As her phone buzzes from inside one of her pockets, she fumbles to find it, then looks at the screen. 'I'm so sorry, but it's my daughter. Would you excuse me?'

She turns and walks a little away from us. When she's out of earshot I ask Hollie directly. 'What are you hiding, Hollie?'

She starts. 'Nothing.'

From the flush of colour on her pale cheeks, I know she's lying.

★

Hollie fills my head for the rest of my run, then back at home while I shower and change. I try to imagine why she's upset, what she could be hiding, feeling an obligation to tell her father about our conversation. It gives me a dual reason to go to the florist this morning as Stephanie's salon is next door.

It's a ten-minute drive along quiet roads through open countryside to the outskirts of the next village, where a range of stylishly converted farm buildings are premises to a few small businesses.

After turning into the yard, I park in one of the cobbled spaces in front of the salon. Sitting there for a moment, I look through the window. Inside, Stephanie's talking on her phone. She's attractive in a deliberate sort of way, with angular features and a hardness that even heavy makeup doesn't soften. She's clearly agitated today, her face flustered as she speaks on her phone. As she ends the call, she stands in the window, not moving. When she notices my car, she makes an obvious attempt to compose herself.

As I go into the empty salon, Stephanie's behind her desk, going through what looks like her diary.

She looks up briefly. 'Elise . . . I won't be a moment. How are you?' There's no trace of the agitation I witnessed when I pulled up just now. As always, she's perfectly groomed, in control, her every movement measured.

'I'm good.' I wait for her to put her pen down. 'But I wish the weather wasn't so grey.'

Closing her diary, her eyes meet mine. 'At least you occasionally get to see the sun.'

'Not so much at the moment. I'm on a short-haul block.' Though, on a good day, I still get a hit of sunlight through the aircraft windows as we break through the clouds. 'Actually, I wanted to talk to you — about Hollie.' I pause. 'I saw her this morning.'

As I watch, a shadow crosses her face.

I frown. 'Is everything OK? It's just that she seemed quite upset.'

This time Stephanie looks straight at me. 'Since you ask, no. It really isn't.' Her voice is tearful. 'Hollie flits around doing as she pleases, not thinking how her behaviour affects all of us . . . I try so hard, Elise. To give her stability, to understand her. But she gives nothing back. It's difficult.'

It's the first I've heard of anything like this. 'Does James know about this?'

'He doesn't see it.' Stephanie's words are hollow. 'When it comes to Hollie, he has a complete blind spot.'

I hesitate. 'It can't be easy for you. And I suppose Hollie losing her mother the way she did . . . It's so sad.' I pause, not wanting to get drawn in any further. 'I just thought you'd want to know she was upset, that was all.' I glance around, looking for a way to change the subject, my eyes alighting on a row of small plants, with dark green fern-like leaves, arranged on a shelf. 'Those are unusual.'

'I got them next door.' She sighs. 'Look, Hollie is angry — I've no idea why. I won't bore you with the details but I was on the phone to the school just before you came in. It isn't just today. She's missing too many classes. James needs to be firmer with her, but he never confronts her.' She breaks off.

31

'I'm sorry. You don't need to know all this. None of our lives are perfect, are they?'

Her eyes hold mine a little too long and, in that moment, I wonder if she knows about Andrew. Could Stephanie be the woman he's having an affair with? I stare at her, trying to imagine them together, then snap myself out of it. I can't go on suspecting everyone I meet. To the best of my knowledge, Andrew goes for younger, less subtle women – Stephanie isn't his type. 'I always thought you and Hollie got on well.'

'So did I. We used to.' Stephanie's voice wavers, then she glances through the window as a car pulls up. 'My next client. I should get ready. Was there anything else?'

'Oh.' I'd almost forgotten. 'Yes. My highlights . . . I don't suppose you could fit me in sometime?'

Opening her diary again, she scans the page. 'I'm busy the rest of today. But how about Monday? First thing?'

Today is Friday. 'Perfect. Thank you.' The door opens and her next client comes in. 'I'll let you get on.'

As Stephanie pins on a smile to welcome her client, I go next door to the florist. The shop is filled with the scent of eucalyptus as I peruse the buckets of spring flowers, my spirits already lifting as I gather bunches of tulips, ranunculi and tiny white narcissi, in my indulgent attempt to bring beauty into our toxic house – not that anyone else will notice.

But as I drive home, I'm thinking about what Stephanie said. *None of our lives are perfect, are they?* I imagine the unspoken message beneath her words. *You have enough problems of your own, Elise.* Does she know what Andrew's up to, and if so, how?

But then everyone knows hairdressers are privy to all kinds of secrets. Stephanie probably knows better than anyone about what goes on around here. I feel myself frown. Except, apparently, when it comes to Hollie.

Niamh

Hollie was friends with Dylan first. But now he's gone, she only has me.

'People are so horrible, Niamh . . .' She couldn't stop sobbing after my parents had gone to the pub last night. It took ages for me to get the truth out of her, that one of her teachers had phoned her father because the school is worried about her.

'The teacher said I wasn't eating. They think I'm anorexic. But I don't eat because I *can't*.' She spoke theatrically through the river of tears pouring down her face.

I could understand her being upset about a teacher poking her nose in, but her hysteria left me mystified.

But it's always the same. Like her clothes, Hollie's defences are paper-thin, every barbed word piercing her skin. She has no armour against a world she believes is set against her.

★

The following day, when I come back from school, I see Hollie from the bus window. She's sitting on the wall, stroking the cat as she waits for me, and her eyes are red, as though she's been crying. As the bus slows and I get off, she jumps down and falls into step beside me. Even before she speaks, I feel her restlessness. 'I hate this place,' she tells me, meaning the village. 'Is your mum home?'

'I don't know.' I lose track of when she's flying. Every week, my mother's roster is different. 'You can come in, if you like.'

Hollie looks wary.

I frown at her. Hollie doesn't usually mind my mum. 'What's the matter?'

'I just don't want to see anyone. OK?' Her voice is fierce.

At the bottom of the drive, I glance towards the house. My father's car is there, which is odd. 'She's out. That's my dad's car but he won't be home.' I look at Hollie. 'Are you coming in?'

But she doesn't budge. 'How do you know he's not there?'

'Because he'll be at work.' I'm starting to feel impatient.

She hesitates, an odd look on her face. 'OK. But if they come back I'll have to leave . . .'

Whatever it is that's on her mind, I know she'll get round to telling me if she wants to badly enough. It's the reason she comes here. She doesn't have anyone else. Trying the back door, I turn to Hollie. 'Don't worry. They're out.' After I unlock it, Hollie follows me in.

I sling my bag on the floor, while Hollie goes over to the huge vase on the table. Usually empty, today it's filled with all kinds of flowers. 'D'you want a drink?' I ask.

She buries her face in the flowers, as if she's inhaling them. 'What is there?'

Shrugging, I go to the fridge, frowning as I pass the sink and see it's filled with several more bunches. What is it with my mother and all these flowers? 'Orange juice, milk, Coke . . .'

'Is it diet?'

Hollie's skinny – that her teacher phoned her dad doesn't

34

surprise me – and though I hardly ever see her eat, when she does, she wolfs down food as though she's been starved for a month. Checking the can, I nod and pass it to her before getting another for myself, then going to the pantry for a bag of crisps.

'Let's go to your room.' Hollie's more on edge than usual, constantly glancing through doorways and windows, as if expecting someone to appear.

'OK.' I shrug, watching her run ahead up the stairs as I pick up my bag and follow her.

In my room, Hollie collapses on my bed, lying on her back and gazing at the ceiling. 'This is the only place I feel safe.' It's the kind of overly dramatic thing she often says.

I half listen, wondering why she's avoiding my mum. Then, suddenly, she sits up. 'I saw your mum this morning. I bunked school.'

I'd already guessed it had to be something like that, otherwise she wouldn't have been waiting for me at the bus stop.

'She gave me one of those mother talks about not missing school. I thought she was different but she's just like everyone else.' Hollie sounds tearful.

Suddenly I'm irritated. It's like last night all over again. Hollie tells me something terrible is going on, something she can't talk about, and I'm supposed to just let her lie on my bed and wallow. Folding my arms, I stare at her, for some reason convinced there's something she hasn't told me yet. 'I can't help you if you don't tell me what's happened.'

Before she can reply, there's the scrunch of car tyres on gravel. Hollie leaps up and runs to the landing window. I follow more slowly.

'She's back. I have to go. Shit.' She sounds hysterical again. 'I don't want to see her.'

She runs back to my room, going to the window and

opening it. It's the craziest overreaction, and it's far too high for her to jump from. I put my hand on her arm. 'Wait. She might go into the garden or to the bathroom or something.'

I hear the back door open as my mother enters the kitchen, then cupboards opening and closing before she runs the tap and turns on the kettle. Then I hear her boots on the wooden floor as she comes to the bottom of the stairs.

'Are you up there, Niamh?' Behind me, Hollie shrinks back. I stand in the doorway. 'Yeah.'

'I've put the kettle on. Would you like tea?'

'No, thanks. I'm doing homework.'

As I push the door closed and turn around, Hollie is distraught. 'Why are you so upset? Does it matter that you're here?'

'Ssshhh . . .' Hollie's eyes are wide as she shakes her head. 'She'll know you're talking to someone. You have to help me. I have to get out of here.'

Hearing my mother coming up the stairs, I hold my breath, my eyes glued to Hollie's. Then as I hear the door to my parents' bedroom open, followed by the door to the en suite, I exhale.

'Now,' I tell Hollie urgently. 'She's in the bathroom. Just be really quiet.'

Without speaking, Hollie flies down the stairs. I don't hear the back door open, just glimpse her running across the grass from an upstairs window before I go back to my room and get my homework out. Five minutes later, there's a knock on my door, and my mother pushes it open.

There's a frown on her face. 'I just saw Hollie running across the garden.'

I look away. 'Yeah. She suddenly remembered something she had to do.'

My mother gives me an odd look. 'Be careful, Niamh. I

know you and Hollie are close, but there's something going on. I'm worried about her.'

My mother is now an expert on Hollie? I don't think so.

In the doorway, she hesitates. 'Did you hear anything last night? Outside?'

'No. Why?'

'It's just that someone slashed your father's tyres.'

I frown. 'Who would do that?'

'I've no idea.' She hovers.

I raise my eyebrows at her. 'I have homework,' I say pointedly.

Heat rises in my cheeks as she glances towards my unopened schoolbooks. 'No doubt you do.' Her voice is cool. 'In that case, I'll let you get on.'

Chapter Five

Elise

In this house of charades, Niamh pretends to do her homework while I arrange the rest of the flowers, then start dinner for my disunited family. On the outside looking in, there's nothing to set us apart from anyone else: soft grey curtains are drawn against the darkness, the smell of caramelising onions fills the house, the serene sound of Classic FM floats in the air, the teenaged daughter reluctantly studies in her bedroom, the wife cooks dinner for the doctor husband, who'll soon be home after another day of healing people. Ludicrous façades when, underneath, we barely speak to each other.

For a moment I imagine a different kind of life – one with honesty, laughter, and lightness, where love is demonstrated, not withheld or wielded with intent. My daydream is interrupted by the sound of a car outside. It pauses and a door slams before it drives away, the sound of footsteps on gravel drawing nearer. When the back door opens, it's clear the day hasn't improved Andrew's mood. If anything, it's worse.

'You're early.' I'm icily polite, imagining he's been stood up by his lover. He wouldn't be here otherwise.

'Hardly,' he snaps. 'But I might have been, if I hadn't had to sort the car out.'

'Is it fixed?'

'For Christ's sake,' he bellows. 'Didn't you see it when you came in? You don't give a shit, Elise. Why are there flowers everywhere?'

Because there is more to life than vile deception and anger. Remember beauty, Andrew? How the gentlest of touches feels? How it is to love and be loved?

'I wanted to cheer up the house. You know I hate winter. Dinner will be about twenty minutes.' Speaking as calmly as I can, I go to the fridge and pour a glass of white wine, but he's already storming through to the living room. He comes back seconds later, slamming something down on the counter behind me; I hear the splintering of glass.

'Can't we have one fucking room without fucking flowers?' As he marches out, I turn to see the vase that used to belong to my grandmother, its crystal dulled by age. There's a jagged crack down one side, from which water is seeping. It pools on the counter before running onto the floor.

Ripping out the flowers I arranged only a little while ago, I drop them on the worktop, then empty the vase and throw it away, trying to ignore my rush of anger. The flowers are still scattered and my fury with my husband barely muted by the time Niamh comes downstairs. Her cool eyes skim over the stems before settling on me, her face impenetrable. I wonder if she heard the way Andrew spoke to me just now, or the shattering of glass. Of course she did. How could she possibly not have?

'Can you lay the table, honey?' My tone is light.

Without speaking, Niamh sets three places at the kitchen table then fetches the peppermill and water glasses.

'Do you have much homework?'

'Not really.' Niamh's voice is expressionless as she comes over and peers into the pan I'm stirring.

It pulls at my heartstrings to see her like this, to know that the poisonous exchanges between me and Andrew reach her ears, too. 'Pork,' I tell her, suddenly aching for connection, for a joking aside, an affectionate exchange, but Niamh and I are not like that. She's inherited the same detached coldness that's my defence against Andrew. 'Would you like to tell him it's ready?'

Without speaking, Niamh wanders out of the kitchen to find her father, and I wonder what's going through her mind as I start serving food onto plates. She comes back then, followed by Andrew. After pouring himself a glass of wine, he picks up a plate and a fork and goes back to the living room.

It's a pattern I've grown used to, but today rage flares inside me at his deliberate contempt. Stifling the urge to tell him what I think, I take the two remaining plates over to the table as Niamh joins me. Sitting there, picking at my food, I watch her eat. I'm filled with resentment that Andrew's behaviour dominates everything in this house – including Niamh. He doesn't care about either of us.

Until now, I've forced myself to tolerate his behaviour, wanting to hold our marriage together for Niamh, believing it's better for her that Andrew and I are together, hoping that he might miraculously change. I've refused to accept that he isn't going to, because once I do that, I become a woman who knowingly chooses to remain in an abusive marriage.

So you're not denying it? That Andrew's bullied away what love there was, betrayed your trust. How much longer can you keep this up? There is only contempt between you. He doesn't care about your marriage any more than you do.

For the first time I see myself as others might see me, and

something snaps. After eating, I wait for Niamh to go up to her bedroom, for the sound of her TV to filter through her cracked-open door, and then I go to find Andrew in the living room.

It's a large room with high ceilings and a row of three sash windows that look out onto the garden. He's slouched on the sofa, his empty plate on the coffee table, his shoes kicked off, his attention focused on his phone. In the home we share, having eaten the meal I cooked for him, he's blatantly ignoring me and texting *her*.

Pushing the door closed behind me, I walk over and stand in front of him.

'Not now,' he says sharply.

'Yes now.' I don't budge. 'For fuck's sake, Andrew. Why are we doing this?'

As he laughs cynically, I stare at him, trying to discern even the faintest trace of the man I fell in love with twenty years ago. But he doesn't exist anymore. 'Oh, I think you know the answer to that.'

Leaning down, I snatch his phone away. 'The very least you could do is show me some respect,' I hiss, keeping my voice low to prevent Niamh from hearing. 'I know you don't care about me, but what about Niamh? She sees the way you treat me. She sees everything. You could make an effort for once, for her sake, instead of texting one of your sluts.' The word is unfamiliar on my tongue, but I'm driven by the desire for a reaction from him.

Standing up, he twists his phone out of my hand. 'You have no idea what you're talking about.'

His words are loaded with contempt and I stand there a moment longer, unfairness washing over me, followed by frustration that we can't even hold a civil conversation, before I

42

give up and walk away. On my way back to the kitchen, I glimpse a movement at the top of the stairs and look up to catch the back of Niamh's head before she closes her bedroom door. If there was any closeness between us, I would go up there and talk to her, reassure her that everything's fine, that Andrew's
just cross about what happened to the car tyres this morning. We could even laugh about it – a shared moment between a mother and her daughter. *We both know what he's like.*

But as well as fuelling self-doubt, my abusive marriage has destroyed our mother–child relationship. I can't lie to her, can't tell her platitudes that neither of us believe, because Niamh's smart and she'd see through it. She knows what's going on, but we're too distanced for me to talk to her about it. Far easier for us both to extend this silence.

Niamh

My parents' marriage falls another step towards ruin, and I wonder again why they stay together. But, as always, my mother says nothing.

I don't see Hollie again until Saturday, when she comes over after making sure my parents won't be there. Her eyes hold mine, making contact yet telling me nothing.

'D'you want a Coke?' When she nods, I get a couple from the fridge, passing one to her.

She pulls out one of the kitchen chairs and perches on it. 'I don't know what to do.' For once, she isn't theatrical. 'Too many things are too wrong.'

Not sure what to say, I watch her.

'Do you really know your dad?' Her eyes are huge. 'Or your mum? Like, really know? Do you ever think they might be this person with all this stuff in their life they've been hiding from you?'

I'm silent. There's so much my parents don't say. I try not to think about it.

'If I tell you . . .' Hollie's bottom lip wobbles as she goes on.

'You have to swear, Niamh. On your life. You can't tell anyone. Not ever.'

I stare at her. Is she actually going to tell me? 'I swear.'

Hollie's eyes dart around, and then she blurts out. 'I've found out something about my dad.'

I take a swig of Coke. 'What about him?'

I wait for her to tell me, but then she changes her mind. 'I can't.' She puts down her can.

'But you've started. And it can't be that bad . . .' It's so annoying when she does this.

She gazes at me for a moment and I look for the answer in the depths of her wide brown eyes. The horror, sadness, sense of betrayal she feels are all there, clear as day, but she breaks our connection as she jumps up.

'Let's get out of here.'

'Hollie, it's raining. And there isn't anywhere to go.'

'I know somewhere,' she says as she pulls on her jacket and does up her boots.

There's nowhere around here – just scattered big houses behind garden walls and a village church – but under her spell, I pull on my boots and follow her.

There's a rawness in the air as we step outside. Hollie's introspective mood is replaced by recklessness as she runs across the garden into the lane.

'Wait . . .' Zipping up my jacket, I run after her. 'Where are we going?'

She doesn't answer me, instead hissing, 'Oh my God . . . Ida Jones has seen us. Run!'

As I glance at Ida's window, I see that she seems to be beckoning me. Pausing, I'm momentarily torn between finding out what she wants and following Hollie's retreating figure. Deciding to follow my friend, I break into a run.

Catching up to her, we turn up Furze Lane side by side, moving past the row of terraced flint cottages with their small, dimly lit windows, and coils of wood smoke coming from the chimneys. Further on, beneath tall trees on either side, the lane narrows before there's a left-hand bend, looping it back towards the village. Most of the lanes in our village are single tracks off which large houses are set back, hidden behind walls and hedges, their gardens mostly obscured from one another.

'Over here.' Hollie points towards a metal farm gate, the top bar of which is wrapped in barbed wire. Undeterred, she climbs over into a field, waiting for me to join her before heading towards the middle of the thick grass. 'There's a back way.'

My head fills with questions, but I don't ask any of them. Being with Hollie is like how it always was with Dylan – an escape into a world so different from mine that I don't question anything, just let myself be swept along with her.

At the other side of the field, there's a post and rail fence, which we slip through.

'This way.' Hollie skips through an orchard where most of last year's apples lie rotting underfoot. As we reach the other side, she stops and gestures dramatically at the stark hedges, beyond which a sweep of lawn slopes uphill towards Deeprose House. Set behind heavy gates and high stone walls, it can't be seen from the road. 'Crazy, isn't it?' She shakes her head. 'The Penns have a place like this, but they're not even here half the time.'

If I had a house like this, I'd never want to leave it. The gardens have a wildness about them, from being untouched, and there are dead flowers and fallen leaves everywhere I look. As I glance towards the house, taking in its cold walls and dark windows, I shiver. 'We shouldn't be here, Hollie.'

Gazing at the windows, I imagine someone watching us. 'If someone's there, they'll easily see us.'

She stares. 'No-one's home. The Penns are away for three weeks.'

Suddenly, I'm freaked out. 'Why have we come here?'

But it's as if someone's walked over her grave. There's a look of desolation on Hollie's face. 'Let's go,' she mumbles, turning back towards the field.

I've no desire to change her mind. Spooked by the empty house and the darkening sky, I follow.

★

When we get home, my father's car is in the drive. Refusing to come in, Hollie runs off up the lane.

Chapter Six

Elise

On the way to Stephanie's salon on Monday morning, I'm curious to know what she might have heard about Andrew. Villages like ours are hotbeds for gossip, but as she starts on my hair I get the sense that she's distracted, our conversation stilted until I ask her a direct question.

'Tell me, Stephanie. Do you like living here?'

'Like?' She looks surprised. 'Of course I do. It's a lovely place, don't you think?' Her words aren't convincing.

'No.' I've no reason to lie to her. 'It's pretty enough, but it's too quiet. And I can't bear the gossip.' I watch her face in the mirror. 'Though I suppose as a hairdresser, you're the agony aunt for all the local villages.'

'It can be a bit like that.' She hesitates, her face seeming too close. 'I don't much like it, either, if I'm honest. You'd be surprised what people say sometimes.'

'I don't think I would.' My expectations of human nature are not high. 'I try to stay away from most of the gossip.'

'It isn't so easy in here.' Stephanie's voice is flat. 'People come in and like to make out that their lives are perfect,

when I happen to know that most of them are not. But then
. . .' She pauses. 'Most of us don't want the world to know
about the less-than-perfect parts of ourselves – or our lives.
By the time you reach our age, you become expert at hiding
them, don't you?'

As our eyes meet in the mirror, a slight frown crosses
her face and I wonder if she's talking about herself or me. 'Is
everything OK?'

'No different to any other family with a wayward teenaged
daughter!' She pretends to make light of it, but a worried look
crosses her face. 'Not always easy, is it?'

'No.' I've often wondered how Hollie felt about her
father remarrying so soon after they'd lost her mother. On the
brink of asking Stephanie if she's heard any rumours about
Andrew, I change my mind. As it always does, fear gets in my
way that it would get back to him.

*

I rarely sleep well and after an early start yesterday for work,
I'm exhausted when my alarm goes off on Wednesday morning.
The room is in darkness and Andrew doesn't stir as I shower
and dress. I wonder how it feels to have no conscience. Pulling
a cardigan on over my uniform, I tiptoe downstairs, glancing
towards Niamh's room, hoping I haven't disturbed her.

In the kitchen, I glance at the clock. It's nearly six, giving
me time to make a mug of tea and a bowl of muesli, a tenuous
layer of peace settling around me that comes from the certainty
that it's too early to be interrupted by Andrew. Unable to stop
my mind from wandering, I imagine how different this house
would be, how free my life would feel, without him.

Having finished my muesli, I check my schedule on my
phone. I'm rostered on a flight to Athens. At this time of year,

it should be an easy day with only a few passengers, on their way to a beautiful place where the winter sun shines, where life could be so different. A yearning fills me to be free of my life here – of Andrew – followed by a grim determination. I need to get through these intolerable years and let Niamh grow up, while doing my best to mute the effect her father has on her.

It's still pitch-dark as I go outside and get into my car. Starting the engine, I let it idle while the layer of ice on the windscreen clears before setting off down the drive. When I turn onto the lane, frost sparkles in the beam from my headlights as they pick up an otherworldly landscape, one in which each branch of every tree is dusted white where freezing fog has touched it, the grass verges glinting silver.

Reaching the main road, I glance at the road sign. The airport is clearly marked, ten miles away, to the left. But this morning, there's something else I need to do. Slowing down and pulling over, I pick up my phone and make a call. Then flicking on my indicator and pulling out, I turn right.

*

With the disruption caused by ice and snow, my schedule changes at short notice and on Thursday, my flight is cancelled. That I am at home that evening, instead of conveniently out of his way, means the tension between me and Andrew escalates.

'I thought you were in Zurich tonight.' When he comes in, he doesn't attempt to hide his irritation. As always, he gives no thought to Niamh. Home early, he'd clearly planned to shower and change before going out again, leaving her here alone.

'My flight was cancelled because of the weather. Does it make any difference to anything?' It's an innocent enough question but he chooses not to answer, instead storming upstairs and reappearing ten minutes later wearing different clothes. Grabbing his jacket, he walks out without speaking to me. When I hear a car pull up outside minutes later, my heart sinks as I imagine Andrew coming back for some reason, preparing myself for another verbal onslaught, but instead, there's a knock at the door.

To my surprise, James is there when I open it. 'Hello.'

'Sorry to bother you like this.' His face is pale in the outside light, his eyes flitting about nervously.

I frown slightly. 'Is something wrong? Would you like to come in?'

'I won't stop, Elise. I just wanted to ask if you've seen Hollie.'

'Not since . . .' I think back, remembering seeing Hollie run across the garden from an upstairs window. 'Well, she was here one evening last week, but I didn't talk to her. I have a feeling she was avoiding me.'

His face wrinkles into a frown. 'Why would you say that?'

'Oh . . .' I try to remember our conversation. 'To be honest, I think she'd skipped school that day. I think she was embarrassed that I'd seen her and caught her out – I made some comment about it being important that she didn't get behind.'

James nods. 'The school called me a while ago. Seems she's skipped a few days recently.' He hesitates. 'Do you know if Niamh's seen her over the last couple of days?'

Hollie's absence is in line with what Stephanie told me, but warning bells are ringing. 'I don't think so, but if you can wait, I'll go and ask her.'

Leaving him alone, I go upstairs to Niamh's bedroom. 'Niamh?' When I push her door open, I find she's engrossed in one of her schoolbooks. 'Have you seen Hollie at all the last couple of days?'

Her face is blank as she shakes her head. 'Why?'

'Her dad wondered, that's all. I'll tell him.' Not wanting her to worry unnecessarily, I say no more and go back downstairs. James is still waiting by the door. 'She hasn't. Is Hollie OK, James?'

There are dark circles under his eyes, as though he hasn't been sleeping. 'To be honest, I don't know. We've just been in touch with the police. Look, I need to get going. I'm trying to talk to everyone in the village before it gets too late.'

'Let me know, won't you?' At the thought that something might have happened to Hollie, my heart thuds in my chest. 'When she comes back?'

He nods before turning to walk away. I close the door and seconds later hear his car start, then its tyres on the gravel as he drives away.

Niamh's voice from the doorway startles me. 'Why was he here?'

'It seems Hollie's gone missing.' I pause. I hadn't wanted to worry Niamh, but she and Hollie are friends. She should know.

Niamh starts, shock registering in her eyes. 'When?'

'They last saw her a couple of days ago. Do you remember the last time you heard from her?'

Niamh's eyes hold mine as she shakes her head. 'I'm not sure. I think it was Saturday when she last came here.'

'Would you have any idea where she might go?'

'No.' Her voice is quiet, her brow wrinkled with a trace of a frown.

I fight off unwanted emotions, imagining how I'd feel if it was Niamh who had gone out one day and hadn't come back. 'If you hear from her, can you tell me? Even if she doesn't want James to know where she is, he needs to know she's OK.'

Niamh nods slowly; then fear crosses her face. 'What if she's not?'

I feel the urge to protect my daughter from the horrific possibility that something could have happened to Hollie. 'I'm sure she's fine, Niamh . . . We both know she's a little bit unpredictable. Maybe she had an argument with James and she's punishing him.'

But from the way Niamh stands there, I know she isn't convinced. 'Try not to worry. I'll call James later – just to see if there's any news.'

That seems to satisfy Niamh for now and she goes back upstairs. Seconds later, I hear her door close, then music drifting through the gap underneath it. Not the usual upbeat tracks she plays, but a haunting instrumental that tells me what my daughter can't put into words.

She's frightened.

*

I leave it until later to call James. 'I'm sorry to call so late. I was just wondering if you'd heard from Hollie.'

'No. No-one's seen her.' He sounds worried sick – and defeated. 'I've spoken to the police again and they're on their way round now. They may well call in on you tomorrow.'

'Tomorrow?' Slightly shocked, I'm thinking on my feet. 'I'm working, James. I have to go out early.'

'Can I give them your mobile number? Hollie's spent so much time at your place recently, I'm sure they'll want to talk to you – and Niamh.'

'Of course.' I pause. 'But let's hope it doesn't come to that.'

Chapter Seven

Jo

It's late, the end of a long first day back at work after a month's compassionate leave – supposedly long enough to get over my husband walking out. I imagine some naïve psychologist calculating the number of days before shock subsides, grief levels out, and the new normality of being left starts to settle. They've got it massively wrong, of course, because anyone can tell you that after ten years in a dysfunctional marriage, a month is nothing.

About to leave the office when the phone rings, I think about letting it go to voicemail. But habit wins out. 'Joanna May.' I listen to the detective inspector's voice at the other end, my stomach suddenly lurching when he tells me that a teenage girl has disappeared in the village of Abingworth, not far from here. My heart sinks as I think about facing distraught parents right now, when my own emotions are still raw. 'Look, I wouldn't normally ask, sir, but isn't there someone else who could do this?'

He hesitates. 'I need someone good. And you're up to speed with Operation Rainbow. This is our chance to get someone into the village without suspicions being aroused.' He pauses again. 'But I'll understand if you'd rather not. I'll see if Robson's around.'

I pause. Operation Rainbow is the name of an investigation into a suspected porn ring that's been linked to the area around Abingworth, albeit tenuously so far. The DI knows I've been off work, but this is an opportunity we need to take for the police to get closer without arousing the suspicion of the villagers. Now that I'm back I have to rise to the challenge, or else people will start asking questions. 'It's fine, sir. I'll go over there.'

'You're sure? Thank you, Jo.' The DI sounds relieved.

After he hangs up, I take a deep breath. Minutes ago, I thought I was about to leave for home. But when a teenage girl goes missing, there is no time to waste. The sooner I get over to Abingworth, the better.

*

Even though the roads are mostly clear, the drive takes longer than I'd expected, the traffic brought to a stop by an accident that's closed one of the lanes on the dual carriageway. Finally clear of it, I drive too fast, and as I take the exit my car skids briefly on black ice.

Slowing down, I gather my thoughts. All I know about Hollie Hampton is that she hasn't been seen for two days. Two days is a long time for a teenager to be missing. That her father didn't call us straight away speaks volumes; that he's used to her disappearing now and then already setting off alarm bells. Hollie is sixteen years old. If she were my daughter, I wouldn't have waited.

Following my GPS, I turn into a narrow lane without road markings, edged with crisply frosted grass. A row of cottages comes into view before I pass a number of larger houses set back behind flint walls, slowing down as the lane bends sharply left. A hundred yards ahead, through the trees, a flashing blue light alerts me to the location of the Hamptons' house.

As far as I can tell in the darkness, it's a long rambling house set in a shallow valley, surrounded by trees. Pulling over, I park on the sloping drive, then get out and take the rough steps down to what looks like the front door. When I knock, it's opened straight away by a man who I imagine to be Hollie's father, judging by his raddled face.

'Mr Hampton? I'm DS May. May I come in?'

Hollie's father nods. 'Yes. Of course.' After closing the door behind me, he says, 'I'll take you to the others.'

I assume he's talking about the local police. 'You still haven't heard anything from your daughter?'

'No,' he mutters, his head down as he leads the way.

Inside, it's obvious the house is old, with wide, uneven floor-boards, the timber frame and old brickwork exposed here and there. I take in the air of shabbiness – the poor lighting, the dated wallpaper that's seen better days – as I follow him to a small sitting room where I recognise one of my colleagues, Sergeant Sarah Collins. She's with another uniformed police-woman and a fair-haired woman who's clearly been crying. I assume she must be Hollie's mother. 'Mrs Hampton? I'm Detective Sergeant May. I'm going to ask Sergeant Collins to update me and then I'd like to talk to you and your husband. Can you give us five minutes?'

Fear, uncertainty, and dread hang in the air, just as they did the last time I worked on a similar case, where every question, every phone call, had the potential to reveal a truth no-one wanted to hear.

Getting up, she goes over to her husband, resting a hand on

57

one of his shoulders as she turns towards me. 'Can I make you all a cup of tea?'

'Yes, please.' Her offer will keep them out of the room so that we can talk openly. As they leave, I turn to Sarah Collins. 'Tell me what you've got.'

She glances at her notes. 'Not much. Hollie was last here two days ago – on Tuesday. Her parents – actually, it's worth mentioning that Mrs Hampton is her stepmother – anyway, they both say it isn't unheard of for Hollie to disappear for a night without telling them, but she's never been gone for longer than that. Also, they've always been able to get hold of her at some point by phone, but this time, they haven't been able to.'

'You have Hollie's mobile number?'

Sarah Collins nods. 'We're already checking it out.'

'What about her birth mother?'

'She died eight years ago.' Sarah pauses. 'We also have the contact details for her school. According to Hollie's father, they called him recently. Apparently she's missed quite a few days, but he seems to think it wasn't anything unusual. We've also got the details for her friend, Niamh Buckley, and Niamh's mother, Elise. Mr Hampton called around to see them earlier. We need to check with Hollie's school, but apart from her parents, it's possible that Niamh was the last person to see Hollie.'

A sinking feeling fills me as I look at her. We really are starting with nothing. 'Is there anything else I should know?'

As Sarah shakes her head, I know that in this extreme cold, too much time has already gone by. 'I'll go and talk to her parents.'

Just then, the Hamptons come back in with a tray of mugs. 'Thank you.' I take one. 'Shall we sit down?' I pause. 'If you don't mind, I'd like to ask you about Hollie.'

Mrs Hampton's face is white as a sheet, tears tracing trails through her makeup. Her hands are shaking as she places the tray on the coffee table.

While they pull up chairs, I get out my electronic notebook. Looking up at them, I do my best to be reassuring. 'We'll be starting a search at dawn tomorrow. It'll be centred on the village, but we'll continue to widen the search area until we find her. Unless there's anywhere specific you think she might be?'

When they both shake their heads, I go on. 'Can you tell me about Hollie? And do you have a photograph I could take?'

Sarah Collins passes me a six-by-four colour photo. 'It was taken six months ago.'

'Thanks.' I pause, taking in Hollie's huge eyes and long dark hair, which look so much more striking than in the small photo the DI had sent me. She's a beautiful girl – slightly ethereal-looking. 'Outside school, was there anywhere she went, any friends she saw, any clubs she took part in?'

I watch their faces carefully as James speaks. 'As we've told your colleagues, she's friends with Niamh Buckley in the village. We don't really know her school friends. She doesn't bring them back here.'

It's not unusual for teenagers who have reached a certain age, though I can't help thinking that sometimes there's a reason why they keep their friends from their parents. 'How would you describe her?' I know as I voice the question that the answer depends on who you ask. Parents are not always entirely objective.

'She's spirited and very bright, but she has demons. Hollie's fragile – her mother died eight years ago and I don't think she's ever come to terms with losing her. I think that because I'm not related by blood, I see her a little differently to James.' She glances at her husband. 'I'd describe her as ferociously loyal,

artistic, given to drama . . . but in short, she's a tortured soul.'
Maybe it's because Hollie isn't her birth daughter that I'm
inclined to believe Stephanie Hampton's assessment.

I turn to James Hampton. 'Do you think that's a fair description? Would you like to add anything?'

He shakes his head slowly. 'No.'

I turn back to Stephanie. 'As her stepmother, did you get
on well? I'm sure it isn't always easy.'

'It wasn't – not at first. I knew I couldn't replace Kathryn
– James's first wife – but I thought that if I was someone
Hollie knew she could rely on, it would be the best basis for
a relationship with her. That's what I've tried to be.'

It sounds a sensible enough approach to the minefield of
step-parenting. 'Has Hollie seemed upset lately? Or different in
any way?'

'It's hard to say.' As Stephanie looks at James, something
flickers between them. 'She could be quite up and down.'

James looks haunted. 'Hollie's always been a bit of a drama
queen.'

Their words make it clear that even if something was going
on with Hollie, they wouldn't have flagged it up as anything
unusual. And yet . . . there was something about the way
Stephanie looked at James that makes me wonder if there's
something she isn't saying. I move on to the facts for now. 'You
last saw her when?'

'Tuesday.' Stephanie's voice is sharp.

It's now Thursday. 'Was that Tuesday night?'

Stephanie nods. 'Yes, at tea. We assume she spent the night
here but neither of us saw her on Wednesday morning. When
it got to breakfast time, she didn't come downstairs and so
James went to wake her, but her bed was empty. It looked as
though she'd slept in it, though.'

'So she left here sometime between Tuesday night and early Wednesday morning. Do you know if she went to school on Wednesday?'

'She didn't.' As James Hampton shakes his head, his face is racked with guilt.

'What time do you generally get up in the morning? Just so that I can get a picture of when Hollie may have left without you seeing her.'

'I'm usually up around seven.' Stephanie glances at her husband. 'James is later, as a rule.'

'So it's reasonable to assume that Hollie had gone before then?'

Stephanie nods. 'She could have slipped out while I was getting up, without me noticing, but it's unlikely. Usually I hear her.'

But not impossible . . . I make a note. 'So, that morning, when you went to wake her for breakfast, you wouldn't have been concerned that she wasn't in her room?'

'No.' James Hampton frowns at me. 'I really don't see how this is helping anything.'

I hesitate, looking at both of them. 'It may seem trivial, but I need to establish what Hollie's routine usually was − what was and wasn't normal. When did you think about calling the police?'

'I wanted to call that first night.' Stephanie sounds resentful and my ears prick up. 'But James thought we should wait. He thought Hollie was probably at a friend's house. On Thursday, we gave her until the end of the school day, but when she still didn't come home, we couldn't leave it any longer.'

'We should have called you sooner. I thought . . .' James Hampton's voice is shaking. *I never thought she wouldn't come back.'*

Placing her hand on his shoulder, Stephanie looks just as guilty.

'Does she have a bank account?'

'She does.' James Hampton looks hesitant.

'So does she have a Saturday job? Or an allowance?'

'Occasionally she's helped me in the salon – but not for a while.' Stephanie glances from me to her husband.

'Would you happen to know if she would have enough money if, say . . . she'd decided to run away? I'm sorry, but we have to consider the possibility.'

James shakes his head slightly as Stephanie speaks. 'I'm not sure where she'd go.'

I pause, trying to think, wondering how sure they are that she hasn't run away. Where teenagers are concerned, parents don't always know them as well as they think. 'Would you have any idea what she may have been wearing, or could you identify clothes that are missing?'

Again, it's Stephanie who speaks. 'Probably jeans. There's a pair I can't find. Her parka jacket is also missing – it's one of those oversized ones that they all seem to wear. Hers is green with a fur-lined hood.'

It's more detail than I'd expected. 'Would you mind if I had a look in her bedroom?'

James Hampton is tight-lipped as he gets up and walks towards the door. I follow him upstairs, then along the landing at the top, until he stops outside a half-open door. Feeling inside for the light switch, I turn it on. At first glance, it's a typical teenage girl's room – messy, with items of clothing strewn here and there, drawers not closed properly, the doors to the wardrobe left ajar. Along one of the walls is a white metal-framed bed, its pale pink covers disturbed, almost as though she's just got out of it.

This is the one part of this house that's Hollie's, and the smallest clue could help find her. Without moving anything, my eyes scan the bits of paper left on the pine desk where her laptop sits, then a few that she's stuck to the wall – photos and quotes alongside reminders to herself about homework.

After taking a few photos, I turn to James Hampton. 'Do you know if Hollie keeps a diary?'

When he shakes his head, I ask, 'Does she have a boyfriend?'

James Hampton hesitates, but only briefly. 'No.'

Going further in, I scrutinise the shelves that hold a range of books – young adult, classics, poetry, fantasy . . . One or two I recognise but the rest are unfamiliar. Taking more photographs, my eyes settle on what looks like one of James's books. Picking it up, I turn towards him. 'One of yours?'

He looks uncomfortable as he nods. 'Yes.'

My eyes linger on the laptop. 'It might help if we were to take this. Is that OK?' Not that it's optional. If Hollie's in danger, we need all the help we can get.

'Fine.' James speaks abruptly, then he adds, 'I don't have her phone. We think she must have it with her.'

'So I understand.' I pick up the laptop. 'Thank you. I think that's all – at least, for now.'

After reassuring the Hamptons that we'll be in touch, we leave them for the night. There's a covering of frost on my car and, as I get in and drive away, I feel myself shiver. James was on edge, haunted and stressed, while Stephanie was brittle. Judging from the size of the house, they must have once had a lot of money, but there are now signs of work needing doing – the wallpaper I noticed when I went in, the threadbare carpet on the stairs. But people have different priorities and maybe these things aren't important to them. Then I think about the dynamic between them. They were at odds over something – and in spite of what Stephanie said, I don't think it's about when they should have called the police.

The feeling in my gut grows stronger. James was too quiet, as though he was frightened of saying the wrong thing. He was awkward when I pulled out his book. There's also the reality none of us talked about. In this brutal cold, each passing hour without any word from Hollie makes it more and more likely something bad has happened to her.

Chapter Eight

Elise

Later that night, I'm unable to sleep, angry that Andrew hasn't returned, envisaging him in bed with *her*, before my thoughts turn back to Hollie. I try to imagine what could have happened to her. Losing her mother when she did, Hollie's had enough difficulties to deal with in her life. It seems incomprehensible that anyone would wish such a fragile girl harm. But I can't shake the feeling of foreboding that hangs over me. It was in James's face – and his voice, too, when he came here. He's used to Hollie's comings and goings, but even so, he's clearly worried.

I'm drifting off to sleep when the sound of Andrew's car coming up the drive stirs me. Rolling over so that my back is to him, I feign sleep when he comes in and gets undressed. After getting into bed, he starts to snore almost immediately. I wonder if he even knows that Hollie is missing.

As I lie in bed, sleep is impossible, my thoughts racing unstoppably, more worried than ever that something's happened to Hollie. It's another early start, a flight to Paris, this time.

Outside as I defrost my car, I imagine Hollie out in this cold, then James out of his mind with worry. I drive through the village slowly, looking out for her, even though I know it's unlikely I'll see her.

Chapter Nine

Jo

The next morning, the search gets under way at first light. It begins close to the Hamptons' home, which in daylight shows more evidence of the shabbiness I detected last night. The paint on the window frames is peeling, the garden overgrown, the unswept paths slippery with moss.

Beyond the house are a number of outbuildings – an unused stable block and another stone building it turns out has been crudely converted into an office that James uses. If she'd wanted to, Hollie could have been hiding in any one of these. No-one would have known.

But why would she hide? Searching each area meticulously takes most of the morning but uncovers nothing. In the stable block are unpacked boxes and old furniture, damp and coated with dust. James's office is no tidier. When he shows us in, he has the same uncomfortable look I saw last night.

'Hollie rarely comes in here.' He pauses, frowning. 'Have you spoken to her friend yet? Niamh Buckley?'

'Not yet.' My eyes scan the books and papers piled messily

on the shelves. 'I'll go round there later when she's back from school.'

'The schools are closed.' Clearly beside himself with worry, he speaks abruptly. 'There's too much black ice – the roads are dangerous.'

I hadn't known, but given the freezing temperatures, it makes sense. 'Did Hollie and Niamh go to the same school?'

'No.' He speaks tersely. 'Niamh goes to a private school outside the village. But all the closures were announced on the radio earlier.'

'I see. I will talk to Niamh, Mr Hampton,' I try to reassure him. 'Just as soon as I've finished here.'

*

It's an hour later when I turn into the Buckleys' drive. On first appearance, it's clear they live in one of the grander houses in the village. Grey and imposing behind the frost-covered garden, it looks stark and unwelcoming. There are no lights on, no signs of life inside, until a sudden movement catches my eye. Framed in an upstairs window, I see a face.

Niamh

The arctic air clings on, lowering temperatures and producing a fine layer of snow to carpet the ground, while freezing fog blankets out the sun, so that the world is silent for a few days, wrapped in bone-chilling cold. With the roads too icy to be safe, my school is closed.

After pulling on layers of warm clothes, I go for a walk through the village, thinking of a hundred places Hollie would have run off to – like her mother's grave, or with one of her school friends. As I think of her out in this cold, tears fill my eyes.

There are no lights in any of the windows. Even Ida Jones's cottage is in darkness. It's as though the village has descended into an eternal night. Then as I pass some of the villagers on the other side of the road, I realise. Anyone who isn't at work is probably helping look for Hollie.

Taking the path to the church, all the while I'm thinking of her, frozen leaves crunching under my footsteps as I walk. Then, as I come to the churchyard, my shiver isn't because of the cold. It's the rows of frozen headstones, frosted grey against the snow; the motionless bell in the tower, its single tone waiting to announce the passing of another soul; the knowledge that I'm surrounded by ghosts.

I force myself to open the church door. The latch is frozen shut, so that at first I think it's been locked, but then it opens suddenly. Inside there is no welcoming light, no hope, just the same dank cold and the sound of mice, as I imagine the ghosts closing in around me. Leaving the church without closing the door behind me, I run.

★

It's later when, from an upstairs window, I watch the police car pull into our drive. When the knock comes, I open the front door to find a policewoman and a younger policeman looking at me. The older woman, with brown hair, shows me her ID.

'I'm Detective Sergeant May. We're from Chichester Police.' She seems to look past me into the house. 'Are your parents at home?'

I shake my head. 'They're both at work.'

She nods. 'We're making inquiries into the whereabouts of Hollie Hampton. Can you tell us when you last saw her?'

I frown at her. Before I can answer, I hear a car turn into the drive. 'That's my mother.'

Both police officers turn to look as she parks, and DS May nods again. 'We'll wait here.'

Closing the door, I watch from the kitchen window as my mother gets out of her car. I frown. She had a flight today – it must have been a short one for her to be back so early. As she walks towards the police, her big woollen cardigan falls open, revealing her navy uniform dress and patterned scarf underneath.

As they come inside, I go upstairs. From the top of the staircase, I listen to them in the kitchen, hearing chairs being pulled out, jackets taken off, the kettle being switched on followed by the clink of mugs. Then there are voices, but they're too low to make out the words.

Ten minutes later, I'm in my bedroom when my mother's voice calls up to me. 'Niamh? Could you come downstairs?'

I'm gripped by nervousness as I make my way down, wondering why they want to talk to me, what they want to ask.

My mother's face is pale when I go into the kitchen. 'This is Detective Sergeant May and Constable Emerson. They're looking for Hollie, Niamh. They just want to ask you one or two questions.'

Their eyes follow me as I pull out an empty chair and sit down.

'Thank you, Niamh.' It's the woman, DS May, who speaks. 'I understand you and Hollie spend quite a bit of time together.'

I nod.

'When did you last see her?'

I think back to the last time Hollie was here. 'It was last weekend.' I glance at my mother.

'Did she mention anything unusual? Or talk about running away, perhaps? Was she behaving strangely?'

I frown, not sure how to explain that Hollie isn't like most people; that a lot of the time her behaviour can seem strange to others. At the same time, I'm frightened of saying the wrong thing, of them getting the wrong idea about her. 'Not especially. I mean, she didn't suggest she was about to do anything.'

My mother looks at me. 'I was working that day. The last time I saw her here was the same day I found her skipping school. She seemed upset about something. Do you know what it was, Niamh?'

There's an edge to her voice, as if she thinks I'm hiding something. Shaking my head, I keep my face blank. 'She didn't tell me.'

DS May frowns as she looks at me. 'This could be important, Niamh. Do you have any idea at all what might have been upsetting her?'

I shake my head. 'It's easy to tell when she's upset about something, but there's a lot Hollie keeps to herself.'

DS May is quiet for a moment. 'So what do the two of you like to talk about?'

I shrug. 'Stuff. School. Music.'

DS May nods slowly. 'Do you know if she has any other friends in the village?'

I shake my head again as my mother says quickly, 'There aren't any other teenagers in the village. There were the Morby twins, but they're nineteen now and at university.'

Turning to her electronic notebook, I watch DS May scrutinise a list, then pause with her finger under a line. 'The Morbys live at Apple Tree House?'

My mother nods.

DS May turns to my mother. 'Your husband, Mrs Buckley . . . He's a doctor, isn't he?'

'He's a GP at the Meadowside practice.'

I feel a flicker of anxiety as I watch the policewoman make a note against her list. Why does she need to speak to my father? Why does she need to speak to any of us? Then, as if she can read my mind, her eyes meet mine. 'It's routine, Niamh. There isn't any need for you to worry. We have to talk to everyone. It's surprising how the smallest detail can help.'

★

72

When the police drive away, my mother looks at me. 'You still haven't heard anything from Hollie?' Under her uniform-standard makeup, her skin is pale, her eyes anxious.

I shake my head. Doesn't she realise I'd have told her? But as I take in her face, I see that she's clinging to hope that the police are unnecessary, that Hollie is just going to turn up; that the nightmare will be over. But as my mother well knows, some nightmares are never over.

Chapter Ten

Elise

'The police were here earlier.' When Andrew comes in that evening, I watch his face carefully for a reaction to my announcement, and I see the split-second freeze before he continues as though the visit meant nothing. 'They wanted to know when we last saw Hollie. It isn't at all like her to run off like this.'

'That's nonsense, Elise, as you well know. That girl doesn't care who she upsets. Look at her now – wasting police time when they have better things to do.'

That he could be so utterly callous in the face of a teenage girl's disappearance appals me. But before I can respond, my phone buzzes. Seeing an unknown number flash up on my screen, my heart is in my mouth. Turning away, I answer it.

'Elise Buckley.' I listen for a moment, glance at Andrew, then walk a few steps away from him. 'I'm sorry . . . I can't talk right now. Can I call you back?' I speak as quietly as I can. Ending the call, I put my phone down, but when I turn around I find Andrew standing just behind me.

'My God.' His words are mocking, a look of faked disbelief

on his face. Surely he knows I see it for what it is, a deflection of attention away from him and onto me.

'Whatever you're thinking, it isn't that,' I say wearily, knowing there's nothing Andrew would like more than to point his finger and find me guilty, as if my having an affair would somehow validate his own extra-marital activities.

'Tell me who that was, then.' He barks it out, an order he expects me to obey. As he steps closer, his presence is suddenly menacing.

'No.' Shaking my head, I hold my phone behind my back.

'Give me your phone.' Holding his hand out, he tries to snatch it from me.

Slipping it into in my pocket, I manage to evade him. 'It's nothing to do with you, Andrew. I am not having an affair, as you very well know.' Summoning all my dignity, I turn away. 'Now if you'll excuse me . . .' As I start to walk away from him, I'm tense, holding my breath, knowing how much he hates being crossed. I've taken barely two steps before he grabs my arm, his fingers closing tightly, roughly pinching my skin. I spin around. 'How dare you!' Up close, his breath stinks of wine as I stand my ground. 'You're the one who's screwing around. You don't even care who knows it. You're despicable.' Hearing Niamh move around upstairs, I shake my arm free of his grip. 'There's only one reason I'm here – and that's Niamh,' I hiss. 'You do know that, don't you?'

'Lying bitch,' he mutters. 'There's no way you'd cope without me. And you love people knowing you're married to a doctor and living in this big, expensive house. Admit it, Elise.'

Hearing Niamh's footsteps on the stairs, I step back, flashing him a warning look. Then, as she comes into the kitchen, I muster the rigid self-control that comes from years of practice. 'I was just telling your father about the police being here earlier.'

My tone is deliberately light as I glance at Andrew. 'Oh – they asked where you work, so I gave them the address of the practice. I'm sure they'll be in touch at some point.'

I turn to Niamh again. 'I've made chicken curry. Can you set the table?'

Under my mask of calm, a torrent of anger is raging; at Andrew's threatening ways, his complete lack of respect for me. I should be upstairs packing, removing myself and Niamh from this toxic household, from Andrew's life, then calling the police, listing the abuse he inflicts on us. Being here isn't good for Niamh.

But then I remind myself why I've stayed, a sense of power-lessness overwhelming me. Andrew will do anything to wrestle Niamh away from me. He won't let her go. He's made that clear more than once. And to leave her with him . . . It will never be an option, meaning that as long as she's at home, I'm trapped.

*

It isn't until the next day, while Andrew's at work and Niamh is upstairs in her room, that I return the call that came yesterday, dialling the number with shaking hands, trying to sound matter-of-fact when an unfamiliar voice answers, waiting as I'm connected.

'Hello. It's Elise Buckley. I'm sorry I didn't get back to you before.' As the voice at the other end speaks, I feel my world slip sideways. 'Oh. Friday? I think that's fine.' Swallowing, I rack my brains as I try to remember when I'm working. 'Yes. Thank you.'

After ending the call, I turn to find Niamh standing there, watching me. I wonder how much of the conversation she's overheard, but I can't read her face. 'Are you OK, Niamh?'

Going to the fridge, she nods. After getting out a can of Coke, she says quietly, 'Are you and Dad getting a divorce?'

My response is too quick, my gasp too loud. 'Of course we're not. What makes you think that?'

She shrugs and then turns towards me in a single fluid movement that reminds me of Hollie. 'So what was that phone call?' When I don't reply, she goes on. 'It isn't just that. You argue all the time, Dad's never here, and when he is, he eats on his own.' I'm astonished when I see tears glitter in her eyes.

Walking towards her, I put my hands firmly on her shoulders. 'We are not getting a divorce.' Hating that she's upset, I try to reassure her. 'I know things seem a bit difficult just now. But we'll get over it. You mustn't worry.' Then I pause. 'Have you spoken to your father about this?'

'Yes.' Her answer shocks me. I can't believe that she's talked to Andrew at all, let alone that she's talked to him before me.

I stare at her, incredulous. 'What did he say?'

She shrugs again. 'Not much . . .' She breaks off and her grey eyes look piercingly into mine. 'He laughed. Then he said you'd never leave him.'

As she says that, I feel something break inside me. He's her father, yet he uses her mercilessly, doing what I've always dreaded he'd do – drawing Niamh into his cat-and-mouse games with me. In that moment, I've never hated him more. I imagine him laughing, unkindly, cruelly, knowing he doesn't care what Niamh sees, how she feels. He doesn't protect her or look out for her. The only person who can do that is me. 'He's right. I won't.' As I gaze steadily at my daughter, the web I'm caught in tightens.

Niamh's nod is barely perceptible as I change the subject. 'I had an email from your school. If the roads don't freeze again, they'll open the day after tomorrow.' I pause. 'Have you heard anything from Hollie?'

'No.' Niamh walks over to the window, gazing out. 'Where do you think she is?'

Seeing her body start to shake, I go over and put an arm around her, both of us standing there watching a flurry of snowflakes in the glow of the outside light. 'I don't know. It's only been four days. Most likely she's at someone's house somewhere, if she's run away.' I break off because no-one knows for sure where Hollie is and because in these freezing temperatures if she's without shelter, the more time that passes, the more worrying her absence becomes.

'I'm scared.' Niamh's voice trembles as she wraps skinny arms around her body. 'I want to know where she is.'

'I know.' I feel exactly the same. 'How do you and Hollie usually keep in touch?'

'Messenger,' Niamh says briefly. 'Sometimes Instagram. But, you know . . . Mostly, she just turns up.'

'Yes.' That's exactly how it is with Hollie. She'll just arrive, unplanned, staying a few minutes or a few hours. 'Listen, I know you're worried. We all are. But the police are doing everything they can.' I place an arm around her shoulders. 'She'll be OK. We have to believe that she will turn up.'

But it's getting less likely. And not all missing teenagers are found. The headline I read on one of my last flights comes back to me. *Only Ten Per Cent of People are Good.* If it's anywhere near accurate, it's a chilling assessment of humanity and what it's capable of. People can be cruel and ruthless, thinking only of their own needs, while too many lives are cut short for the most hideous reasons. I swallow, not liking how that makes me feel. Right now, Hollie's life could be in anyone's hands.

Chapter Eleven

Jo

And so it goes on, officers knocking on doors throughout the village and searching gardens, woods, fields, and farmyards; finding nothing of any significance.

After leaving the Buckleys' house, I turn to Emerson. 'Everyone's hinting – though no-one's actually saying – that something was going on with Hollie. What Elise Buckley said, about her missing school and coming around to their house upset. Then Niamh Buckley saying how Hollie often didn't want to talk about things . . . If she's telling the truth, that is.' I'm thoughtful for a moment. 'We're talking about a teenaged girl who lost her mother and whose relationship with her stepmother is adequate, though it doesn't sound like it's any stronger than that. It sounds like Hollie's emotionally fragile.' I think back to her photograph, and to Stephanie Hampton's assessment of Hollie as a tortured soul. 'We need to talk to more of the villagers. In places like this, it's impossible to keep secrets. Someone somewhere will know something.'

'Maybe she decided to move away for reasons we don't yet

know? Either way, if she'd decided to run off, she could be miles away by now,' Emerson says.

I look at Emerson. 'How? There are no buses through here.'

'A friend could have picked her up. Or she could have walked and caught a bus.'

I shake my head. 'It doesn't seem that she had any close friends. And it's too cold for her to have walked far. My guess is she's still around here somewhere. But we should check out the buses. Can you get the DI on the phone?' Pulling over in a lay-by, I'm silent as he dials.

I take Emerson's phone, waiting for the DI to answer. 'Sir? Nothing yet. I think it's likely she's still somewhere around here – otherwise one of the villagers would have seen her – and it's probably a long shot, but we need to check out which buses come near Abingworth.'

'I'll get someone to check. Have you said anything to the Hamptons about a press release?'

'Not yet.' It's a fine line to tread, gauging whether it would turn anything up, because once the news is out that a teenage girl has disappeared, the press will be all over the village.

'Maybe have a word? If we don't find anything soon, we need to get on it.'

'Yes, sir.'

Switching off the phone, I turn to Emerson and notice the footpath marked a little ahead of the car, where a sign points to the church. I nod towards it. 'The village church. Shall we take a look?'

Getting out, Emerson turns up the collar of his coat as I lock the car, then do the same. The air is sharp, the path frozen as we make our way along it towards the churchyard. As the trees open out, ahead of us the headstones are grey against the white of the frost.

The church is small, dating back about eight hundred years according to a small metal plaque, with a narrow tower in which a single bell hangs. I try the door, surprised when I find it unlocked, but a search of the sparse interior yields nothing. Closing the door behind me as we exit, we've started walking back towards the car when my phone buzzes.

'May.' As the voice at the other end speaks, the blood drains from my face.

I turn to Emerson. 'They've found her.'

★

To get to Park House on the opposite edge of the village, we double back past the Buckleys' house before taking a right turn into Greyfriars Lane. Almost immediately, a police car comes into view parked up ahead. After pulling over behind it, we get out.

Sarah Collins is waiting by the intercom in front of locked metal gates. 'The owners are away. There's a caretaker who has a key, apparently, so we're trying to get in touch with him.'

Shivering in the cold, I pull my coat tightly around me. 'Where is she?'

Sarah's voice is grim. 'In the gardens. When we couldn't get any reply from the house, Milsom and Edwards found a way in through the woods – there's a fence that's easy to climb over. I assume that's how Hollie got in.'

'Can you show us?'

We walk in silence further down the lane, and then Sarah turns in to a stretch of woodland. After a couple of minutes, we reach a fence. We climb over into the large gardens, and I try to establish where we are in relation to the rest of the village.

Glimpsing a roof through the trees, I frown. 'Is that the Buckleys' house?'

'I think so. She's just through here,' Sarah says quietly.

All the time we were searching, there'd been hope. But as I cross the gardens in front of the old farmhouse, then follow Sarah through a hedge into a smaller enclosed part of the garden, all hope is gone. I notice her hair first – long and spread out around her as she lies face down in the pool in front of us.

'She was under the leaves, ma'am.' As Milsom speaks, I notice the piles of leaves scraped back around the edges of the pool. 'She must have fallen in. She was invisible until we cleared them as the water had frozen over her and the leaves had settled on top.'

As I stand there, I shiver. She's wearing the jeans and jacket Stephanie described, but only as Milsom speaks do I notice the ice encasing her body, her hair, so that only the back of her head protrudes above it.

'We should inform her parents.' Sarah's voice is flat.

'Not yet. We need to be sure of how this happened.' Hearing voices, I turn towards the house where I see two more officers making their way across the garden towards us. 'They must have found a key.' Two more men come into view carrying a stretcher.

There's silence as we stand there while Hollie's body is photographed before the ice is broken and it's removed from the water.

'I'll go and see her parents.' Sarah nods as I speak, her eyes grave.

Emerson comes with me as I make my way back to my car, steeling myself. Many things about this job aren't easy, but the worst of all is breaking bad news. When you tell a parent that their child isn't coming back, you know that you're destroying their life as they knew it – their hopes, their dreams for the future.

When we pull up outside the Hamptons' house, I turn to Emerson. 'I'll do this alone.' The Hamptons don't need an audience for their grief. Getting out, I walk down the path to the front door, but Stephanie opens it before I get there. When she takes in my silence, then my expression, a stricken look crosses her face and her hand goes to her mouth. Turning around, she runs back in, calling out to her husband.

'James. James . . .'

Going inside, I find them huddled together in the hallway. 'Please,' I say quietly, closing the door behind me. 'Can we sit down?' I gesture towards the sitting room, where only last night they were telling me about Hollie. All of us clinging on to hope that we'd find her alive, little knowing that hope was futile, because from the way the ice had frozen over her, it was clear Hollie had been dead for some while.

'Where is she?' James's voice is harsh and shaky at the same time.

'We found her in the grounds of Park House.' I speak slowly, quietly. 'She was in the pool.'

Stephanie's in denial. 'No . . . She's not . . .'

'I'm so sorry.' I pause to let my words sink in, at the same time watching for any sign they already know. If Hollie's death turns out to be suspicious, they will be suspects. 'She'd obviously been there for a while. There was nothing we could do.' We've all considered worst-case scenarios, but when it happens, nothing prepares you for the shock. Their faces are disbelieving, stricken with pain as they struggle to take it in, trying to twist my words, make them into anything other than the truth.

When James gets up, it's as though he's physically shrunk. 'I want to see her.' His face is ashen. 'Please take me to her.'

'We'll need you to identify her body in due course but not just now. We'll be carrying out an investigation into how she died and exactly when. It's entirely possible that it was accidental, but we have to rule out the possibility that it wasn't.'

'But why was she there?' Stephanie cries. 'She doesn't even know the Marinos. She had no reason to be in their garden.'

'It's my fault.' James's face is grey, his body rigid with shock as he stares at me. 'It's all my fault.'

I watch him, knowing this is a natural response when a parent loses a child, that self-blame and guilt are common emotions at times like this. 'I think we'll find it was an accident,' I say gently, feeling my heart twist as Stephanie takes his arm. As always, imagining how it would feel to be a parent who'd have done anything they could to protect their child.

'But I knew something was going on,' he mutters.

Tears roll down Stephanie's face as she tries to reason with him. 'Hollie could be impossible,' she says desolately. 'We both know that. You didn't do anything wrong. You couldn't have known anything like this would happen.'

★

When I get out to the car, Emerson's sitting in the driving seat. 'You told them?'

I nod. 'They're devastated. Heartbroken.' How can they be anything else, when in the last few minutes, their entire lives have been shattered? 'We have to find out what happened.' Experience has taught me that when you're faced with such a pointless, tragic death, with a broken, grieving family, you have to focus on finding answers.

Niamh

I know before anyone tells me. Hollie isn't coming back.

From my window, I see the single police car pass slowly through the village, the unmarked van directly behind it sending a chill rippling through me.

I've seen one before.

It's the kind of van they send when someone's died.

Chapter Twelve

Elise

It's Ida Jones who tells me, later that evening, that the police have found Hollie's body.

'I'm so terribly sorry to be calling you, Elise.' Ida sounds distressed. 'But I thought you'd want to know, what with her and young Niamh being so close. It's such a tragedy.'

'*No . . .*' Shock hits me, followed by a rushing in my ears. As Ida goes on talking, I interrupt. 'Wait . . . I can't take this in.'

'Such a terrible thing . . .' Ida's voice trembles. 'To think of that poor young girl . . .'

'I have to go.' My hands are shaking. 'I'm sorry, Ida. I need to tell Niamh.'

In a daze, I go to find Niamh. She's upstairs, lying on her bed with her iPad in front of her, earphones plugged in, but when she sees me, she takes them out.

'Niamh? Honey?'

Whether it's the *honey*, or the tone of my voice, I can tell from the way she stiffens, she knows something's very wrong. As her eyes meet mine, I contemplate the enormity of what

I'm about to tell her, saying it as gently as I can. 'The police have found Hollie.'

I watch her eyes widen as my words sink in; her gasp of shock followed by denial. 'Is she OK?'

But I'm shaking my head. 'Niamh . . . She isn't. I don't know what happened . . .' Going over to the bed, I sit next to her, the words sticking in my throat. 'I'm so sorry. Hollie's dead.'

'No.' Niamh springs up, her voice tight, high-pitched. 'She can't be.' Going over to the window, she stands with her back to me, her shoulders hunched, her denial absolute, but then, it's her bed that Hollie was sprawled on just days ago, her company Hollie sought out when she needed an ally. Even to me, what's happened is incomprehensible. As she starts to shake, I go over and put my arms around her, trying to absorb the sobs racking her.

'I need to know what happened,' she mumbles through her tears. 'Poor Hollie . . .'

I keep my arms around Niamh, tears rolling down my face onto her hair. 'Ida didn't say. She probably didn't know.' Pausing, I wipe my face with one of my hands. 'It's terrible, Niamh . . . So sad . . .'

As Niamh's shaking intensifies, I realise she's in shock. 'Why don't you come downstairs with me? I'll make us some tea,' I say anxiously, not wanting to leave her alone. Hollie's death is too close. I can't help thinking – as no doubt every other parent would – *what if it had been my child*?

I think of James, trying to imagine what he's going through. After losing his wife, it seems unthinkable that he's lost his daughter, too.

★

Later, I'm in the kitchen when Andrew comes in. After taking off his coat, he pours himself a large whisky instead of his usual glass of wine.

'I imagine you've heard about Hollie, Andrew?'

He takes a large slug from his glass. 'Yes. Her body was picked up this afternoon.'

I'm incredulous. It stands to reason that the medical practice would have heard, but at the very least, I'd have expected him to call me. 'And you didn't think to tell me? What if Niamh had heard from someone else?'

'I was too busy.' Speaking impatiently, he starts towards the door. 'I've had a hell of a day. If you don't mind, I'm going to sit down.'

'Just a minute, Andrew.' My voice is sharp. 'Do you know what happened to her?'

I watch warily as he stiffens, then slowly turns around. 'She drowned,' he says curtly. 'There'll be a post-mortem. Until then, there's no way of knowing whether it was an accident or not.'

An image of Hollie's lifeless body comes to me, her long hair fanned out around her under the water. I feel the blood drain from my face. 'Where did it happen?'

'In the grounds of Park House, apparently. The Marinos are in Italy, so God only knows what she was doing there.'

But as he speaks, my skin prickles. From one of our spare rooms, you can just about make that house out through the trees. 'I've told Niamh that Hollie's been found, but none of the details.'

Andrew raises his eyebrows. 'I suppose you ought to tell her, then. Or I will. But not right now.'

'I'll talk to her.' I don't trust Andrew to break it to her gently. Heavy-hearted, I go up to her room again, knocking softly on the door before pushing it open. As I tell her what Andrew told me, it feels as though I'm peeling away a layer of her childhood.

I sit with her, my arm around her shoulders as more tears pour down her cheeks. I'm guessing the police will be back at some point, that there will be more questions about Hollie that only Niamh can answer. 'Niamh?' I stroke her hair off her face. 'Do you have any idea why Hollie might have gone there?'

Niamh shakes her head. 'I've no idea,' she says tearfully. 'But it doesn't matter, does it? She's gone. Nothing can bring her back.' She collapses into more heart-rending sobbing.

★

Shock ricochets through the village as the news spreads the next day. Everyone here has children in their lives – grandchildren, nieces, nephews – and teenagers aren't supposed to be found dead. Meanwhile, the press start arriving, wandering around the lanes in search of the story behind Hollie's death.

'If anyone approaches you, just tell them you don't know anything. Or walk away,' I tell Niamh. 'And if you're here alone, don't answer the door to anyone you don't know.'

Niamh's face is pale as she nods. 'OK.'

Fortunately, I'm there later on, when a couple of strangers I guess are probably reporters walk up the drive and knock at the door. As Niamh appears at the top of the stairs, they knock again, then one of their faces peers in through the kitchen window. Seeing Niamh's look of fear as she shrinks back is the last straw.

Going to the door, I open it to find a middle-aged man holding his phone, obviously ready to record me, a younger woman standing behind him. 'You're both trespassing. I'd like you to leave.'

He ignores me. 'We'd just like a quick chat about the missing girl. They've found her body, haven't they? Can you tell us a little about . . .'

Folding my arms, I glare at him, incensed by their invasion of our privacy. 'If you don't leave right now, I'm calling the police. Get out.'

'All right . . .' Holding up his hands, he nods to his colleague and the pair of them slope away.

Once they've gone, I close the gates onto the drive. They're heavy, and inconvenient, but the least of my concerns. Knowing they'll keep the press out, I lock them.

★

The next day, I call work and arrange to take a couple of days' unpaid leave. I can't go away, leaving Niamh here alone. It isn't just the thought of the press hanging around, it's the noticeable impact of Hollie's death. While Niamh's never been demonstrative, she seems to have closed up completely, the extent of her silent calm unnerving me.

I have the strangest sensation, as though time itself has been paused. It's a morning when I should have been on my way to Zurich, when Niamh should have gone back to school; a morning that, in the aftermath of Hollie's death, the minutes have slowed, our lives changing around us invisibly – irrevocably – as we wait to hear more. It takes until the afternoon for the police to arrive. Opening the door, I hesitate before I recognise DS May from last time. Instead of a uniform, she's wearing a black, well-cut coat and lace-up boots.

'Mrs Buckley? May we come in?' Behind her is a uniformed police officer.

'Of course.' I stand back to let them in, then close the door behind them. 'Would you like to come through to the kitchen?'

'Thank you. This is Sergeant Collins.' DS May gestures towards her colleague. 'I appreciate this probably isn't an easy time, but could we talk to you and your daughter?'

'By all means.' I gesture towards the kitchen table. 'Do you want to take a seat? I'll find Niamh.'

'Before you do, Mrs Buckley . . .' DS May speaks quietly '. . . I'm not sure whether you know, but Hollie drowned. You might want to tell her first, as she might find the news rather distressing.'

'We do know.' Taking in their surprised glances, I add, 'My husband is the local GP. He told me the night before last.' I start walking towards the stairs, calling up. 'Niamh? Could you come down here for a minute?'

As I look up, her pinched face appears in her bedroom doorway.

'The police are here again.'

Niamh comes closer, a worried look on her face as she peers through the bannisters. 'Have they said any more about what happened to her?'

Shaking my head, I go up the stairs towards her. 'No more than we already know. They just said they'd like to talk to both of us.'

Niamh's intake of breath is sharp and I wonder if it's too much for her.

'If you're up to it?' I look at her anxiously. 'I can tell them if you're not.'

Wordlessly she nods, then slowly comes downstairs. When we go into the kitchen, I pull out a chair near mine for her to sit on. 'This is Sergeant Collins and Detective Sergeant May – you met last time?' I remind Niamh, nodding towards the woman.

'Hello, Niamh.' DS May speaks gently. 'I'm so very sorry about your friend. We hoped we could talk to you some more about her as you might know something that could help us find out what happened to her.'

'OK.' In front of the two policewomen, Niamh seems younger, smaller, as though the news of Hollie's death has reduced her in some way. Then I realise she has been reduced; in a village of adults, the two who were allies are now one.

DS May's digital pen hovers above her notebook. 'How long were the two of you friends?'

Niamh glances towards me. 'Two years?'

I nod. 'About that.'

DS May frowns slightly. 'You didn't go to the same school, did you?'

'No.' Niamh's discomfort is obvious, her hands in little fists, clenched on the table in front of her.

'Did you know any of Hollie's other friends?' DS May's eyes scan her notes.

Niamh shakes her head. 'She didn't talk about anyone. I don't think she had that many.'

'Any boyfriends?'

Niamh glances at me quickly before shaking her head. 'She didn't have one.'

'How about old boyfriends? Was there anyone she might have upset, or who wanted her back?'

'No.' An anxious look crosses Niamh's face.

DS May turns to look at me. 'Mrs Buckley, I know we've been over some of this last time, but how well would you say you knew Hollie?'

How well do any of us know each other – and how do you measure a relationship? 'I've known her for years – and she's spent a fair amount of time at our house since she and Niamh became friends. I also used to see her around the village. I go running,' I explain. 'Sometimes, weeks could go by without a sign of her. But she's a teenager. I never thought of it as strange.'

'You know her parents?'

I nod. 'Not particularly well, but enough to talk to them in the pub, if our paths happen to cross. Stephanie – her stepmother – is a hairdresser and now and then I've been to her salon. I've been there recently, as it happens – but like I said, we're acquaintances rather than friends.'

'Hollie got on well with them?'

I frown. If she wants a window into their family life, she's asking the wrong person. 'As far as I know, but I'm probably not the best person to ask.'

DS May looks at Niamh. 'Niamh? Did Hollie say anything to you about her relationships with her father and stepmother?'

Niamh shakes her head.

DS May is silent for a moment. 'Hollie's body was found in the grounds of Park House. Do you have any idea what she might have been doing there?'

Niamh's gaze drifts towards the window before she looks back at the policewoman. 'She used to go into everyone's gardens. She liked to find her own way in. She never did anything bad. It was more like she was doing it because she could.'

DS May looks interested. 'You think she got a kick out of it?'

'Kind of.' Niamh pauses, thinking. 'Part of it was she didn't like being told what to do. But mostly, I think she just wanted to feel free.'

DS May looks at her closely. 'Did you ever go with her?'

The hint of pink in her cheeks and Niamh's look of alarm give her away.

DS May tries to reassure her. 'Niamh . . . you're not in any trouble, I promise you. All we're trying to establish is what Hollie was like, what she did, who she saw . . .'

Niamh hesitates, then speaks quickly. 'The other day, when I was with her, she climbed a gate up Furze Lane into a field. But that's all we did. I did try to stop her,' Niamh adds. 'The gate said "private" on it. She said we weren't doing any harm. And we weren't.' Glancing at me, she folds her arms.

'Can you tell us when that was?'

Niamh frowns. 'About ten days ago? I'm not sure.'

DS May turns to me. 'Mrs Buckley, you said earlier you sometimes saw Hollie when you were out running . . . Where was that, usually?'

'I don't always run along the same route, Detective Sergeant.' I pause. 'But quite often, I'd see her in the churchyard.'

DS May pushes a strand of her long hair behind her ear. 'Didn't that strike you as a macabre place for a teenager to hang out?'

'Yes . . .' I hesitate. 'I suppose it was. But Hollie had a vivid imagination. She lost her birth mother eight years ago and though she isn't buried there, I think there was something comforting to Hollie about the idea of being among ghosts.'

It's the same reason any of us go there. To remind ourselves of loved ones who have gone before us. 'It isn't as strange as it may sound,' I add, then falter as she looks at me oddly. 'I'm not sure what else I can tell you.'

It seems as though we've reached an impasse; DS May stands up. 'Just to warn you, the press are hanging around. Unfortunately it's what happens when a story gets out. I strongly advise against talking to them.'

'They've already been here,' I tell her. 'I told them they were trespassing and asked them to leave.'

DS May nods. 'Good. I'll leave you my card. Should you

think of anything about Hollie, however small, I'd appreciate you calling me.'

After they go out to their car, Niamh stands at the kitchen window watching them leave, then, without saying anything, turns and goes upstairs to her room. Left alone, I swallow the lump in my throat. It's hard for her, and even harder for Hollie's parents. Hollie's death will affect all of us.

Chapter Thirteen

Elise

With Hollie's body being held until a post-mortem has been carried out, no date for her funeral has been set and so a week and a day after she was found, instead of the handful of regulars, most of the villagers make their way down the frozen footpaths to gather in the church, while parishioners from outside the village join us and I'm relieved when Mia, one of Niamh's school friends, squeezes into the pew next to her. The church is packed and the service poignant, a reminder of how transient life is, after which the vicar delivers a more personal message.

'More than ever, we need to look out for one another. Small communities like ours are rare places. At times like this, we must stand united. We should all feel safe enough to let our children roam the footpaths. Our children should, in turn, feel safe doing so. We have to find a way to not let this tragic accident destroy the sense of security that's always existed here.'

It's a naïvely optimistic message – and inappropriate, I can't help thinking. We don't yet know if Hollie's death was an accident. Whether or not it was, it will be time, rather than faith, that will lead people to feeling safe around here again.

As we file outside, Della catches my arm. 'Andrew not here?' Raising a questioning eyebrow, she seems to lack her usual sparkle.

'He's playing golf.' He's the only person I know who hasn't felt the impact of Hollie's death. I watch surprise register on Della's face.

Now and then I've come close to confiding in her, but it's impossible to explain, even to her, why I tolerate Andrew. My heart twists in sympathy as I see James across the churchyard, his face shadowed with grief. But it seems that even here, there is no escape from the press and as he stands there, a man walks towards him, raising a camera. James turns away in the nick of time but then another man I vaguely recognise, smartly dressed in a dark coat, steps in and after what looks like a confrontation, the cameraman leaves.

'Bloody press.' As the man in the coat turns back towards James, I'm curious. 'Who is that talking to James?'

'Phil Mason.' Della's silent for a moment. 'You'd think the press would have the decency to stay away, wouldn't you?'

'I'm not sure they have a moral code.' I frown as I study this Phil Mason. He's of average height, younger than James, and like many people around here, wealthy, judging from the winter tan and neatly styled hair, the cut of his coat, his polished shoes. After a brief exchange with James, Mason walks away. 'Poor James. It makes you wonder how much pain one person can bear.'

'He isn't the only person who's lost someone.' Della's eyes drift towards Stephanie, standing a few feet behind him. 'I hope it isn't much longer before we find out what happened to Hollie. The police are treating her death as suspicious, aren't they?'

'All I know is they're carrying out a post-mortem. I suppose we have to wait and see what that shows.' I glance at my watch, glad to have an excuse to get away. 'I should go. I'm working this afternoon. I'll catch you another time.' Kissing her on the cheek, I start looking for Niamh, finding her with Mia. 'I'm sorry, Niamh – I have to go home and get ready for work. I check in at one. Do you want to walk back with me?'

'Can I go to Mia's?' Niamh looks at me anxiously.

'Of course – if that's OK with your mother, Mia?' I'm grateful not to be leaving her alone. She and Mia aren't particularly close, but right now, Niamh needs company.

Mia nods. 'She did say it would be OK. I asked her on the way here.'

'OK . . .' I glance at Niamh. 'I'll call your father – he can text you to arrange a time to pick you up.'

*

Three hours later, I'm sitting on my crew seat as the aircraft takes off for Nice. Thankfully, the short flight is unadventurous, the passengers undemanding, and for the few hours in the calm of the half-empty cabin, Hollie's death seems far away. In the south of France, the sky is blue and we open the aircraft door to warm air and French accents, but as I drive home after the return flight, and turn into the village, it comes flooding back.

Andrew's car is in the drive. After I park and go inside, the sound of the television filters through from the sitting room. I slip off my shoes and am on my way upstairs to look for Niamh when I hear Andrew's voice.

'For God's sake, you know I can't.' His voice is scathing as he talks on his phone, seemingly unaware I've just come in.

'She won't say anything.' There's a silence before he laughs

101

cynically. 'How do I know? For Christ's sake, I'm married to her. Of course I know!'

Unable to stop myself, I walk over to the sitting room and push the door open, pretending I don't know he's on the phone. 'Did you collect Niamh, Andrew?' I speak louder than usual, deliberately interrupting.

Turning around, frowning, he points to his phone. I ignore him. 'Niamh?'

'Just a moment,' he mutters into his phone, then covers the mouthpiece with his hand. 'How dare you!'

'I would have thought our daughter's whereabouts would be your highest priority right now.' I stare at him coolly, my meaning clear. 'Particularly in light of Hollie's death. Did you even read my text?'

I've caught him out. He hasn't bothered. 'One of us needs to go and get her,' I say pointedly, gazing at the almost empty bottle of wine on the table in front of him. 'I imagine that's going to be me.'

I was hoping to have a bath and put on pyjamas, but suddenly I've no desire to be in the same house as Andrew. Without waiting for a reply, I walk out to the kitchen and put on my shoes just as a car pulls up outside. Hearing a door slam, dread fills me that it could be the press again, but seconds later, Niamh appears through the door. 'Mia's dad dropped me. He said he didn't mind.' Her face is brighter than this morning, pink from the cold, her voice lighter and less troubled than it has been in days, weeks even. My stomach churns at how obvious it is that even for a few hours, it's been good for her to be away from this house.

'Your father got held up.' As always, I make an excuse for Andrew's selfishness. 'Have you had a good day?'

'Yeah.' But at the mention of Andrew, her face clouds over.

'I'm so sorry he didn't text you. I only got in a few minutes ago and I was just about to come out and get you.'

'It's OK.'

I watch her eyes lower. She knows I'm lying about Andrew, that I'm pretending everything is fine, even though, especially in light of Hollie's death, Andrew's selfishness is breath-taking. My stomach twists more tightly. Niamh misses none of it. Two minutes in this house, and the lightness is already leaving her.

*

On Monday morning, life resumes a semblance of normality when Andrew goes to work and Niamh goes to school. For once, there are no harsh words or arguments. Instead, an odd sense of calm pervades the house – one that fills me with unease.

Pulling on a sweatshirt over my running gear, I head out for a run, taking a route that brings me past the Hamptons' house. There are no lights on in the windows. Closed and dark, the only sign of life is the single police car parked outside.

Just beyond their drive, the press are lurking. Anger flares in me that they can be so insensitive. Crossing the road to get away from them, one of them calls out to me as I pass. I make out one word – *Hollie* – running faster, not bothering to reply.

Further away from the village, I turn into the pine woods, taking the wide path between trees that stretch either side of me as far as I can see in neat, regimented rows. The air is cold and dry, without wind; just the occasional cry from a passing bird breaking the silence.

Beneath my feet, the ground is cushioned by a carpet of pine needles and I run faster for a couple of miles before slowing to a walk, pausing to catch my breath and stretch for a couple of minutes.

Breaking into a run again, I see a car parked a few hundred yards ahead. It's familiar and as I watch the driver get out, I recognise James. Hanging back, I watch another car come into sight, one I don't recognise. Not the press again, surely?

As the car slows down and stops, James goes over, leaning down to talk through the open window with the driver. I'm too far away to hear what they're saying, but from his body language, the exchange appears to become hostile. Suddenly it escalates further and James starts shouting obscenities, then thumps his fist several times on the top of the car.

Behind me, a pheasant takes flight, shattering the silence with its distinctive call. Momentarily distracted, James fleetingly glances towards me. Quickly shrinking back into the shadows, I stay out of sight as I carry on watching.

After a couple of minutes, James is forced to step back as the other car drives away. As he paces back to his car, I wonder if this could in some way be connected to Hollie's death. But if James suspected anyone, he'd have talked to the police. This must be about something else. But the question is, what?

Uncertain, I stay out of sight. I haven't spoken to James since Hollie died and after what I just witnessed, now isn't the time. As he gets into his car and drives away, I slowly come out from under the trees, then as his car disappears out of sight, I break into a run.

Carrying on, I head in the same direction the two cars took. Then, just before the track meets the main road, I see James's car again, parked to one side. Through the window it looks as though he's on his phone – pleading with someone – clearly upset. But then, he's lost his daughter and has every reason to be. As I run past, I raise a hand in greeting, but when he sees me, he looks horrified, lifting his hand briefly in response before looking away.

Living in a house the press are hanging around, with the police omnipresent, in a village where suddenly everyone's watching him, he's clearly come out here to find privacy, not expecting anyone to see him. It's understandable.

There could be any number of explanations for what I saw – and anyway, it's none of my business. There's every reason for his behaviour to be erratic. The death of their child breaks a parent's belief in the order of everything. For a moment I imagine how broken-hearted he must feel. Despite the flurry of well-wishers and neighbourly support around them in these early days, in their grief, James and Stephanie are alone.

Chapter Fourteen

Jo

For the Hamptons, as for us all, it's been over a week of waiting to find out more about how Hollie died. I try to imagine how James Hampton must be feeling. I've never lost a child, but I do know how it feels when the unthinkable happens and your life shatters into a million pieces. For him, however, I imagine it's far worse.

First thing on Monday morning, I wake up to overcast skies from which the first drops of rain are falling as I get into my car. By the time I reach the office, it's become a downpour.

Shaking the rain off my coat, I make my way to my office. I've been there less than five minutes when the DI calls, and my blood runs cold as he explains that the injuries to Hollie's head don't correspond with bruising she would have sustained from a fall.

'We're still checking it out, but there's a wound to the front of her head that couldn't possibly have come from falling against the edge of the pool. It doesn't look like her death was an accident. You'd better get back to the Hampton house. It's likely we're looking for a murderer.'

Chapter Fifteen

Elise

The cause of Hollie's death has yet to be announced, but when news of the post-mortem findings slip out, Andrew at least has the grace to call me.

'I had a call from the coroner's office. Apparently Hollie had injuries to her head. They're opening a murder inquiry.'

'God.' Shock hits me, just as it did when her body was found, only this time, it's laced with fear. I'd imagined Hollie missing her step, hitting her head on the side of the pool as she fell. Not someone killing her. 'How can they be sure?'

'There's an injury to the side of her head, which would be likely if she'd simply fallen, but they've found a second. It's most likely someone struck her with a sharp object, then she hit her head a second time as she fell into the pool. I have to go, Elise.' He speaks coldly. 'I have patients.'

★

I'm still struggling to take in the news of Hollie's death when it's time for me to tell Niamh later on. She listens in silence,

109

then gets up and pushes past me on her way to the bathroom, making it just in time before she throws up.

When she comes back, her face is ashen, her body slumped as I put my arms around her, wishing I could take the pain away. Lowering my head to rest against hers, I hate what this is doing to her, but there's nothing I can say to change this most brutal of realities.

She should be going to school tomorrow, but after this latest shock, knowing that word will soon get around, I want to protect her. As we stand there, the breeze ripples through her open window, the silence only broken by the gradual crescendo from outside as the rain starts.

★

Wanting to be home for Niamh, I take another week's unpaid leave. As the rain falls relentlessly in the days that follow, I realise how little I know about the people around me. I've spoken to Ida Jones now and then, but never about anything other than the most trivial matters, and when I see our other neighbours, conversation is superficial, the briefest of exchanges. None of us open our hearts, bare our souls. Each of us has our own lives, just as each of us has secrets. Even Della, whom I'm closest to, only sees what I choose to share with her, as I hide the miserable truth from everyone.

Nearly two weeks after Hollie's body was found, a police car pulls up outside the house. As DS May gets out and hurries through the rain, I go to open the door.

This time, she's alone. 'Sorry to turn up without warning. Do you mind if I come in?'

'Of course.' I'm already standing back to let her in. 'Can I take your jacket?'

'Thanks.'

I wait as she slips it off before I hang it near a radiator, then lead her through to the kitchen. 'Do sit down.' Her long hair is rolled into a twist, and in a pale blouse and black trousers, she appears coolly confident. As I sit across the table from her, I feel I'm under scrutiny, uncomfortable even before she speaks.

'What a day. Still, at least it puts the press off. Have they been back here since last time?'

'No.' I frown. She didn't come here to talk about the press.

Leaning forward in her chair, she looks at me. 'I wanted to talk to you about Niamh's friendship with Hollie. Was there anything about Hollie that made you concerned about them spending so much time together? It's just that we're getting a picture of quite a troubled teenager.'

I'd never considered Hollie as anything but harmless, but I understand DS May is trying to establish her own picture of a girl she'll never meet. 'No more than anyone else.' I meet her eyes. 'I liked that she had a friend in the village. Hollie could be flighty, I suppose, but I didn't worry about them spending time together. Niamh's fourteen. You can't watch over children forever – you have to let them grow up, be themselves. I think that's one of the reasons she and Hollie got on. However unhappy she was feeling, Hollie was always herself. I think Niamh admired that.'

DS May frowns. 'Would you say she was often unhappy?'

I sigh. 'Not particularly. We're all different, Detective Sergeant. Hollie could be volatile, emotional, high-strung. She was smart, too, but I think it's fair to say she thrived on having a degree of drama in her life.' It's how I'd always seen her. She wasn't the kind of person to be content with a quiet life. She should have been an actress.

'What about her father?' This time, DS May looks openly

111

curious. 'Can you tell me anything about him? He wrote a bestseller, didn't he?'

I nod. 'He's written other books since, though I don't think they've done so well. But the family seems to have a nice lifestyle – and Stephanie has her salon.'

DS May nods thoughtfully. 'Hollie got on well with Stephanie?'

I shrug. 'As I told you before, I didn't really spend time with them as a family, though I've been to Stephanie's salon a couple of times. The last was just before Hollie disappeared.' Pausing, I remember Stephanie seemed distracted. 'I wasn't aware of any animosity between them, but she said she was finding Hollie difficult. Stephanie meant well, but when she married James, she took on a grieving stepdaughter. Something like that doesn't come without its challenges.'

'You sound as though you knew Hollie quite well.' DS May watches me carefully.

'It's a village.' I sit back, looking at her. 'There aren't many of us here, and because Hollie spent so much time with Niamh, there was a certain familiarity between us. I don't think there's anything unusual about that.'

She shakes her head. 'Of course not. To be honest, I'm struggling to find anyone other than her father who knows Hollie more than just in passing.'

I try to recall how Hollie was, the last few times I saw her. 'I'm sure something was going on. It wasn't just what Stephanie said. The last time I saw Hollie in the churchyard, she was definitely upset. She'd taken the day off school. In fact, I even asked her what she was hiding . . .' I look at DS May, remembering Hollie's agitation. 'She said there was nothing. But she was lying. I'm sure of it.'

DS May nods. 'I'm seeing her form teacher tomorrow. She

may be able to shed some light on whatever was going on. We need to speak to Niamh again, too, especially now that we're looking at a murder inquiry. If Hollie was afraid of anyone, she may have confided in her.'

Knowing Niamh doesn't find it easy talking to the police, I'm torn between protecting her and wanting to help. I nod. 'I'll ask her. She's very upset – she tends to bottle things inside.' It's happened even more so as she's got older, but then, Andrew and I are hardly a shining example.

'It might be really helpful.' DS May gets up. 'Perhaps I could come back later on? When she's back from school?'

My heart sinks. None of this is easy for Niamh. 'She's usually home around four.'

★

After DS May leaves, I stand at the kitchen window, watching her hurry across the drive and get into her car. As she drives away, I wonder who else in the village she's talking to about Hollie. Shivering, I glance at the sky, heavy with rain that shows no signs of easing.

In the quiet of the house, I wonder if I should have told her about seeing James in the woods. No matter, I can tell her later, when she comes back. But unwanted thoughts fill my head, until finally I have to get out. It's raining too hard to go for a run, so I pull on my coat, dash to my car and set off for Della's.

The road has flooded in places and I drive slowly through the water overflowing from the streams on either side. A torrent of water pours down the drive outside the Calders' house. Managing to sidestep it, I get to the door.

Julian opens it. 'Elise! How are you?' He speaks with his usual air of bonhomie, but he looks surprised to see me. 'You must come in. Dreadful, isn't it?'

Unsure whether he's talking about Hollie or the weather, I hover on the doorstep. 'I was hoping to catch Della – is she around?'

'Hasn't double-booked again has she?' Julian looks at me curiously. 'She went to Chichester. Something to do with a fundraising lunch . . .' Breaking off, he frowns. 'At least, I think that's what she said. I don't know. I lose track of what she's up to.' He pauses. 'Are you coming in?'

I'm not in the mood for Julian's small talk. 'Don't worry. She wasn't expecting me. I was just passing. I'll catch her another time.' I start backing away towards my car. 'Tell her I called?'

Back in my car, I watch him close the front door as I start the engine. Pulling away, I avoid the worst of the puddles, but even with my windscreen wipers on full, I have no choice but to crawl along, barely able to see the road ahead until I reach the dual carriageway. Accelerating, I drive aimlessly for a while, playing loud music, trying to shake off the uneasiness I feel. Hollie's death has got under my skin, dredging up emotions I don't want to face even as I try to bury them.

I end up at Stephanie's salon, driven there by a need to be anywhere other than my home. But when I go inside, I stop thinking about myself. Stephanie's eyes are red, her shoulders slumped, the salon filled with an atmosphere of sadness. Her efforts to rally herself evaporate when she sees it's me.

'Elise.' Even her heavier than usual makeup doesn't hide the paleness of her skin.

'How are you holding up?' Instantly I regret asking. 'I'm sorry, that's a stupid question. It's such a horrible day, and as I was driving past, I thought I'd just pop in.'

She nods. 'It's nice of you. Everyone else is staying away. I haven't had a customer for days. I could put the kettle on – if you have time?'

It's what people do – stay away – because they don't know what to say, when what's needed most is basic human contact. Being up close to someone else's grief can be too much of a reminder that death can happen, at any time, to any one of us. 'Thanks.'

She looks mildly surprised. 'The kettle's through here.'

I follow her through a doorway behind her desk into a smaller room. There are photos on the walls of brides with elaborately styled hair, presumably some of Stephanie's work. In one corner, there's a compact kitchenette, with a long table covered in buckets of spring flowers set against the wall.

Stephanie sees me looking at them. 'I got them from next door. They're for the funeral.'

'They're beautiful.' The flowers are fresh shades of lemon, white, pale blue and pink, and I recognise the scent of narcissi and hyacinths. But at the mention of a funeral, shock hits me. After Hollie's disappearance, the discovery of her body, then the police involvement, and now her funeral, everything's moving so fast. 'Have you set a date?'

'Next Thursday. It's early to get the flowers in, but the florist said it would take a few days for them to open . . .' Her voice wavers. 'She's going to help me take them to the church. Oh God . . . Hollie's dead and I'm talking about flowers.' As she looks at me, her face is etched with grief.

Going over to the worktop, I finish making the tea. 'Why don't you sit down? I can do this.' Wiping away her tears, she doesn't argue as she goes and perches on one of the chairs. A minute later, I hand her one of her mugs.

'Thank you.' She takes a sip of tea. 'The day after her body was found, I had to come in early to do a bride's hair – and her bridesmaids'. She was having the kind of fairy-tale wedding that every girl dreams of. All I could think was, Hollie will

115

never get married, never have children . . .' Her voice breaks as more tears stream down her cheeks.

Hollie may not have been her daughter by blood, but Stephanie's clearly heartbroken. A feeling of powerlessness overwhelms me that I have no words of comfort to offer, but at times like this, there is nothing to say, nor is there anything I or anyone else can do to help her. I gently touch her arm. 'I'm so sorry.' I'm silent as she drinks her tea, then quietly ask, 'How is James bearing up?'

'Honestly?' She raises her tear-stained face to look at me. 'He's a mess. I'm trying to be there for him, but he's all over the place. Losing his first wife when she was so young, now Hollie . . . it's too much for anyone.'

'He has you,' I say gently. But she's right. Hollie's death is too much; the worst, most unnatural kind of loss.

'I don't know how he'll get over this.' More tears roll down her face.

I don't say anything, because I don't believe people do get over a loss like this. What happens is that you get used to living with the grief as time passes, somehow assimilating it into your life, as it changes the way you see everything.

Then Stephanie shocks me. 'The thing is . . .' Breaking off, she's tense as she looks at me. 'Please don't tell anyone this, will you? It isn't just Hollie – though that's terrible enough.' Swallowing, she shakes her head. 'I think there's something else going on. It might sound paranoid, but I'm sure James is hiding something.'

Thinking of the day I saw him in the woods, my ears prick up. 'To do with Hollie, you mean?'

Her eyes widen, then she tries to backtrack. 'Oh no . . . Nothing like that. I shouldn't have said anything. I'm probably just on edge. We both are.'

116

I think about telling her that I saw James while I was running, but I don't want to add to her burden when I don't know what the exchange I saw was about. There's no question Stephanie suspects something – and I know from experience that there are gut instincts you can't ignore. 'What makes you think that?'

'Oh, I don't know.' She looks evasive. 'Why does anyone suspect someone's keeping something from them? Private phone calls, hiding what he's looking at on his laptop . . . he's drinking far more than he used to, too. But this all started a long time before Hollie disappeared.'

A chill comes over me. 'Have you asked him about it?'

'I've tried . . .' Her voice wavers. 'He pushes me away. Tells me more lies.' She shakes her head sadly. 'James and I used to be so close. But that's gone. And now poor Hollie . . .' She pauses. 'I've tried so hard to make up for Hollie losing her mother. To be a rock for James. For a while, I even thought the three of us were happy, but nothing ever stays the same.'

I think back to something Stephanie said the last time I was in the salon. *We become expert at hiding things.* Maybe even then she was alluding to what James is keeping from her.

As for being happy . . . I try to remember when my life was happy – when Andrew was faithful, when there wasn't anything to hide. Before Niamh was born? Days after, I'd discovered Andrew was having an affair – his second, as far as I know. Having forgiven him for the first, it had cast a shadow over the joy of Niamh's birth. Thinking back further, I stop myself, because for as long as I can remember, life's been dominated by Andrew's bullying and infidelity.

I turn to Stephanie. 'You need to talk to James. Ask him what he's hiding from you. But you have Hollie's funeral coming up. Maybe it would be better to wait. If you and James are

117

good, as you hope you are, you'll get through this.' I watch her take it in. 'Try to take one day at a time, Stephanie. This is the hardest part – for both of you.' I pause for a few seconds. 'If I can do anything, you know where I am. Call me – or come over. Any time.'

I'm already regretting my offer as I leave the salon. Not just because I instinctively protect my privacy, but because Andrew hates people turning up uninvited. The more people who know his whereabouts, the harder it becomes to hide his indiscretions. He likes to maintain the illusion that we're the epitome of the perfect family. He has no intention of letting that image slip.

Niamh

In death, as in life, Hollie takes centre stage in my mind. On the bus, everyone's talking about her. At school, it's the same. But bad news travels faster than good.

Through the bus window, I stare at the rain painting everything grey, settling on the roads in oily puddles, while all I can think of is Hollie.

Hollie standing in the churchyard among the headstones, staring at the ghosts. Hollie running across a field, her long hair flying out behind her. Hollie's lifeless, floating body, cold in death.

In the time it takes to run from the bus stop to my house, my clothes are soaked through. In the kitchen, my mother's talking on her phone, looking up briefly as I go upstairs and change. When I come down, she's waiting for me.

'How was your day?' She looks anxious.

'OK.' I shrug, then go to the fridge for a drink.

My mother's voice comes from behind me. 'Niamh, the police want to talk to you again. They have this idea that Hollie may have told you something that might help them get to the bottom of what's happened to her.'

Opening the can, I take a mouthful, turning around as my mother goes on.

'DS May was here earlier. She wondered if Hollie might have confided in you.'

Raindrops on the window scatter the beam from a car's headlights into a thousand tiny shards, as it turns into our drive. My mother says from behind me, 'That's probably her.'

I feel myself frown. She has no idea how impossible this is. That I have to lie to the police because I made a promise. There's stuff Hollie told me I can't tell anyone.

By the time they come inside, DS May and Sergeant Collins look as though they've been standing in the rain for hours. I feel my insides twisting as they take off their coats, accepting my mother's offer of tea before sitting at the kitchen table.

DS May gets out her electronic notebook. 'Thank you for talking to us again, Niamh. It's just that you're one of a very small number of people Hollie was close to and we need to make sure we haven't missed something.'

Coming over, my mother places mugs on the table, then pulls out the chair next to mine.

DS May goes on. 'We're trying to establish if there might be someone out there who wished to harm Hollie. Did she ever mention anyone she was frightened of? Or had she met anyone new recently?'

Gazing at her, I bite my lip. She doesn't understand. There are things I can't repeat, as well as so much I don't know. The only person who knows what happened is Hollie.

'I can't tell you anything,' I say at last, looking between them.

'Niamh.' There's a warning tone in my mother's voice.

I turn to her. 'It's true. Hollie and I used to watch movies. Sometimes we went for a walk.' I shrug. 'She mentioned there

120

was stuff wrong at home, but she never actually said what it was.'

DS May's frowning at me. 'Was this recent, Niamh? Hollie telling you something was wrong?'

I nod.

'And you've no idea what it was?'

I try to remember Hollie's exact words. 'It was something like she couldn't trust the one person she should have been able to depend on.' I stare at DS May.

'Who was it? A close friend? Family?'

I shake my head. 'She didn't tell me who – or why. I don't know anything else.' I wonder if she believes me. Then, suddenly, it gets to be too much. Pushing back my chair, I get up and go upstairs.

In my room, I lie on my bed the way Hollie used to – on my back, hands clasped behind my head, staring at the ceiling – before rolling over and pushing myself up with my elbows, so that I can see the window. I'm still lying like that, watching the trees blowing in the wind, when my mother comes in.

'Niamh, you really shouldn't have walked off like that. The police need your help.'

I shake my head. She still doesn't understand. 'I can't tell them anything.'

My mother comes over and sits next to me on the bed. 'Look, I know this is upsetting. But surely you want to help the police find whoever did this to Hollie?'

Sliding off the bed, I get up and walk over to the window. It's almost dark, the rain still beating on the glass. I turn to face my mother. 'She made me promise.'

There's a moment of silence before my mother reacts. This time, she doesn't hide her irritation with me. 'She's dead, Niamh. Don't you think this is more important than a promise?'

I stare at her. I'm not the only one who's holding something back. Then I say it. 'Have *you* told them everything?'

Watching my mother's face pale, I know she hasn't. But I'd known that before I asked the question. When she goes downstairs, I know it's the last time she'll try to push me to talk. She's worried what will happen if she does.

★

From the top of the stairs, I listen as she talks to the policewomen in the kitchen, fobbing them off. 'I'm sorry. Niamh isn't feeling well. She's finding this incredibly traumatic – we all are. Maybe it would be better to come back another day. But I will talk to her. And I'll let you know if I find anything out.'

'Of course. It's a difficult time. I understand that.' DS May's voice carries up the stairs. 'You have my number. If Niamh changes her mind and wants to talk to us, give me a call.'

'Of course.'

Even from my room, I can hear the obvious relief in my mother's voice. There's a further murmur of voices before the back door opens and closes, followed by the sound of a car starting and then driving away. I hear my mother's footsteps as she comes back upstairs.

Pushing my door open, her face is anxious as she pauses in the doorway. 'Are you OK, Niamh?'

I nod.

'I know how difficult this must be.' She hesitates. 'It's difficult for all of us. All that matters is that the police find out what happened to Hollie.'

Silently, I gaze behind her through the window at the top of the stairs as a pair of headlights swing into the drive.

'Your father's back.' My mother's eyes shift anxiously. 'I'll tell him the police have been here, but it's up to you if you want to tell him about them questioning you.'

I nod. We both know he won't ask. He never asks me anything, but I don't mind that. It means I don't have to cobble together satisfying answers to his pointless questions. Silence makes everything so much easier.

Chapter Sixteen

Elise

'Don't bother cooking. I have to go out at seven.' Andrew's voice is abrupt as he comes into the kitchen, dropping his bag by the table before putting the kettle on. 'I won't have time to eat.'

I don't usually ask him what he's doing, but I've had enough of walking on eggshells around him, and this is my home, too. 'Where to?' I make no attempt to hide the sarcasm in my voice.

'What's this?' he mocks, getting a mug out of the cupboard. He doesn't ask me if I'd like a cup of anything. 'Have you suddenly decided you care?'

'Let me see.' I stare him in the eyes, deliberately taunting him. 'Is it the golf club, Andrew? Or the pub? Oh, silly Elise. It's Friday, isn't it. Everyone knows where Andrew goes on Fridays – everyone except his stupid wife. But do you know what, Andrew? She isn't as stupid as you—'

But before I finish speaking, he comes over, stopping inches in front of me. 'Bitch,' he mutters through gritted teeth. Then he raises his arm and slaps me. Above the sound of his hand on my cheek, I hear a gasp of breath. Through the kitchen door, at the top of the stairs, I see Niamh watching.

Anger courses through me, followed by humiliation, my face throbbing painfully. It's months since he's done anything like this. 'You need to watch it, Andrew,' I mutter under my breath as I walk away from him. Near the door, I stop. 'Emotional distance and infidelity are one thing. But I'm not sure how physical abuse would sit with your practice manager.'

'Prove it.' His eyes are like lasers boring into me. It seems he's forgotten that we have a witness. 'But I'm warning you. One mention, Elise, and I'll dredge up those notes from two years ago. I bet your airline would love to read them. Not to mention the police.'

His words hit me harder than any blow delivered by his hand. He's talking about the circumstances that, in my desperate state, triggered me to start drinking heavily in an attempt to numb my pain. Andrew had it all documented by the time I stopped, and he held it over me for months afterwards, reminding me constantly that if I'd been thinking of Niamh, I would have asked for help, but instead, I'd been utterly selfish.

Desperately unhappy at the time, I told him I wanted us to separate. I can still remember his look of contempt, his cruel smile as he told me that I could leave, but it would be alone. No-one in their right mind would give me custody of a child – he'd make sure of that. I knew he'd stop at nothing, not caring what it did to me, or to Niamh. I remember how my blood had run cold as I'd realised he didn't care even slightly about either of us. All he was interested in was controlling us.

I tried to talk to him several times, each time getting progressively more upset; only affirming in Andrew's mind the hold he had over me. The only way of staying sane became to stop fighting him. Tell myself I'd ride it out. Stay until I could find a way past him. What was most important was that Niamh had both parents, rather than just him.

'Fuck you.' I turn away so that he can't see my face. However it looks to anyone else, I'm trapped, married to a monster.

At the top of the stairs, I hesitate outside Niamh's closed door, trying to think what to say to her. *He didn't mean to hurt me. It was an argument that got a little too heated. It looks worse than it is. It's nothing to worry about.*

But there's nothing I can say to make it right. Closing the door to my bedroom, I gaze at my reflection. In the mirror, my eyes are huge, the side of my face an ugly red. Going to the bathroom, I splash cold water on my cheeks, then dry them before I start applying makeup.

★

Three days later, on a morning when I'm alone, Stephanie turns up unexpectedly, clearly distraught, her tears blending with the rain on her face as she stands on the doorstep.

Her eyes are desperate as she looks at me. 'I'm so sorry, Elise . . . After what you said, I didn't know who else to turn to.'

'Come in. You're soaked.' Only when I close the door and she starts to sob does the extent of her distress become clear. 'What's happened? Let me hang up your coat.'

Wiping her face, she awkwardly shrugs off her coat and passes it to me. Underneath, her sweater is also soaked. 'Come and stand by the radiator. I'll go and get you something to change into.'

Upstairs, I find a lamb's wool sweater in a dull shade of blue and take it down to her. 'The cloakroom's through there.' I indicate a door just beyond the kitchen. While she goes to change, I put the kettle on.

When she comes back, she's slightly more composed, but as

her eyes flit around, it's clear she needs to talk about something. As she sits down, I get out two mugs. 'I've made a pot of coffee. But if you'd prefer tea, it's no trouble.'

She shakes her head. 'Coffee would be good.' She hesitates. 'Thank you, Elise. I'm so sorry to turn up here like this.'

'It really isn't a problem. Let me finish making this; then we'll talk.'

Taking the coffee pot and milk over to the small table by the sofa under the window, she sits down. There's a wood burner, which I hadn't bothered to light earlier, but even without it, the sofa is soft and it's the cosiest corner of this house. I pour the coffee and pass her a mug before sitting next to her with mine. 'Now, tell me what's happened.'

As she starts to talk, what little composure she's managed to muster evaporates. 'James will kill me if he knows I've talked to you.' Her voice cracks.

'James doesn't need to find out,' I tell her firmly.

Mopping her face, she sighs shakily. 'We're in trouble, Elise. I mean James is, but it affects both of us. He's massively in debt. The mortgage is in arrears – I only found out yesterday. Unless a miracle happens, I think we're going to lose the house.'

I listen, horrified, as the words pour out of her, thinking how desperately unfair it seems that after losing Hollie, they're now faced with this. 'Have you spoken to the bank? They might give you some time – especially if they know you've just lost Hollie. They can't repossess it overnight.'

She shakes her head, blinking away her tears. 'It's hardly overnight. This has been going on for a year. You know how I said I thought James was hiding something from me? I should have listened to my instincts. But I'm never there when the post arrives and emails always go straight to him . . . It was irresponsible of me, but I've never thought anything of it. Now, of course, I feel completely stupid for trusting him, but I've never had any reason not to. Anyway, it's too late. I've no idea what we're going to do.' There's despair in her voice as she wipes her face again. 'We're going to lose everything.'

I'm puzzled. 'But you have your salon . . . And what about the books he's written? Surely they must make some money?'

'They do. It used to be enough.' Her voice shakes. 'But not now.'

Something in her voice makes me frown. 'What's changed?' I watch her closely, convinced there's something she isn't saying.

For a moment, she doesn't speak. Then she sighs heavily. 'James invested in a business and he owes them money.'

I frown at her. 'So why doesn't he sell?'

'It seems he can't.' She doesn't look at me. 'He's up to his neck in something. It took me ages to get anything out of him and he still hasn't told me the details.' Instead of sympathetic, she sounds bitter. 'The only thing I can say in his defence is that he didn't know what he was getting into. There was supposed to be a contract. And he was led to believe he'd make a lot of money . . . but he was conned.'

I stare at her. 'There has to be something he can do. Have you had legal advice?'

Stephanie shakes her head. 'It's not that simple. James was desperate, Elise. His last book was rejected by his publisher.' She pauses, as though she's trying to work out whether to tell me more, before raising her eyes to meet mine again. 'It was a massive blow to him. Then he met someone who told him about a sure-fire way to make a lot of money. What the man didn't tell him was how, exactly . . .' She breaks off, then sighs. 'I may as well tell you.' Her eyes rest on mine before glancing away. 'It's a porn site. Whoever got James into this, conned him by telling him they were looking for investors in an app they're developing. Only, once someone's looked up the website on their laptop, they're immediately on a list – and the website is in their search history. You can imagine, can't you?' Her voice is shaky. 'Finding out what you've got yourself involved in, but if you want your investment back – like James does – you end up being blackmailed.'

'James actually bought into a porn site?' I'm not easily shocked but the thought of someone I thought I knew getting into something like that is utterly abhorrent.

'I know.' Stephanie covers her face with her hands. 'It's completely vile, Elise. He can't sell, and now he's being forced to pay huge amounts – more than we can afford – just to remain anonymous. It's a nightmare.'

But as she speaks, I'm thinking of the exchange I saw between James and the man in the woods that day. Maybe it was connected to this. It would explain why James looked so desperate. 'The man who's conning him, do you know who he is?'

'James won't tell me his name, but I know he got swept into this circle out of pride – and vanity. James likes to impress people. I think he thought this man was a doorway into a circle of wealthy, powerful men – which he was, of course – but they are the worst kind of people, wealthy for the worst possible reasons.'

I stare at her in disbelief. 'James should go to the police.'

She looks up sharply. 'You won't tell them, will you?'

'No, but you or James have to.' I pause, frowning again. 'Why on earth hasn't he?'

'Because he'll be arrested,' Stephanie whispers. 'They produce images – of young girls. Some of the photos . . . they're of children, Elise.'

'God.' Suddenly I feel sick. How could he get involved in

child porn? 'That's even more reason to get the police involved. You can't protect him, Stephanie. There's no excuse for something like this.'

'I know.' As her eyes meet mine, she looks old, prematurely aged by worry and shame. 'But he swears he didn't know there were children involved when he invested. It will be the end of his writing career . . .'

It will be far more than that, but it doesn't mean she should protect him. 'That's his problem. He should have thought of that before he got involved.'

She shakes her head sadly. 'The irony is, he's just finished a new book. He was about to send it to his agent, but then Hollie went missing.'

Suddenly, I shiver. I'm thinking of how Hollie was in the days before she disappeared. She'd seemed more erratic, more distracted than usual, even for her. 'What if Hollie had found out?' There's a look of horror in Stephanie's eyes as I go on. 'She definitely seemed upset about something. What if her death is connected in some way? I don't see how you can rule it out.'

'You're right.' Her voice is low but she doesn't meet my eyes. Then, as I watch her, I feel myself shiver again, realising she's thought of this already and she still hasn't told the police. Her voice shakes. 'I need to ask you one favour.'

While I sympathise with Stephanie and James over Hollie's loss, I can't feel anything other than disgust about what she's told me today. 'What?'

She hesitates. 'I know it's a lot to ask . . .' Her eyes fill with tears. 'But can you wait a few days before telling the police? If we could just have Hollie's funeral . . . I don't want her memory tainted by whatever mess her stupid father is caught up in. For that one last day, I want everyone to be thinking about her.

After that, the police can arrest James, for all I care. I won't be around to see it.'

Her words surprise me. 'Where are you going? What about the salon?'

'I've given notice on the lease.' Her voice is emotionless. 'As for where I'll go . . . I don't know yet. There's nothing for me here. I need a clean break. To somehow start again, somewhere – anywhere – far away from here.'

If the police question me directly about what I know, I'm not prepared to lie. They need to know what James is involved in, just as I need to tell them I saw him arguing with someone. But putting myself in her shoes, I can understand why she's asked me. 'I won't tell them unless they ask. But after the funeral . . . If you don't tell them, I'll have to, Stephanie. For Hollie's sake.'

If she was hoping for more from me, she doesn't say. She stays long enough to finish her coffee, putting her mug down now and then, as if she wants to say more, before thinking better of it. As she leaves, cowed by grief and shame, she seems smaller somehow, and I think about how desperation drives people to extremes. First James and his investment, and now Stephanie, prepared to lie to the police; each with motives they've somehow justified to themselves.

I think of the headline I read on the flight before all of this started. The more I talk to my neighbours, the harder it becomes to find anyone at all good in this village.

Chapter Seventeen

Jo

We have few facts around Hollie Hampton's death, and with the lack of answers from the villagers – and the failure of the press to extract anything more than we have – my hunch grows that the community is closing ranks.

Meanwhile, there's been a breakthrough with Operation Rainbow, the case I was meant to be working on before Hollie's death – a covert investigation into a child porn ring that's been tenuously linked to Abingworth. Hollie's death will explain the police presence in the village, but two such high-stakes investigations running side by side has stretched our force to its limits.

Spending most of the morning in the office, I catch up with new evidence that's come to light, most of which has come from two fifteen-year-old girls who were invited to a party by a man they met in a pub on the outskirts of Chichester. Fortunately, one of them became suspicious when she saw a text message on his phone, and they left the pub without him. He came after them, but they managed to get away thanks to the intervention of a couple who happened to be passing by.

Worried about being caught for underage drinking, they didn't come forward until a week later, when two other girls went missing from the area, right around the same time that Hollie disappeared. They provided a generic description of the man in the pub – dark-haired, about six foot, in his late twenties – but given the fact that it's a week later and they had spent that night drinking, anything more detailed would be questionable. Apparently, he plied them with drinks he may have spiked – one of the girls described herself as feeling dizzy and faint – before the other girl read the text and got them out of there. All they knew about the party he invited them to was that it was that same night, at a house in Abingworth.

Operation Rainbow has been running for the last two years, since photographs of abducted teenagers started appearing on online porn sites, weeks after they've disappeared. Unfortunately, most of them have never been found.

It's crossed my mind more than once since Hollie was found that her death might be connected. Maybe she stumbled across some information she shouldn't have? Or said the wrong thing to the wrong person?

Reading through the notes again, I sigh. We have to be missing something.

*

At home that night, I close the curtains and light the fire. Apart from the crackle of the flames, the house is quiet in a way that takes getting used to after ten years of marriage. So does the reality that when you love someone, when they gradually start undermining you, shredding your self-esteem until you believe everything they tell you, it can be impossible to recognise that what they're showing you is no longer love. It's abuse.

Even now, it's hard to shed the sense of shame I feel that I was a victim. Objectively, I know how it happens – the behaviour changes slowly, the episodes of cruelty followed by passionate declarations of regret and overblown apologies. He didn't mean to hurt me . . . Anyone would want to believe the man they love simply made an error of judgement – none of us are perfect. We tell ourselves these and other lies while the vision of our pale, drawn faces becomes familiar to us, along with walking on eggshells to tiptoe around the next explosion. And as we gradually withdraw from life, the light slowly fades from our eyes.

Getting up, I go to the kitchen and pour myself a glass of wine.

And for some reason, I think of Elise Buckley.

Chapter Eighteen

Elise

In light of what Stephanie's told me, I start to wonder how many other people are embroiled the way James is, in an immoral, illegal business that they're too frightened to blow the whistle on. I wonder if Andrew's got wind of what's going on, too, not that he'd care. He isn't a doctor out of compassion for other people. It's for the aura of authority and integrity that accompanies his title – his cloak of infallibility – and the fact that his words carry more weight than other people's. It astonishes me how, even now, so many people don't question their doctors, even though doctors are human, as capable of making mistakes as anyone else.

I keep thinking about James, still regretting my promise to Stephanie. It isn't right that the police don't know about his so-called business venture.

But I keep my word. Two days before the funeral, I go back to work, reporting early in the morning for a flight to Barcelona. The flight is busy and I don't get time to look out of the window until much later, by which time we're flying over the south of France. The cloud carpeting the landscape as we left the UK is far behind us and I view the snow-capped Pyrenees from the small window in the forward door before the land flattens out to meet the sea.

As we start our descent into the city, I make a final check of the cabin and by the time I return to my view, we're low enough to make out buildings and the network of streets bathed in winter sun.

After landing, I find myself hankering for another life as I study the rows of faces in front of me, imagining lives so very different from mine, unencumbered by an abusive marriage and the knowledge of a murdered teenager. As the last of the passengers disembarks, I'm gripped by an urge to make an excuse to follow them to the terminal building, imagining myself merging into the crowd of thousands before disappearing from everything I know. I come close – for a moment believing I really could do it – but then I think of Niamh.

The reality check causes my mood to slump. Life is too bound by my responsibilities – as a member of the cabin crew required to get this flight home, as Niamh's mother, and now, in light of what's happened to Hollie and what Stephanie has told me, by the additional burden of secrets.

★

I push it all to the back of my mind for the flight back, but as we make our approach into Gatwick two hours later, I think of the hold Andrew has over me. Am I really so different from Stephanie? Playing along with Andrew's game for my own reasons, instead of exposing what he's doing to me and letting the truth come out? But as the aircraft wheels touch down, I realise I'm not like Stephanie. She isn't weak. After the funeral, she's leaving.

I make a promise to myself that one day, in the not-so-distant future, I'll find a way to do the same.

After we taxi in and park on our stand, the return passengers start to disembark and my eyes fix on a man speaking angrily to his wife. Instead of looking upset or anxious, she humours him, touching his arm with affection. I watch his anger evaporate; his quiet laugh, the way he kisses her cheek. It's a brief moment that reminds me of everything that's wrong in my marriage; that happy relationships do exist.

While I drive home, I feel uncertainty escalating around me. *I need to get the funeral out of the way,* I remind myself. *Then, at the first opportunity, I'll talk to the police.* Taking a deep breath, I try to calm my mind. But it's as though unstoppable change is all around me.

*

The feeling is heightened that afternoon when I drive into Chichester for an appointment; and again, later, when I'm back home switching on the radio and turning the music up. Out of character for me, I open a bottle of Prosecco and pour myself a large glass. I don't care what anyone else thinks. There's no reason why I should, when the world around me is increasingly unpredictable.

Finishing the glass, I pour another as an upbeat track comes on the radio. Caught in a moment of recklessness, I start to dance uninhibitedly – because no-one's watching and because I feel like it. It isn't until the track comes to an end that I hear the knock at the door.

Catching my breath, I smooth my hair behind my ears before opening it to find Sergeant Collins and DS May standing there.

'Mrs Buckley? I hope we're not disturbing you. Would you mind if we came in for a moment?' Their faces are impassive. If they saw me dancing through the window, it doesn't show.

Standing back, I open the door wider. 'Of course not.' The cloud of uncertainty I briefly danced away is back again. 'Come through.'

They follow me inside, hovering until I gesture towards the table. 'Would you like to sit down?'

DS May nods. 'Thank you.'

I watch her eyes glance around the kitchen, taking in my half-drunk glass, then glancing at the clock, before sitting at the table.

'Can you remember where you were the day Hollie died?'

I gasp. Am I a suspect? Suddenly my mind is racing.

'The date was Wednesday the 4th of February.'

'OK.' The date's engrained in my mind. 'I think I was at work – on a flight. I'll have to check where I went.'

'If you wouldn't mind?'

My feeling of uncertainty grows stronger as I get my phone, logging into the crew portal before bringing up my flight schedule. 'I went to Athens.'

Making a note, she nods before going on. 'I wondered if you knew Niamh was with Hollie the day before she disappeared?'

Shaking my head, I frown at her. 'You must be mistaken. It isn't possible. She would have been at school.' But I was flying that day, too, and can't be certain. 'I've always trusted that she goes to school – I've no reason not to. There's a portal parents can access that records attendance, but I haven't checked it recently. I didn't have any reason to, though it's possible I missed a call from the school – I switch my phone off while I'm working.'

The expression on DS May's face is grave. 'We have reason to believe that Niamh took the day off. We've checked with the school. According to them, you emailed the office to tell them she had a dental appointment.'

As I stare at her, I feel my grip on reality loosen.

'Did you email the school, Mrs Buckley?'

In that moment, I'm paralysed, torn between needing to protect Niamh from whatever Hollie might have been involved in and telling the truth. Except that the truth is I don't know where Niamh was that day. My voice is hoarse. 'I can't be sure. I'd have to check the calendar . . . Maybe the school made a mistake. Did they say if she'd missed any other days?'

To my relief, she says, 'To the best of our knowledge, this was the only one, which makes it all the more important. Did Hollie have some kind of hold over your daughter? Enough to make her take a day off school, for whatever reason?'

'I wouldn't have put it like that. I think it's best if I talk to Niamh.'

DS May and Sergeant Collins glance at each other. 'She's usually home around four, isn't she? Would you mind if we wait?'

141

Niamh

When I get off the bus, I look for the cat as always, but I haven't seen him since the day Hollie disappeared. Back home, I think about turning around and going somewhere else – anywhere else – when I see the police car parked on the drive outside my house and my mother standing at the kitchen window. Seeing me, she raises a hand.

As I go inside, I see the two policewomen sitting at our kitchen table. I know they're waiting for me – why else would they be here?

'Niamh? The police want to talk to you again.' My mother sounds jittery. 'They say you were with Hollie on one of the days she was missing from school.'

'Yes.' I'm not going to lie. 'But there's a reason I didn't tell you.' I glance at her. 'Before, I mean.'

Shaking her head, she looks furious for a moment. Then she looks worried. In a flash, I get why. She thinks I know more than I'm saying about what happened to Hollie.

After putting down my school bag, I go over to the table. 'I made Hollie a promise,' I try to explain to DS May and

Sergeant Collins. 'Just because she's dead, doesn't mean a promise should be broken.'

DS May looks slightly thrown. 'If Hollie told you something that could help us find out what happened to her, you should tell us, Niamh.' When I don't reply, she goes on. 'So you're saying Hollie was upset that day? Upset enough that she persuaded you to take the day off school? Wasn't there anyone else she went to when she needed to talk to someone?'

I shake my head. 'She didn't have anyone else. I went to get the bus and she was waiting for me. She was desperate.'

'So what happened after you didn't get on the bus?'

'We came back here. I got changed, and we went out again.'

DS May nods. 'But first, you emailed your school, telling them you had a dental appointment.'

I pause. Has she rung my school? 'It was Hollie's idea. I didn't want to.'

'Niamh.' My mother sounds shocked.

DS May's eyes don't leave my face. 'So what did you and Hollie do after that?'

★

There are things you don't tell your parents, that they don't need to know or wouldn't understand.

'Please don't go to school today.' I found her waiting for me at the bus stop, her eyes huge with dark circles under them, as though she hadn't slept in days. 'I'm going mad, Niamh. I need you.' The words broke out of her in a kind of sob.

I thought about the classes I'd miss, the trouble I'd get into when my mother found out. 'If I don't go to registration, they'll call my mother.'

Her eyes didn't leave mine. 'Can't you tell them you have a

dentist's appointment? I'll never ask you to do anything like this again.'

I paused, thinking of the school's online portal for parents. I'd memorised the login details they sent my mother. 'I suppose I could. What are we going to do?'

'I don't know. I don't care. Your bus is coming, Niamh. You have to decide. Please . . .'

The desperation in her voice swayed me. One day off school wouldn't make any difference to anyone. 'OK.'

'Is your mum at work?' Hollie spoke hurriedly as we walked away down the road. When I nodded, she said, 'Can we go back to yours? Shouldn't you change?' She looked at my uniform anxiously. As the bus came into sight, Hollie grabbed my arm. 'Quick. Before the driver sees us.'

By the time it reached the bus stop, we were out of sight. From the garden, I heard the bus slow down, and then – when the driver saw I wasn't there – it gradually accelerated and pulled away. Running ahead of me across the garden towards the house, Hollie seemed more anxious than usual. 'Hurry up, Niamh. You need to email the school before they try to call your parents.'

Unlocking the back door, I closed it behind both of us, then got my laptop, logging in and sending the email to the school before shutting it down again. I turned to Hollie. 'What now?'

There was a strange look on her face. Then she said, 'My dad's done something.'

'What?' Before she could speak, I added, 'You're right, I need to change. Come upstairs.'

She was restless while I changed, flitting around my room and I tried to imagine what her dad might have done. Then, as I pulled on a sweater, she said, 'I have to show you something.'

145

'What?'

But she was already going downstairs again. In the kitchen, she picked up my jacket and handed it to me.

'Where are we going?'

Shaking her head, she opened the back door, and then stood outside impatiently. 'Come on, Niamh. It has to be now, or someone will see us.'

As the same urgency that gripped her filtered into me, I closed the door and hurried to catch up, jogging to keep pace with her quick steps. As we reached the lane, she glanced around, as if making sure we weren't being watched. When she broke into an easy run, I did the same, following her along the pavement, watching her unzipped jacket flapping behind her. 'Hollie.' When she didn't slow down, I shouted after her. 'Hollie . . . stop.'

There was a mystified look on her face as she turned round. For some reason, I was annoyed. 'What are we doing out here? Someone will see me. I'm supposed to be at school, remember?'

Jogging back to me, she grabbed my hand, then stroked a strand of hair off my face. 'It'll be OK, Niamh. But I have to show you something. It's important.'

Passing Greyfriars Lane, we crossed the road to the woods, where we took an unmarked path, relief filling me when no cars had passed us.

'It takes longer this way, but no-one will see us.'

Clouds were rolling across the sky, threatening rain, and the woods were dark under the canopy of branches as we followed the path that looped around the edge of the village. It took fifteen minutes for us to reach the house Hollie wanted me to see.

'Where are we?' I looked around for somewhere I recognised.

'Your house is over there.' Hollie pointed towards some trees.

Squinting, I followed her gaze, unable to see it, taking her word for it.

'Stay here, Niamh. I won't be a minute.' She hurried around the front to check the drive before coming back.

'No-one's home.'

I followed her across the garden to a window and we peered through it, seeing a small room that looked like someone's office, with photos on the desk. Photos of young girls. Then she told me what she'd been keeping from me and everyone else, and made me swear on my life never to tell anyone.

'Everyone has secrets, Niamh. And now, mine is one of yours.'

★

Knowing, even now, I can't go back on the promise I made her, I give the police a slightly looser version of the truth. 'She made me walk a long way to this house that belonged to someone she didn't know. But that was it.' It seems an age ago that it happened, but that's how it feels when someone dies. It's the difference between life with and without; before and after.

'Where was the house?' DS May's voice is sharp, her pen poised, ready to write it down.

I look at her blankly. 'Through the woods somewhere.'

'Was it Park House?'

'Park House?' I glance at my mother.

'Up Greyfriars Lane, Niamh.' My mother's voice is quiet. 'One of the bigger houses – where the Marinos live.'

I've seen that house – when I've been out with Hollie. I shake my head.

Then DS May asks, 'Would you be able to take us the way you went with Hollie?'

147

Can I remember the twisting path Hollie took? 'I'm not sure I could.'

'It's really important, Niamh. If I come with you, could we try to find it?'

Chapter Nineteen

Elise

Unfortunately, DS May hasn't finished. She's frowning as she fiddles with her pen. 'Niamh, you told us before that Hollie used to go into other people's properties.'

Niamh nods. 'She didn't do any harm. She just walked around.'

'Did the two of you go anywhere else in the village?'

As Niamh's pale cheeks tinge with pink, shock washes over me. After the forged email to the school, what else don't I know about my daughter?

'We went to Deeprose House once. It was a while before she disappeared. We were only there a few minutes and we didn't do anything. I told Hollie I didn't think we should be there.' Niamh looks at me. 'I've told you . . . I really don't know anything else. I wish I'd gone to school that day.'

'Hollie could be very persuasive,' I tell DS May and Sergeant Collins.

'So it seems. What was it about the house through the woods that made Hollie want to take you there?' DS May's voice is gentler as she addresses Niamh.

Niamh's silent for a moment. 'She didn't say. And there wasn't anything to see there.' She shrugs. 'It was just a house.'

'Can you describe it?'

'It was big.' Niamh frowns. 'The garden was massive. Hollie said you could see our house from there – but I couldn't.'

DS May makes a note. 'You're sure?' When Niamh nods, she goes on. 'Can you remember anything unusual about it?'

'Not really. Only that it seemed really big. Otherwise it was like the other houses around here.'

DS May changes track. 'Hollie always came here, didn't she? Rather than you going to her house?'

'Hollie's father works from home,' I supply. 'The girls weren't bothering anyone here – both Andrew and I are out most days.'

She turns her attention to me. 'How often are you away, Mrs Buckley?'

Her scrutiny makes me uncomfortable. 'It varies. Mostly, my flights are short haul. Sometimes I'm away overnight, but it's rare.'

'I see.' Nodding, she goes on. 'And what about the Monday, the day before Hollie disappeared? Did you see her?'

I watch as Niamh starts.

'I think I was working. I need to check my flight schedule again.' Getting up, I go to get my phone, clicking on my calendar. 'I had an eight thirty check-in for a flight to Malaga. I would have left the house by six thirty and got home around five that evening.'

'Could you send us a copy of your schedule for our records? That way, we can rule out the need to question you further.'

I realise that everyone is potentially a suspect at this stage but with the spotlight turned on me, I feel uneasy. 'Yes. Of course. You're questioning everyone in the village, I assume?'

DS May leans forward. 'Yes, Mrs Buckley. Until Hollie's

murderer is found, we will continue talking to everyone in this village and in her life. Somebody, somewhere, must know something.'

Her words make me uncomfortable. Both Stephanie and I are keeping information from the police, information they need. Hollie's funeral is two days away. Two days – after that, I'll tell them everything.

DS May turns to Niamh again. 'We have about an hour of daylight. Can you try to take us to the house Hollie took you to?'

*

We follow Niamh through the village, past the turning into Greyfriars Lane. Reaching the woods, she stops.

'I think it was this path.' She sounds far from certain.

DS May nods. 'Shall we carry on?'

The ground is damp underfoot as we take a narrow path through the trees, their canopy of branches blocking out the light. When we come to where the path intersects with others, Niamh stops again, a frown crossing her face. 'I can't remember which way she went.'

DS May looks at me. 'Do you know these woods?'

I shake my head. 'I don't.' These paths are too narrow and dark. When I run, I like to have space around me.

She gets out her phone. 'I'll save the location. We'll come back in daylight and check this out.'

*

After the police have gone, I turn to Niamh. 'I can't believe you and Hollie went onto other people's properties. How many other times have there been?'

She shakes her head. 'None. And like I said, we didn't do

151

any harm. It's not like there's anything else to do around here.'

'Niamh, that doesn't mean it's OK to trespass on private land—'

But our conversation ends prematurely. As I'm speaking, Andrew's car swings into the drive and Niamh gets up and runs upstairs.

★

Thursday arrives, the day of Hollie's funeral, and for a short while the rain lets up, leaving a watery sky broken by rays of weak sunlight. The path to the churchyard is sodden underfoot as we join the small crowd assembled outside the church, all of us pausing our lives to spend this hour to remember Hollie, while the thought occurs to me. Hollie's killer could be among us and no-one would know.

We wait while Hollie's coffin is carried into the church, and as it passes, I notice the posy on top, made up of the spring flowers in delicate shades I saw at Stephanie's salon last Friday, that seem somehow befitting of Hollie's ethereal beauty and free spirit.

Inside, my eyes wander towards the front of the congregation, where I catch a glimpse of the back of Stephanie's head as she stands next to James. I think of her determination not to let anything get in the way of today happening the way she wanted it to. Each step of the way, she's held her husband's hand, her show of solidarity with James unfaltering, as though united in their grief. No-one would guess what's really going on between them.

When it's time for the eulogy, James stands up. You could hear a pin drop as he walks to the front of the church and talks about the pain of losing the daughter he'll always miss, then

152

asks for everyone to be patient and give them time to grieve. His eyes flicker over the congregation, pausing on me. In that second, I know Stephanie's told him that she confided in me.

Whatever the circumstances, whatever wrong James may have done, I can't help but imagine how he's feeling today. Around me, the service leaves no-one unmoved – well, almost no-one. To my right, Andrew is tall and sombre in his black suit and tie, an expression of sorrow on his face that only I know he isn't capable of feeling. As I glance at Niamh's fair head on my other side, there's a lump in my throat as I wish yet again that I could protect her from all of this.

★

As everyone files outside after the funeral, I see DS May and Sergeant Collins standing together on the fringes of the small crowd. On the other side of the churchyard are two more uniformed officers. Whether they're expecting trouble and playing it safe, or merely observing us, their presence is nonetheless unnerving.

While Andrew plays the concerned mourner, I pause, watching DS May's eyes fix on James, with his head bowed and shoulders slumped, before her gaze moves to Stephanie, with her hair newly coloured and wearing an understated navy dress, as she stands at her husband's side. Despite her confession to me, it doesn't at all look like she's about to leave him.

Della walks towards me. 'God-awful day, isn't it, Elise?' Leaning forward, she kisses me on both cheeks. 'Sorry I missed you when you came round. Julian was a bit worried, actually. He said he thought you were upset.'

'It was one of those days,' I say evasively. 'I can't even remember what was going through my mind. You're right, though. Today's a terrible day. It doesn't get much worse.'

Della gives me an odd look. 'Are you coming to the pub? James and Stephanie have invited everyone.'

I shake my head. 'I don't think so.' After the funeral, the last thing I feel like doing is being in a crowded pub with people I don't want to talk to. Across the churchyard, I catch sight of Phil Mason – the man James was speaking to at the service two Sundays ago – now talking to someone I don't know. Then I notice James glance towards Mason, his face clouding over as he takes Stephanie's arm and steers her away.

It could be something or nothing, but James clearly doesn't want anything to do with Mason. 'James doesn't seem too pleased to see Phil Mason. Do you know him?'

Della stares at him. 'Julian does. Actually, you may have met him, Elise. A year ago – at our summer party. Why?'

As she says this, pieces start falling into place. I remember drinking too much wine to numb the stultifying boredom of another village social gathering, drifting away from everyone else to pour another glass.

I shrug. 'I don't remember seeing him around before, that's all. What does he do?' My voice is purposefully casual.

Della frowns. 'He works for some software company. Don't ask me for details – you know what I'm like with anything technical. But he's done well out of it. It's made him quite a wealthy man.'

I'm silent as I study him, wondering if it's him who's blackmailing James. But if that were the case, surely Mason wouldn't show his face here?

I feel myself shiver as Stephanie's voice comes from behind me. 'Are you joining us at the pub, Elise?'

Turning, I realise what today is taking from her; that however united she and James may appear, the truth of what she's going through is in the desperation flickering in her eyes. 'I'm sorry,'

I hedge, floundering around for a believable excuse. 'I won't be able to. To be honest, I don't want to leave Niamh alone.'

'Niamh is welcome, too.' It's a mixed message. She wants me close – but not too close. I know too much.

'Thank you. But I think I'll take her home. It's a difficult day for her, as it is for everyone – especially you and James . . .'

Stephanie's eyes fill with tears. 'Thank you for coming.'

'Your flowers were beautiful,' I say quietly. 'I'll come over to the salon in the next few days, if you'll be there?'

As she starts, I realise she's worried I'm giving away what she told me in confidence. 'I'll be there. I'm hardly going to be anywhere else.' Her voice is overly bright.

I know the lie is for Della's benefit, as well as for anyone else who might be eavesdropping, and as her eyes catch mine, I again see the depth of her desperation.

'I should go and find James,' she mutters, already turning to walk away.

There's a strange atmosphere as Della and I stand there, but I'm not prepared for what happens next. Over everyone's heads, I glimpse Andrew in what appears to be an amicable enough conversation with Phil Mason across the churchyard. I then notice James watching them. Shaking hands with Mason, Andrew turns and walks away just as Stephanie reaches James's side. He takes her hand as he glares at Andrew, the look in his eyes one of pure hatred.

Knowing Andrew will go to the pub with everyone else, Niamh and I leave the church, my sense of unease building. As we walk home, it begins to rain, the force of it rapidly intensifying so that we only just make it back before it becomes a downpour. Niamh goes upstairs to change while I put the kettle on and make a pot of coffee, my head buzzing with thoughts of Hollie's funeral.

As I go back over what I saw, I become more convinced there's something going on between James and Phil Mason. I already know from Stephanie what James is embroiled in. Then there's the argument I stumbled upon that day in the woods, between James and some unidentified person. Could that have been Mason? There's also Mason's wealth, which Della hinted at, to consider. But quite how this all adds up, I'm not sure.

Thinking back to what Stephanie told me about James's so-called investment and how it's bankrupted them, my blood runs cold. If Andrew had got involved in something similar, would I know?

The truth is, I wouldn't. I don't know half of what he does.

With Niamh up in her bedroom, I go quietly to Andrew's study, closing the door behind me before sitting at his desk. Opening the drawers, I glance at the few letters inside, which appear innocuous. But there isn't a lot to find – if Andrew was involved in anything nefarious, he'd be meticulous about covering his tracks.

My eyes scan the shelves behind his desk, but if I do find anything here, I know it will be because he wants me to. I wonder if he knows about the mess James has got himself into. Judging from the look James gave him, there's clearly ill-feeling between them. Maybe I should ask Stephanie if she knows why.

Leaving everything as I found it, I close the study door behind me. But my suspicions have taken root and even though it's risking Andrew's temper, I want to know more. It's late when he comes back from the pub stinking of whisky and cigarette smoke, slurring his words.

'What's for dinner, Elise?'

Dinner's long gone. Niamh and I ate two hours ago. 'I assumed you were eating at the pub.' I watch him get a glass and pour himself a large Scotch. 'I didn't realise you knew Phil

Mason,' I say calmly. 'Are he and James friends? I assumed they must be, otherwise why else would he have been at the funeral?'

Turning around, he puts his glass down, his eyes narrowing as he comes over and stands in front of me. 'It's a small village, Elise. Of course I know him. What exactly are you trying to say?'

I don't miss the warning note in his voice, but before I can speak, he goes on. 'A word to the wise: Phil's a powerful man. He's not the kind of person you go around asking questions about.' His voice is menacing. 'Do I make myself clear?'

I stare at him. Is he saying Mason's the person who involved James in this scam? But if there's something going on, if Andrew's involved too, I want to know. 'That's a little melodramatic, Andrew. This is Abingworth, for God's sake. You're making him sound like a Mafia boss.'

But he's too drunk for rational conversation. His eyes flash dangerously. 'You have no idea, do you?' he sneers. 'But how could you? Face it, Elise, your pathetic little life is so cut off from the real world.'

After years of him talking to me this way, his words bounce off me. Even in this state, he isn't going to tell me what I want to know. Not wishing to escalate things, I cut him short. 'It was an innocent question, Andrew. If you're hungry, there's cold chicken in the fridge. I'm going to bed.' As I walk out, I wait for him to lumber after me, steeling myself for his hand gripping one of my arms then twisting it; for one of his blows.

At the door, I glance back to see him knocking back his whisky, praying that it's one of those nights he'll be too drunk to make it upstairs.

Chapter Twenty

Jo

Hollie Hampton's murder remains unsolved, but it's more than that, that frustrates me. Usually the whole world has an opinion on what's going on with a murder investigation, but not in Abingworth. They're too reticent, too reluctant to talk – about almost anything.

'It's as though there's some unspoken agreement, sir. Either that, or a secret they're all in on.'

The DI looks nonplussed. 'Operation Rainbow, Jo . . . Have you identified the man who tried to lure the two young women?'

I shake my head. 'Not yet.'

'What about the house where the party was supposedly being held? Any clues yet?'

'Nothing.' I pause. 'Niamh Buckley told us Hollie took her to a house on the edge of the village and I think there's more she's not telling us. She says she doesn't know who the house belongs to. Apparently Hollie took her there through some woods. Niamh tried to show me which way they went, but there are paths leading off in every direction and she can't remember which one they took. I've got the approximate location – I'm going to ask Emerson to go back over there and take a look.'

'Good. Right now, Jo, anything's worth trying.'

'What I don't understand is how someone could be getting away with abducting young women and taking them to a house around here without anyone in the village noticing something – unless all of them are involved, which is unlikely.'

'Villages . . .' Going over to the window, the DI stands there for a moment before turning to look at me. 'On the one hand, they're small enough that everyone knows everyone else, but on the other, there are those big, hidden-away houses, plenty of which have no neighbours. If anything was going on behind those hedges and walls, no-one would know. Park House is a good example of that.'

'Sir, there are other houses near Park House. And no other road in.'

'I'm not suggesting anything's going on there specifically, May. It just seems too much of a coincidence that Hollie's body was found in the same area we believe the porn ring to be based.' He frowns. 'The only evidence we do have suggests there was a private party being held in Abingworth . . . Again, hearsay rather than proof. We haven't questioned any of the villagers about this so far, have we?'

'Not yet. We've been trying not to alert whoever's behind this.'

'Perhaps it's time to start asking. Stir things up a bit.'

'It's always possible there is no link between Hollie's death and Operation Rainbow, sir.'

'Yes.' He doesn't sound convinced, and like him, I have my doubts. 'Niamh Buckley . . . So you think she knows more about Hollie's death than she's saying?'

'I suspect so. Her loyalty to Hollie is commendable, if a little misguided, given the circumstances. But she's fourteen years old and her friend has just died – she's scared.'

'Maybe talk to her again. Win her trust, May. What about the mother?'

'The last time I saw Elise Buckley, she had half a bottle of Prosecco inside her. She's protective of her daughter. But on the whole, she seems fairly black and white.'

'And her husband?'

'Andrew Buckley's the local GP. He's business-like, professional – and busy. I've only spoken to him on the phone so far.'

Leaning back in his chair, the DI clasps his hands behind his head. 'Tell me about the funeral.'

I nod. 'I'd say most of the village was there. The church was packed. It was really sad, as you'd expect, but there was nothing noticeably out of place.'

'And after?'

'Most of them went to the pub,' I tell the DI.

'Keep asking questions,' he orders. 'Someone in that village must know what happened to Hollie Hampton.'

★

People don't always act as you think they might. There's often someone who may not realise they're sitting on a vital piece of information, just as there's always someone in a village who sees what goes on, yet remains in the background.

When I reach Ida Jones's cottage, I wonder if she could be that person, the keeper of the village's secrets. Her lips are pursed as she lets me in, her unruly grey curls scraped back in a bun. She comes up to my shoulder but despite her height and age, looks strong. As she shows me into her sitting room, she gestures to the sofa.

'Do you want to sit down?'

'Thank you.' The heavy dark furniture and dated three-piece suite remind me of my grandmother's house. 'I'm sorry to turn up unexpectedly like this, Mrs Jones. I was hoping to talk to you about Hollie Hampton.'

She nods. 'I thought you might. But I'm not sure there's much I can tell you.'

'Well . . . you could start by telling me about her. How well you knew her. Where you saw her, what you knew about her, her relationships . . .'

'She was quite a sweet young thing. But flighty, I'd say. She was friends with young Niamh, but I expect you know that. It's hard on young ones to lose a friend.' Her eyes mist over.

'How well do you know the Hamptons?'

'As well as I know everyone else in this village.' She smiles. 'You'll know that James is a writer and Stephanie's a hairdresser?'

When I nod, she goes on. 'I might be wrong, but after his first book, I don't think he's had much luck. It's her salon that keeps them going.'

'Is that so?' It would explain the shabbiness of their house if money was tight. 'Do you know the Buckleys?'

'Oh yes.' Ida Jones nods. 'I see Elise from time to time. The doctor though . . .' She seems to stop herself.

My instincts are on full alert. 'What about him?'

'Between you and me, he's not a nice man. I won't say any more than that.'

'Mrs Jones . . . If you know something about Doctor Buckley that could help us, we need to know.'

She's shaking her head, her expression mutinous. 'It won't help you find who killed poor young Hollie.' She hesitates. 'But there are rumours. Villages are full of rumours.' She pauses again. 'He likes women. That's all I'm saying.'

I'm not altogether surprised. If her husband's fooling around, it might explain the slight hostility I sense in Elise Buckley.

Ida frowns. 'I almost forgot. I saw Elise with Hollie not that long back. They were by the church. I think they were arguing about something. I'd just started talking to them when my phone rang – it was my daughter – and by the time we'd finished our chat, they'd sorted it out.'

My ears prick up. 'Did you hear what it was about?'

'They were too far away. And, of course, they stopped once they saw me. I did wonder why Hollie wasn't in school.'

She continues. 'I used to see Hollie and Niamh together all over the place. They didn't take too much notice of boundaries, those two. But they were harmless.'

I think of what Niamh said about the two of them creeping into private gardens together. 'Where did they used to go, Mrs Jones? Do you know?'

'How would I know?' She glares at me. 'Ask young Niamh. She's the only one who could tell you. Wherever Hollie went, Niamh was always right there with her.'

Without knowing how, I've struck a nerve. 'How long have you lived in the village, Mrs Jones?'

'It's gone thirty years, twenty of them without my Derek. I've seen a few folks come and go, you know.'

'Have you seen any strangers hanging around, or noticed anything unusual?' I watch her face for any clues and she smiles.

'Well, of course. It's different these days. Folk drive past in their big cars . . . And the pub is full of outsiders. Even the church . . . folk only seem to go there on high days and holidays. We used to go every week. Shame.' She shakes her head.

High days, holidays . . . and funerals, I can't help thinking. 'So life around here has changed?'

She seems to think for a moment. 'You could say that.' She

speaks quietly. 'It used to be that when something terrible happened, people would rally round. There was a real sense of community.'

'And you don't have that now?' I feel myself frown.

She looks at me sadly. 'It hasn't been like that in a long time.'

*

After what Ida Jones has hinted at about the Hamptons' financial situation, I pay a visit to Stephanie Hampton's salon, hoping to talk to her away from her husband. But when I get there, the door is locked and it's in darkness. Checking the clock in my car, I realise I've timed my visit badly, guessing she's closed for lunch.

Her salon is one of a few businesses arranged in a courtyard of converted farm buildings. From what I can see of the dim interior, it looks as though Stephanie has closed in a hurry. A couple of towels are hung over chairs, and the whole place looks untidy, but it stands to reason that her mind would be on other things after Hollie's death.

Or would it? If Ida Jones is right, this salon is the only thing keeping the Hamptons afloat. Going back down the steps, I walk along to the next building, glancing at the window display filled with wedding paraphernalia. Above the door, gold letters spell out the shop's name: *Tiger Lily*.

I open the door and go inside, taking in the rails of wedding dresses as I'm greeted by a young woman wearing a tape measure slung around her neck. 'Can I help you?'

'I was hoping to catch Stephanie next door.'

Clearly hoping for business, the woman's face falls.

'DS May – Chichester Police. I'm investigating the death of Mrs Hampton's stepdaughter. I don't suppose you know where she is?'

She shakes her head. 'I'm sorry, I don't. Her hours have been a bit erratic lately. Hardly surprising given what's happened . . . Can I help in any way?'

I pause for a moment. 'How well do you know Mrs Hampton?'

'Only on a business level. I used to refer brides to her, to get their hair done.' A shadow crosses the woman's face. 'I don't like saying this, but I think I'm going to be a bit careful now. One of her suppliers came in chasing her for an unpaid bill the other day. I don't want to refer my brides to her if her business is shaky.'

It sounds as though Stephanie's in a downward spiral – when a business isn't doing well, word gets around and customers stay away, making it worse – and of course the situation won't have been helped by Hollie's death.

*

Back at the office, I go over everything we know for the umpteenth time, then check in with Sarah Collins to see if they've got any further with Operation Rainbow.

'We have the lead we've been waiting for – I hope.' Sarah sounds relieved. 'There was a call earlier today from a woman. Apparently her partner had been boasting about a business opportunity that was going to make him a lot of money. He then showed her the adult website he was planning on investing in – he justified it by saying it was the kind of thing that was everywhere. She was horrified, but while he was in the shower, she had another look. This time, she found images of children. She was quite smart, actually. Instead of confronting him, she pretended to go along with the idea and quizzed him about the investment. He told her he'd met someone in a pub in Abingworth – a man who lived around there, apparently,

165

though he didn't say where exactly, and of course, it could have been a front. But it seems to fit too well to be a coincidence.'

'We need to speak to him.'

'There's a problem with that.' Sarah pauses. 'He runs a delivery service and he's away on a job for a couple of days. His partner doesn't know exactly where he is.'

'Get the vehicle registration of the van. Or trace him by his phone.'

'We're already doing it. As soon as we locate him, we'll bring him in.'

Chapter Twenty-One

Elise

Assuming Stephanie will have kept her word and spoken to the police after the funeral, I leave it a couple of days before I go to see her. It's early afternoon when I get to her salon and she looks on edge when I walk in.

'Have you told James?' I ask her.

'That I'm leaving? I suppose it's obvious.' Her voice tight, she glances around the shop. 'It's complicated, Elise. I haven't told him in as many words.'

'I wanted to ask you something.' I hesitate. 'Do you know if James and Andrew have fallen out?'

At the mention of Andrew's name, she looks startled. 'I wasn't aware that they were ever friends.' An odd look crosses her face. 'Why do you ask?'

'I've never thought of them as friends. But they've always seemed to get on reasonably well socially.' I feel myself frown. 'It was just that, at Hollie's funeral, I caught James looking at Andrew and . . . let's just say it wasn't friendly. In fact, I'd describe it as hatred.'

'That's a bit strong.' Stephanie seems to stiffen. 'I've certainly no idea why.' She's silent; then she adds, 'I don't know what you want me to say.'

'Nothing. I thought I'd ask you, that's all.' Slightly puzzled by her response, I change the subject. 'What did the police say when you spoke to them?'

Folding her arms, she looks awkward. 'I haven't.'

I'm shocked. 'Stephanie, you have to. It's bad enough that they don't already know. You need to call them.'

She at least has the grace to look ashamed. 'I know.' Her voice hardens. 'Surely you can understand it's the last thing I feel like doing. After Hollie . . .' Her voice wavers. 'I can't face having to answer more questions from the police. And I'll have to tell them where I'm going.'

'You don't have to tell them you're going anywhere. But they do need to know what James is involved in. If I were you, I'd have everything packed and ready to go, so that once I'd talked to them, I could drive away and never come back. Call them. Tell them what you need to about his "investment", then just get away from here.'

'You think?'

I shrug. It depends what her conscience will let her live with. 'It's his problem, Stephanie, not yours. You have to do the right thing, but after that . . .'

A look of anguish crosses her face. 'I've done what I can for James, but he's a fool. I would never have imagined he'd be so stupid. What kind of a man risks everything the way he has?' Her voice is shaking, but her eyes are blazing as she looks at me. 'I keep asking myself – *why? Why me? Why us?* So much has gone wrong all at once. And if I talk to the police . . .'

In spite of everything, I feel sympathy for her. My circumstances are different, but I've thought the same lately – about

Andrew's infidelity, his abusive ways, Niamh's silence . . . It's so much – sometimes too much.

But then she says pointedly, 'There's no use my trying to explain to you. You have no idea, Elise, how it feels to . . . to have nothing. How could you?'

Taken aback, I stare at her. 'None of us knows what each other's lives are like. You've said it yourself, before. How can we?' I'm challenging her, wanting her to see how wrong she's got it. That appearances are meaningless and her assumptions about me are way off, because she has no idea what my life is really like. No-one does.

But she doesn't get it. 'Yes, but look at you in that big house, married to the local doctor . . . You don't need to work but you do it anyway. For fun, I suppose – getting to wear that uniform, giving you more money to spend and the perfect excuse not to be here.' Her words are loaded with bitterness.

'What are you insinuating?' Quietly seething, I stare at her. 'What makes you so sure you know what my life is like?'

'Do you know how many people would give anything to be in your shoes?' This time, her voice is filled with resentment.

I stare at her, shock hitting me as she makes no attempt to hide her jealousy. It isn't other people she's talking about. It's herself. Stephanie's jealous of my life. Then her mood suddenly changes. 'Oh God.' She looks mortified. 'I'm so sorry. I should never have said that.'

'No, you shouldn't have,' I snap, already turning away and marching out before she can say anything, I close the door hard behind me before almost walking into Ida Jones.

'Elise, my dear. How are you? How's young Niamh?' In a woollen coat with a colourful knitted scarf, Ida looks puzzled as she takes in my mood.

Hastily I try to compose myself, but Stephanie's words are

still ringing in my ears. 'We're fine.' I try to soften my voice. 'We're both fine, thank you . . . I just called in to see Stephanie. It's a difficult time for her.'

Ida's eyes linger on me. 'You look a little upset. Are you sure you're all right? It can't have been easy for you, either, what with—'

But I interrupt. 'I'm fine. Really. Thank you.' I glance up at the shop window. 'I'm sure Stephanie will be pleased to see you.'

'Yes.' It's as though Ida's speaking to herself. 'Come for coffee, Elise dear. So much has happened. I haven't seen you in such a long time.'

I've a sudden need to get away from here, to be alone. I nod. 'I'll call you – when my next flight schedule comes out.'

★

I'm still angry with Stephanie as I drive away. I know her life is collapsing around her, but she has no right to make assumptions about other people. By the time I reach home, my anger hasn't dissipated. In the house, I throw my bag on the table. Then thinking what Stephanie said – *if I talk to the police* – I realise there's every chance she isn't going to. Without hesitating, I grab my phone and call the number DS May gave me.

She answers straight away. 'DS May.'

'Hello. It's Elise Buckley.' I'm floundering, suddenly less sure of what I want to say, terrified I'm opening a Pandora's box. But I can't go back. 'There's something I think you need to know.'

★

In the thirty minutes before DS May's car pulls up in the drive, I swing between fobbing her off and telling her the truth about

170

James, but in the end, duty wins over. James is involved in a business that puts children at risk. I should have gone to the police the moment I found out. But there's Stephanie, too. I saw a different side to her earlier – unstable, poisonous. Whatever she said about calling the police, I don't trust her.

'Come in.' I hold the door open for DS May, who looks like someone's mum rather than a policewoman in her printed cord skirt and suede boots. She follows me into the kitchen.

'What was it you wanted to tell me?'

'Would you like to sit down?' As she goes over to the table and pulls out one of the chairs, I take a deep breath. 'James Hampton is caught up in something he's been hiding from you. Stephanie, his wife, told me about it.' I sit down opposite her.

Switching on her notebook, DS May frowns at me. 'What exactly has he done?'

'Someone offered him the chance to invest in a porn business. Apparently they told him they're developing an app, which is why they were looking for investors.' I hesitate. 'She said he knew what he was investing in was porn – there's a website. But what he didn't know until later was that there are images of children, too.'

She leans forward, her gaze suddenly sharp. 'Do you know the name of it?'

'She didn't say. She was very upset.'

'What else has she told you?'

'Just that they were having money problems and James was told it would make him a lot of money. She didn't know who he's involved with.' I look at DS May, wondering how much of this she already knows. 'What he hadn't realised was that once he'd looked at the site on his laptop, it was there in his search history – and whoever runs this, has a list. When he wanted to withdraw his investment, they started blackmailing him. If he didn't pay, they'd tell the police. Now, they're on the brink of losing everything.'

All the time I've been speaking, DS May has been making notes. 'How long has she known?'

I try to remember if Stephanie told me. 'I'm not sure, but not long. She was horrified when she found out,' I emphasise, not wanting DS May to imagine Stephanie was complicit.

DS May leans back, looking oddly satisfied, rather than shocked, as I go on.

'There's something else. This I'm less sure about.' I hesitate. 'I think I told you before that I regularly go running. One morning, almost two weeks after Hollie was found, I took a different route, which comes out in the woods up the lane.'

'On the way in from the main road?' When I nod, DS May writes it down.

'As I came out of the trees, I saw James's car. I was about to go and speak to him, when another car turned up. It parked next to him and he went over and had an angry conversation with the driver. It ended with James shouting and thumping his fist on the roof of the car before it drove away.'

'Did you hear what was said?'

I shake my head. 'I was too far away. But they were definitely arguing.'

'You didn't see who the other driver was? Or recognise the car?'

I shake my head. 'All I noticed was that it was black and expensive-looking, like a lot of cars around here.' I pause. 'There's one final thing. I don't know if you've met Phil Mason? At Hollie's funeral, I saw James giving him a venomous look I couldn't explain and I also noticed he went out of his way to avoid him. It made me wonder if Phil Mason could have been the person James was yelling at in the car. Then later . . .' I pause again, remembering what Andrew had said. 'I asked my husband if he knew Phil Mason, or if he knew whether Phil and James were friends. He told me he did know him and then he said, *"He's not the kind of person you go around asking questions about"*.'

DS May makes more notes then looks up. 'Are your husband and Mason friends?'

'Acquaintances, yes. Friends, I really don't know.' I shake my head.

'When did Stephanie Hampton tell you about James?'

'Just before the funeral. She asked me to wait a few days. She wanted them to remember Hollie without the funeral being sullied by what James had got involved with.'

Her face is unreadable. 'You didn't think you should tell us right away?'

'Of course I know I should have.' My face feels flushed, and I glance away, trying to remember exactly what I'd been thinking. 'But they'd just lost a child. To me, respecting their grief took precedence over everything. I could understand her wanting to have the funeral without everyone talking about what James had done. Anyway, Stephanie did say she was going to call you – I just thought too much time had already passed and I shouldn't wait any longer.'

'Mrs Buckley . . .' DS May pauses. 'Please don't keep information related to a crime to yourself. You could be charged with perverting the course of justice.' She sounds less than impressed.

Heat rises in my cheeks. 'I did what I thought was right.'

'It wasn't your decision to make. We would have spoken to Mr Hampton but it wouldn't necessarily have interfered with the funeral.' She pauses. 'When did you last see Mrs Hampton?'

'Today.' I look at her. 'I went to her salon.'

'Is she still there now?'

I glance at the clock on the wall. 'If it's quiet, she closes early. You may have missed her for today.'

As DS May gets up, I ask, 'What happens now?'

'Obviously we have to talk to both her and Mr Hampton. Have you told anyone else what you've told me?'

'No.'

'Be careful, Mrs Buckley.' Her face is grave. 'Desperate people are capable of extreme things. If you're concerned at any time, call the police.'

'What's going on?' Registering the seriousness of what she's saying, I feel the blood drain from my face.

'I can't say anything for sure, but there may be other people in the village who are involved in the same . . .' She hesitates before adding, 'The same business as James Hampton. I would be very careful who you mention this to.'

It's only after she's driven away that I realise what I forgot to tell her – that I'm sure Stephanie's told James that I know.

Chapter Twenty-Two

Jo

'Why didn't we know this before?' Getting up, the DI paces over to the window. 'There have been enough police officers poking around the Hamptons' home since Hollie died. All with their bloody eyes closed, by the looks of it.'

'Stephanie Hampton asked her to wait until after Hollie's funeral, and so Elise Buckley decided to keep it to herself.' But he's right. We should have picked up on it.

'Whoever's blackmailing Hampton must have put the fear of God into him for him to believe them. Either that, or they've been very clever about covering any links to the porn site. I assume someone's on their way over to talk to Mrs Hampton?'

'Collins is – she left twenty minutes ago – and I'm going there when I leave here.'

He scratches his head. 'At least we've got a name to follow up now. Philip Mason. We need to bring him in for questioning.'

'I have an address and a photo.' I slide the image across his desk. 'Elise Buckley found it on Google images while I was there. She confirmed it's him. He was at Hollie's funeral.'

The DI frowns. 'Do you think there's anything else she isn't telling us?'

'I don't trust her, that's for sure.' I pause. 'I've just had a thought. The house that Hollie showed Niamh . . . It isn't impossible it was Mason's place. And Mason's land backs onto Park House, where Hollie was found.'

'We need to find him. He could be connected to both the porn ring and Hollie's murder.' The DI speaks through gritted teeth. 'Maybe on one of her free-spirited jaunts, Hollie stumbled across something and Mason felt he had no choice but to get rid of her.'

Niamh

When I think back to Hollie's funeral, all I remember is how wrong it was. The sadness, the hymns, and DS May across the churchyard watching everyone. As I watched James Hampton talking to people afterwards, I wondered if he had any idea what Hollie knew about him. Not that it matters. When you're dead, nothing matters.

It's like I can feel what's happening around me under my skin, in my bones. I think of Hollie's wide, brown eyes, her hair flowing behind her, her constant agitation. Hollie's world was never going to be right. There were too many problems out of her control, things that she couldn't resolve.

Hollie felt more than most people. She lived harder, more intensely, hurt more deeply. I noticed it with Dylan, too, how a light burned between them, dazzling everyone. And then, afterwards, Hollie's world darkened forever.

At the funeral, I wanted to shout at all the villagers. Scream that Hollie should still be here, that her death is yet another that shouldn't have happened. But behind the tears that vanished as soon as they walked out of the church, none of them actually cares.

And it isn't over. The night after the funeral, I overheard my mother ask my father about Phil Mason.

He answered with another of his lies. I know because Hollie told me my father knows Phil Mason very well. Her death isn't the end of this. Nothing will ever be the end of this.

Chapter Twenty-Three

Elise

The greyness of the evening is broken by a single blue light, followed by a siren. My first thought is that it's connected to James Hampton, and I wonder whether the police have arrested him. I don't hear any more until later, when Andrew comes home. Without speaking, he pours himself a drink, downing it in one gulp before pouring another.

'I suppose you should know,' he says at last, dispassionately, unemotionally. 'Stephanie Hampton was in a car accident.'

'God.' Shock hits me. Light-headed, I feel my way to the table, pulling out a chair and sitting down. 'What happened? Is that where you've come from? Is she OK?'

'Actually, I was in the pub at the time. I was supposed to meet James, but he didn't turn up. Then I got a call from the police telling me what had happened – James must have told them where I was and obviously they needed a doctor there immediately. I went straight over – Stephanie's car hit a tree near their home.' He frowns. 'I'm not sure how the police got there so quickly. They must have gone there about something else. Anyway, she's been taken by ambulance to St Richard's.'

'God,' I repeat. After everything else that family has been through, and now this . . . I can't take it in. 'I saw her earlier today – I went to the salon. I can't believe this.'

'Whatever for?' His voice is disdainful.

'To see how she was,' I lie. 'It's called being neighbourly, Andrew.' I pause. 'What are the chances that she'll recover?'

Andrew looks at me. 'You're like everyone else around here, aren't you? Sticking your nose in where it isn't wanted. You really think she'd have wanted to talk to you, of all people? Don't you think the poor woman's been through enough?'

Flabbergasted by his rudeness, I watch him slam his glass down before topping it up.

He goes on. 'If you really want to know, I've no idea if she'll survive. Her pulse was weak, her heart all over the place when she went to the hospital. God knows what speed she was driving at.'

Andrew's voice is cold, disdainful, as if he doesn't care. Meanwhile, guilt creeps up on me because I feel instrumental in what's happened. Stephanie was on edge when I saw her, aware that time was running out. She probably knew that after her outburst this morning, I had no reason not to go to the police. Maybe she decided not to call them in the end. Or maybe, after the conversation I had with DS May, the police went over there because of me.

'Stephanie was worried about James.' I watch Andrew's face, and as he turns around, DS May's warning about being careful comes back to me.

'Did she say why?' His eyes bore into me.

Suddenly uneasy, I shake my head. 'It was a passing comment. I assumed it was because he'd lost Hollie. Stephanie didn't confide in me, Andrew. I don't know her that well.' Pausing, I change the subject, because I want to know something. 'Why were you meeting James tonight?'

'No reason.' He looks away. 'I thought that, after the funeral, he might appreciate the company. I was . . . how did you put it? Being neighbourly?'

'How caring of you, Andrew.' I can't keep the sarcasm out of my voice, knowing he isn't capable of unselfish acts, that there always has to be something in it for Andrew. He's lying. 'You're not even friends with James. In fact, the last time I caught him looking at you, I'd say he seemed positively hostile.'

'You have no idea what you're talking about,' Andrew says smoothly.

He's trying to stifle me, my instincts telling me that I've touched on something he doesn't want me to know.

But I'm wary of pushing him too far. 'Do you know which ward Stephanie's in? I want to see her.'

Andrew takes another swig from his glass. 'She was taken to Accident and Emergency, then admitted to Russet Ward.'

Getting up, I go to find my phone.

'What are you doing?' Andrew sounds annoyed.

'Calling the hospital. I want to know how she is.'

'Don't be ridiculous.' His tone is scathing. 'You're no friend of Stephanie's.'

'Unlike you, Andrew, I'm sympathetic.' And unlike him, I'm being honest. But he snatches my phone away.

'Call them in the morning, Elise, if you must. Right now, you'll be wasting their valuable time when they should be saving lives. It's not as though they'll be able to tell you anything. It's too soon.'

'What about James?'

For a moment, Andrew loses his bluster. 'When I left, the police were with him.'

181

After what I told them earlier, if the police are with James, the chances are they'll be questioning him.

*

The next day, I get up early for a flight to Rome. Apart from a couple of men who've drunk far too much beer for breakfast in the departure lounge, the outbound passengers are quiet. As we touch down, then taxi towards the terminal building, I find I'm suddenly thinking of Stephanie, wishing that she was getting on a flight intending to disappear somewhere like here, in a city rich in history and culture, another world where she could start again. But instead, she's unconscious in a hospital bed.

After the aircraft parks, and all the passengers have disembarked, I quickly check my phone and find a voicemail from Andrew. It's clipped and to the point, no emotion in his voice. *'I thought you'd want to know Stephanie didn't make it.'* As the return passengers board, I'm in shock; on automatic. All I can think is what a waste of a life. The flight back to Gatwick is surreal, life suddenly even more tenuous than usual, no less because I'm at thirty-five thousand feet, where a few millimetres of metal is all there is between life and certain death.

*

I try to call James before driving home, but it goes to voicemail. When Andrew gets home that evening he has little to add to his earlier message, other than citing organ failure as the most probable cause of Stephanie's death.

Whenever I run past the Hamptons' house in the days that follow, the windows are closed and curtains drawn. Even at night, it's in darkness and I wonder how long before the bank forecloses, before what's left of James's life is gone.

Oddly, I find my husband is suddenly home earlier, and

182

around more often, as Stephanie's comment from the last time I saw her comes to mind. *'Do you know how many people would give anything to be in your shoes . . .'* It makes me think about James's hatred, about the jealousy in Stephanie's eyes, and all of a sudden, everything falls into place as I see what's been right under my nose.

I remember the call I picked up ages ago, before Hollie disappeared. No-one had spoken or left a message. After, I'd written the number down, but never called it. Searching in the kitchen drawer where I would have put the piece of paper I'd written it on, I find it, against the odds. Then I dial the number.

After, as I try to take in what I now know to be fact, I take advantage of the fact that Andrew's out. Going to one of the cupboards, I start gathering bottles, pouring away every last drop of his beloved Scotch, then taking the expensive red wine he buys outside and hurling each bottle into the dustbin, listening to the glass shatter. Then back inside, I'm forced to wait, on … mentally preparing what I want to say to him. When he … work and goes to the cupboard where the … empty, he glares at me.

… ks impatientl…

…tly, accusingly.

…rearsing evap-

…otch isn't here.' He speaks…

…Words I've spent most of the afternoon rehearsing.

…orate as I turn to face him. 'You're a fucking liar, Andrew. It

wasn't James you were meeting in the pub the other night.

It was your lover. Don't try to lie your way out of this. I've

worked it out. While James's life has been going down the pan,

you've been fucking his wife.'

Chapter Twenty-Four

Elise

'Me and Stephanie? You really are insane.' Andrew's voice is patronising. 'You need to go back to the specialist, Elise. Maybe there's something he can give you.'

I recognise the first warning sign. Usually it gives way to anger, and if I don't back down now, he'll do whatever it takes to make sure I do. But I'm not backing down when it's so clearly Andrew who's in the wrong here. 'She called the landline. Your lovers usually do, Andrew. Did you know that? Oh, of course you do,' I say sarcastically. 'Silly Elise. It's you who puts them up to it, isn't it? Anyway, this time I wrote the number down, and this afternoon I called it.' It takes all my strength to hold his gaze. I won't let him get to me. 'As you'd expect, it went to voicemail.'

A woman's voice. *'Please leave a message.'* Four words, but it's all you need when it's a voice you know.

It's bad enough to put a face to the mystery woman Andrew's been screwing. But to know that I tried to befriend her, to know that she's now dead after crashing her car. With each passing second, more is becoming clear in m

Hollie's comings and goings here; her agitation, hardly surprising given her father's problems, while her stepmother was shagging Andrew. 'But it got complicated, didn't it, because Hollie found out.'

Poor Hollie, carrying the weight of it alone.

Instead of blustering his way out of it, he shakes his head. 'This is ridiculous, Elise. Yes, I've been seeing someone. It isn't a secret. Hardly surprising when you're so cold towards me.'

Andrew's done this before, twisting the truth, making his behaviour my responsibility. Even so, his audacity is breathtaking. 'I'm not in the habit of sleeping with men who shag around,' I say curtly. 'And we're talking about Stephanie, not me. Maybe it was Hollie who slashed your tyres. Maybe she'd found out.' I shake my head. 'God knows you deserved it.' He'd better hope the police don't make the connection. It would make him a suspect in Hollie's murder.

Andrew's silent for a moment. 'That girl had problems. Hardly surprising given her background.'

I stare at him. It's a staggering example of the way Andrew thinks. 'How can you say that, Andrew?'

Watching his jaw clench, I tense, waiting for a reaction. But today he doesn't explode in anger. Instead, there's a trace of vulnerability I haven't seen in years as he sighs heavily. 'Hollie was completely unstable. There was an incident. Last year.'

'What kind of incident?' My voice is cold. 'And why don't I know about it?'

'It was nothing to do with you,' he says crisply, any impression of vulnerability instantly dispelled. 'But if you must know, now and then, a teenaged girl gets a crush. Usually girls seeking a father figure. Hollie made an appointment to see me at the surgery. She said she had a lump in one of her breasts. I told her I'd ask a chaperone to come in, but she

said she didn't want anyone else in with us. Said she was shy
. . .' A cynical laugh comes from him. 'She made a hell of a
fuss after – accused me of touching her inappropriately. She
even wrote a letter to the practice manager. Of course, they
knew nothing had happened. But even so, it was hugely
embarrassing.'

Damaging to his professional image, too. 'You don't think
you deserved it, Andrew? She'd probably found out about you
and Stephanie.'

'I told you, Elise. She had a crush – one I didn't reciprocate,'
he says sharply. 'You and I both know that Hollie was a mess.
She was all over the place.' He shakes his head. 'I have to say
I'm very happy that Niamh is free of her.' Utterly callous about
Hollie's suffering, he glances at the cupboard. 'Bloody stupid,
throwing away that Scotch.'

It staggers me that he can switch topics like that without so
much as drawing breath. 'You're missing the point, Andrew,' I
say acidly. 'Maybe she knew about you and Stephanie and she
was looking for a way to get back at you.' I shake my head. If
I knew Hollie at all, her first priority would have been to
protect her father. 'Frankly, you deserve far worse.' Then I break
our unspoken agreement. 'How long had you and Stephanie
been seeing each other?'

Without replying, he picks up his jacket and walks out.
Seconds later, I hear his car start. Andrew may believe he can
do what he likes but we've crossed a line tonight and I wonder
if he knows. Fear ripples through me, fear that for years has
been the basis of our relationship; of his silence, his stonewalling,
his anger and humiliation of me perpetually being stepped up
another notch in the escalating scale of his abuse.

It can't go on.

★

The following day, I'm in the garden pruning back last year's growth on the roses that ramble along the wall, enjoying a fragile sense of peace that's long been absent from my life, when DS May and Sergeant Collins arrive. As DS May walks across the garden towards me, I pull off my gardening gloves.

'I'm sorry for turning up like this.' DS May looks apologetic. 'Do you have a moment? I wanted to talk to you about Stephanie Hampton.'

'Will it take long?' I glance at my watch. 'It's just that I have an appointment in an hour's time.'

'We just need to run through a couple of things.' When DS May doesn't offer to come back another time, my heart sinks.

I nod. 'You'd better come in.'

At the back door, I pull off my boots and leave them outside. The kitchen isn't as tidy as it usually is, with unironed clothes piled on the table and this morning's breakfast dishes yet to be cleared. 'I'm a bit behind. But sit down.' I move the pile of washing onto the sofa, stacking the remaining plates and carrying them over to the sink before joining the two policewomen at the kitchen table.

DS May's notebook is already switched on. 'You saw Mrs Hampton very recently didn't you? In fact, you were one of the last people to see her alive. I wanted to ask how she seemed to you.'

'Stephanie?' Given the events that have happened, it seems weeks rather than days since I saw her. 'She was grieving for Hollie. And she was worried about James.'

'Did she say anything to suggest she was thinking of killing herself?'

'No.' I look at her sharply. 'She told me that after she'd spoken to you, she was going away. Somewhere far away from here – I think that's what she said.'

DS May frowns at me. 'She didn't imply anything more sinister?'

'No.' The suggestion that Stephanie would take her own life shocks me. 'You don't think . . .' I tail off.

'We found a letter in her salon. It's almost certain she planned to take her own life. Whether the crash was an accident, we don't know.'

Shocked, I try to take in what DS May is saying. 'I suppose it's easy to interpret her words completely differently now. I was on a flight to Rome the day she died. I was actually thinking of her just before I checked my phone and picked up a message from Andrew, telling me she'd died.'

'Your husband was her doctor.'

I nod. 'Yes. To be honest, he's doctor to half the village. His practice is the only one between here and Chichester.' Then I look at her more closely, suddenly aware there's something she isn't saying. 'Why do you ask?'

As DS May's eyes meet Sergeant Collins's, I realise they know about Andrew and Stephanie. Folding my arms, I sit back, watching them. 'Go on.'

'This is a little awkward.' DS May looks uncomfortable. 'But we have evidence that suggests that your husband and Mrs Hampton were intimate.'

As another layer of dignity is stripped away, I shrug. 'So it would seem. I may as well ask, who told you?'

'No-one. There were text messages on her phone – they made it quite clear what their relationship was. But you knew?'

I feel slightly sick. 'I've only just found out. I worked it out after Stephanie died.' When they look surprised, I add, 'Oh, I knew he was having an affair – just not who with. Andrew's had several affairs. I tolerate them.'

DS May's face is blank. 'Plenty of women turn a blind eye

to their husband's infidelity. But considering Mrs Hampton had confided in you, you must have been shocked.'

'She told me I didn't know how lucky I was.' I shake my head. 'I think she loved James, but he'd screwed things up between them. Maybe she needed someone more solid – like her good old, reliable doctor.' Even I can't believe I'm defending the woman who was sleeping with my husband.

DS May looks at me oddly. 'You were OK with that?'

'Absolutely not. Don't try to understand my marriage, Detective Sergeant. It really doesn't bear scrutiny. I stay for one reason only. My daughter.'

'Why can't you leave him?' She makes no attempt to hide the genuine curiosity in her eyes. 'You're an independent woman. If you separated, half the proceeds from selling this house would buy you a lovely cottage, even around here. Children are often better off with divorced parents, rather than stuck in the middle of a war zone.'

'You have no idea what goes on here.' My response is too sharp. 'Anyway, Andrew would destroy me.' Watching their faces, I try to explain. 'He likes the image. This house.' I gesture around the large proportions of the kitchen. 'His daughter, the private school she goes to . . . The fact that we're together, when so many marriages flounder. Status is important to Andrew. He's a doctor and it's important that his patients believe in him.' It's about control, too, but I don't tell them that.

From their expressions, I know I've painted enough of a picture for them to understand how he is. Then I add carefully, 'None of us know how it is to be someone else, so I don't believe any of us should judge.' I'm thinking of Stephanie, obviously, but myself, too. Still watching them, I lean back in my chair again.

'Do you think Hollie knew what was going on between your husband and her stepmother?'

I'm silent for a moment, wondering if they think Andrew is a suspect. 'It's possible. Andrew told me she set him up at the surgery. Accused him of touching her inappropriately. He said she had a crush that he didn't reciprocate, which I find impossible to believe. It would make more sense for her to have been angry with him about something.'

DS May looks puzzled. 'But why would he invent something like that?'

'His ego,' I say briefly. 'Or perhaps, for reasons of his own, he wanted to convince people that Hollie was unstable and irrational.'

She shakes her head slowly. 'But why? Why would he want people to think of her like that?'

I shrug. 'I've no idea.'

'Did your husband say if James Hampton knew about his affair with Mrs Hampton?'

'No, but it's possible.' My frown deepens. 'It would explain the way James looked at him in the churchyard.' I catch sight of the clock, getting to my feet in a hurry. 'I'm sorry, but if there isn't anything else, I have an appointment to get to.'

★

After they drive away, I tidy the kitchen and get ready to go out. Thinking about where I'm going, it seems fitting that the blue skies of earlier are clouding over, that the sunlight has gone; that a minute later, it starts to rain.

Chapter Twenty-Five

Jo

Elise Buckley's revelations about her husband throw up more questions for which there are no answers. His medical practice confirms there was an incident with Hollie and that there had been a note on her file about mental health issues and a suggested referral, which was never followed up.

I try to think. By her own admission, the Buckleys' marriage has problems, backed up by the fact that the husband was having an affair. Not the first, either. As doctor to most of the village, Andrew Buckley has a window into everyone's lives. But it isn't just Elise who's told me what he can be like. Ida Jones had suggested the same.

My instincts are telling me not to trust him. If Hollie knew about Stephanie's affair with Andrew Buckley, it gives him a motive. And if she'd confronted him about it, who knows what may have happened.

The pool where Hollie was found in the grounds of Park House isn't far from the Buckleys' house. Clicking on my laptop, I bring up a map of the village, noticing for the first time that Park House, the Buckleys' house, and Phil Mason's, while physically separated by stone walls and tall trees, form the three corners of a triangle.

★

In the aftermath of Stephanie Hampton's death, we question her husband. With both his wife and daughter dead, James is broken. Even so, on the subject of Phil Mason, he remains frustratingly silent.

When we take a break in the DI's office, I explain where we're at. 'I think he's frightened, sir,' I tell him. 'Either that, or he's hoping we don't have anything concrete on him.'

'Then we need to make him see how misguided that notion is, don't we?' he says impatiently. 'What about Mason's house? Any luck?'

'Apparently, it's locked up, sir, the curtains and blinds drawn. It looks as though he's gone away.'

'Try and find out where he is. We need to speak to him.' The DI sounds frustrated. 'What's the time?'

'Twelve, sir.'

'Right. We'll question Hampton together this afternoon.'

★

When we go into the interview room, James Hampton barely looks up from where he's slumped at the table. Beside him, his lawyer's face is blank. I pull out a chair. 'This is DI Saunders, Mr Hampton. We have a few more questions for you.'

The DI clears his throat. 'I understand you bought into a business through Philip Mason. Is that correct?'

The lawyer looks mildly irritated. 'My client has already confirmed this to your colleague, just as he's confirmed he had no idea what he was getting into.'

194

'I see.' The DI leans back in his chair. 'Didn't know it was porn, is that what you're saying, Mr Hampton?'

When James Hampton shakes his head, the DI says, 'Answer yes or no for the tape, Mr Hampton.'

At Hampton's muttered *'no'*, I glance at his lawyer.

'You're already facing potential charges of the possession and distribution of pornographic images of children. Lying isn't going to look good when you go to court. Nor is the fact that you're perverting the course of a police investigation.' The DI pauses. 'You want us to believe that you invested a substantial amount of money without checking out what you were buying. Is that correct?'

It's clear Hampton's caught somewhere impossible. But the DI's right. No-one invests without knowing where their money's going – or had he been stupid enough, desperate enough, to do just that? And why is he protecting Mason?

'All right. I knew.' He slumps lower in his chair. 'But not about the images of children.'

'And you thought that was a justifiable way to – in your late wife's words – *make a lot of money*?'

'It happens,' James Hampton mutters.

'That doesn't make it morally defensible. Let me get this straight. Even though you had money problems yourself, you handed over all the cash you could get your hands on to a man you took at his word to invest in a questionable business without a contract of any kind. Is that correct?'

Still, Hampton remains silent.

'If you can tell us what Mason's up to, we'll see what we can do about reducing the charges against you. Mason's already in the crosshairs.' The DI's voice is steely. 'Nothing you say can change that. You might as well tell us what you know. After all, Mason hasn't exactly done you any favours, has he?'

James Hampton nods miserably. 'He said that if we had a gentleman's agreement, it would save a fortune in tax.'

The DI glances at me, then back to Hampton. 'Porn and tax evasion, eh? I'd really like to have a chat with your friend. Do you have any idea where he might be?'

He shakes his head. 'I haven't seen him since the funeral.'

'Have you heard from him at all?'

'No.'

'When did you first realise your money was being invested in child porn?'

'Not to start with. He showed me a website.' James Hampton looks haunted. 'Then he told me he was developing an app and he was looking for investors. At first, I was shocked. But then he told me thousands of people make money in the porn industry – and it might as well be us as anyone else. He told me there were safeguards in place and the girls needed to make money . . .' He rests his head in his hands, before looking up again. 'I was desperate. A few days later, he called me. Said he'd like to come over and catch up with what I wanted to do. He came into my office . . . He suggested we take a look at the website together. He'd left his laptop in his car, so of course, I suggested we use mine . . .' He pauses, his face ashen as he remembers. 'He showed me images. He told me they were of teenagers over the age of consent . . . And I wanted to believe him.'

'Go on, please.' The DI's voice is curt.

'I transferred the money into his account. When I received the first return on my investment, I didn't think too much about where it had come from. I was just relieved to have some money coming in. Then, one evening, I'd had a couple of drinks and I took another look at the website. This time, I looked at more pictures than Mason had shown me on my laptop. That was when I discovered images of children.'

I turn to the DI. 'We have the search history, sir.'

The DI's face is implacable, his eyes riveted to James Hampton's. 'What did you do then?'

'I called Mason and told him I wanted my investment back. I offered to repay the money I'd received, but after that, I wanted out.'

'What did he say?'

James Hampton's voice is heavy. 'At first, he tried to charm me around to his way of thinking. When I wouldn't go along with it, he turned nasty. He said that because the site was now in my search history, I could be reported to the police for being in possession of pornographic images of children, unless I paid him off.'

'And you believed him.' The DI doesn't take his eyes off Hampton. 'It didn't occur to you that he wouldn't be able to do that without incriminating himself?'

'He told me how easy it would be to anonymously tip off the police. Then he said that they'd never find anything to link the website to him.' Hampton looks wretched. 'I couldn't take the risk. At that point, I was wishing I'd kept my mouth shut. If I had . . .' He shakes his head. 'I wouldn't have lost anything, would I? I might even have ended up richer.'

For a moment there, I'd almost felt sorry for him. But that last remark reveals the depth of his self-interestedness. Beside me, the DI stiffens.

'Perhaps. But you'd have found yourself in just as much trouble further down the line.' He pauses. 'When did your wife find out?'

At the mention of Stephanie, a look of regret crosses

197

Hampton's face as at last he shows some remorse. 'Recently. I hid it from her.' He says it as though his secrecy makes what he's done less abhorrent. 'But she found a letter from the bank a few weeks before she died.'

He pauses and the DI says, 'So as well as bankrupting you, your deal with Mason has effectively led to the death of your wife.'

'Mr Hampton . . .' I pause, trying to establish if there's a link to Hollie's death. Just as it was with Elise Buckley, there's no easy way to ask this. 'Did you know your wife was having an affair with Andrew Buckley?'

In his chair, he seems to rock slightly. 'It wouldn't surprise me,' he says at last through gritted teeth.

Frowning, I give him a moment before asking again. 'Are you saying you knew about them?'

Unable to control himself this time, he snaps at me, 'No. I didn't.'

So what was behind his hostility towards Andrew Buckley, which Elise witnessed at Hollie's funeral?

'Had you been to your wife's salon recently?' I watch him closely.

'Not for a while.'

I nod. 'I guessed as much. If you had, you'd have noticed business was far from booming. I'd say she was winding it down, with every intention of closing it.'

James looks horrified. 'But she told me the salon was doing fine. Bookings were up. She said we'd get through this.' As he falls silent, I know what he's doing. He's replaying every excuse she made to stay late at work, to be working at weekends. It's clear he'd believed it at the time, but now he's wondering if any of it was true. That's what happens when someone cheats – you question everything.

'I suppose you believed what you wanted to believe.' I pause.

Fists tightly clenched, he holds it together. 'It's this fucking village.' His voice is full of anger, the strain clearly visible on his face. 'Ever since Hollie met Dylan, it's been nothing but a nightmare.'

'Dylan?' My ears prick up. I've never heard his name mentioned before.

He utters a brief, cynical laugh. 'Right there, that one word, tells you how little you know about what's happened around here. Ask Elise Buckley. No, on second thought, ask her bastard of a husband. They know far more than I can tell you.'

'Who is Dylan?' I repeat.

James looks stricken. 'The boy Hollie loved, with all of her heart. But he screwed her up – destroyed her. If you're looking for her murderer, it started with him.'

Chapter Twenty-Six

Elise

I swap a flight to go to my husband's lover's funeral, keeping up the appearance of the smartly dressed, loyal doctor's wife, the cracks in our marriage hidden beneath layers of makeup, trying not to think about how many people know as I take my place at his side. It seems two funerals in the village within a month are too much for most people. The church is only half full, the flowers pitifully lacking.

James sits at the front with two men I've never seen before either side of him. He speaks to no-one. There is nothing uplifting about the service. It's only after it's over that I realise the two men are plain clothes police officers. Their presence confirms my suspicions that the police are holding him. After waiting around only until Stephanie's coffin is carried out through the door and laid to rest next to Hollie's grave, they escort him away.

The villagers may have let her down, but as I walk outside to the churchyard, it's as though nature has done its best for Stephanie. The funeral may have been sparse in every sense, but out here primroses crouch in the shadier corners alongside brave stems of the first bluebells; under our feet, the grass is scattered with violets and the palest lilac wildflowers, the paltry efforts of the congregation during the few hymns outshone by the chorus of birdsong.

As a rule, Andrew avoids touching me. But today, in a gesture that's proprietary rather than affectionate, I feel his hand lightly against my lower back as he nods towards the path. He clearly doesn't want to hang around. 'Shall we go, Elise?' It isn't a question, but I've no more desire than he has to stay here any longer than necessary.

As we walk home, I casually tell him what the police told me. 'They know about you and Stephanie.' Beside me, I feel him tense.

When he speaks, his voice is measured. 'I'm assuming it wasn't you who told them.'

Taking a leaf out of Andrew's book, I avoid answering. 'Do you think I enjoy being made to look stupid?'

He ignores me. 'It rather makes one wonder who did.' I know it's for my benefit that instead of annoyance, there's amusement in his voice.

As I keep walking, pulling my coat tighter around me, nausea rises in my throat. I'm sick of him, of everything he does. 'Have you a new one lined up? A lover, I mean?' My tone is intentionally, inappropriately light, spelling it out that he can do what he likes but I won't let him get to me.

'Don't be ridiculous,' he snarls.

'Me? Ridiculous?' But my emotions are too stretched. In spite of my best intentions, I lose it. 'You're the one who's fucking ridiculous, Andrew. Look at you. Your entire life is a façade. Us, your affairs, your holier than thou act with the villagers. But do you know what? No-one's fooled. And even if they were, they'll soon see through you. It'll catch up with you, Andrew. Don't think it won't.'

I feel his fingers around my arm, knowing that if my coat wasn't thick, there'd be red bruising where he's pinching me. But recklessness seizes me. 'What are you going to do?' I'm deliberately goading him, unable to stop myself. 'This act? The mighty doctor with the wife who's so important to him? Everyone knows it's fake.'

In the split second before he reacts, I know I've pushed him too far. His hands close around my neck as he slams me against a tree. 'Bitch,' he hisses, closer to losing control than I've ever seen him. 'You think you're so clever, don't you? You'll never win, Elise. I know too much about you.' His eyes glint with hatred. 'Do you know how easy it would be for me to kill you?'

Despair overwhelms me in that moment, as I know he's capable of anything. A sob escapes me as I imagine Niamh left motherless and – far worse than that – being left alone with *him*. However much I want to be free of him, however wrong this is, it's this side of him, his physical violence, which means I'm trapped.

Relaxing his grasp, he arranges his face in the facsimile of a smile. 'But that would be too easy.' Pretending to dust off my coat, he tucks my hand under his arm. When he speaks, it's clear he's enjoying himself. 'It's so much more fun watching you suffer.'

*

At home, I lock myself in my bathroom, carefully taking off my clothes and examining the red marks on my neck before applying concealer over them and pulling on a high-necked sweater. Andrew's behaviour is growing more extreme. What will he do next time?

But my question is followed by another. *Could Andrew have*

killed Hollie? Had she goaded him, forced him into a corner, pushed him too far? All those evenings and weekends, when Andrew's been out, I've had no idea where he's been. I've assumed he's been meeting his lover. How convenient then, that the one person who could have verified his whereabouts is now dead.

Or did Hollie find out something about the porn business that James was involved in? Out of everyone in this village, there are two people I can imagine being capable of murder.

Having seen him lose his temper, the first is James Hampton.

The second is my husband.

I think of the way Andrew spoke about Phil Mason. The few times I've seen him, Mason's presence has disturbed me. There's a cold watchfulness about him. He gives the impression of a hunter in a world where the rest of us are fair game. After seeing him with James, then Andrew, and watching his iron self-control at Hollie's funeral, I know he's a man I want nothing to do with.

When I think back to how upset Hollie was the day I met her in the churchyard, I imagine her discovering the porn business James had invested in, what it would have done to her. It would explain why she was so agitated. Maybe she found out that Mason was blackmailing her father, then confronted him and so he killed her? I stop myself. All of this is wild speculation, but Hollie's body *was* found in the grounds of Park House, just a stone's throw from where Mason lives. It's also not far from our house.

Suddenly I'm claustrophobic, thinking of Andrew again, then this village, Hollie's murder . . . All of it is too much. Getting up, I pull on a jacket and go out.

I walk briskly, trying to shake off the feeling that hangs over me. The air is cold but I'm warm by the time I reach Ida Jones's cottage. Thinking of what she said when I saw her last, I pause to knock on her door, instantly regretting it, wishing I'd called her first to check that she isn't busy. But then I hear the latch lift; the door opens and Ida appears.

'Elise! What a lovely surprise.' A smile crosses her face, but then she falters, studying me. 'Would you like to come in?'

'Thank you. I hope I haven't interrupted you? I should have called you but I wasn't working, so thought I'd just pop by – if you're not busy?'

'Oh no, dear. Not at all. I was going through some old photos.' When I follow her through to her sitting room, I see her small dining table is covered in them. 'Young folk these days don't appreciate them, do they? Everything's on their phones. All very well till they lose them.' She sounds wistful. 'Now, come into the kitchen and I'll put the kettle on. Would you like a cup of tea?'

'Thank you.' I'm ridiculously grateful for the warmth, not just of her cottage, but how her presence feels, making me suddenly aware of the absence of warmth in my own life.

Looking around I see that her kitchen is dated and the pine units are in need of a coat of paint, but her curtains are fresh and there are pots of herbs on her windowsill. It's homely in a way I'm suddenly nostalgic for. Hugging my arms around myself, I watch her warm the teapot. I can't remember the last time I saw anyone do that. Then she gets two mugs.

She turns briefly. 'How's young Niamh?'

'She's quiet. Losing Hollie has rocked her. It's impossible for her to understand why anyone would have wanted to kill her.'

'It's difficult for any of us to understand.' Offering me a mug, Ida picks up the other and starts towards the sitting room. 'Let's go through there.'

I sink into the sofa, feeling the tension leave my body, then exhaustion taking over, suddenly aware of the strain I'm under but conscious of Ida watching me.

'These are sad times,' Ida says quietly. 'Those two poor people, and so close together. From the same family, too . . . I don't know how that man is coping.' She goes on. 'Have you seen him at all?'

I nod. 'At the funeral earlier.'

'I didn't make it.' Ida looks sorry. 'I had a hospital appointment this morning. I do hope enough people were there.'

'Not really.' There's a lump in my throat.

Ida hesitates. 'There's no accounting for some folk. You'd think they'd show a little more kindness.' I wonder if word has got around about Stephanie's crash possibly being intentional, *or if Ida knows about Andrew and Stephanie* . . . . But she changes the subject. 'So, what about you, dear? How are you?'

Her question takes me by surprise. It's so long since anyone has asked anything like that. As tears fill my eyes, I try to wipe them away without her noticing. Her frown deepens. 'Elise, dear. What's wrong? Whatever it is, you do know you can talk to me.'

I look at her, touched by her kindness, but where do I start? There's so much she doesn't know – about Andrew, Niamh, Hollie . . .

'Oh, I'm fine.' I pin on a ghost of the mask I wear. 'It's been a difficult time, hasn't it?' I can't burden her with everything that's wrong in my life – because even if I did tell her, nothing would change.

Niamh

I try to remember Hollie alive – free, happy, the way she was when she was with Dylan. If he hadn't gone, none of this would have happened. Dylan abandoning her changed Hollie's life.

But there were consequences for all of us . . .

I avoid the churchyard for a while, until in the end it pulls me back. Hollie's grave doesn't yet have a headstone, but Hollie wouldn't care about that. Her voice is in the air, the wind blowing her words into my mind: 'Remember me as I was, Niamh . . . Don't let anyone forget . . .'

As I stand beside her grave, the sun warming my back, I try to imagine the night she died, Hollie's last minutes. Her body in shock as cold, dark water engulfed her, her fear as it closed over her, the fight to reach the surface and then the realisation that there was nothing she could do; she was dying. I wonder how long it took before she stopped thinking, before oxygen stopped reaching her brain, before her body went limp; how much more time passed before Hollie's spirit left it.

Chapter Twenty-Seven

Jo

The day after Stephanie Hampton's funeral, we finally track down the delivery driver, then question him about the man he met to discuss the porn business when we discover that the man fits Mason's description, confirmed later when we show him a photo of Mason.

As a result, the search for Mason is stepped up, but apart from his passport being traced to a flight he boarded to Paris a week ago, he's become invisible.

Andrew Buckley continues to prey on my mind. I know the power that people like him have to maintain control, force silence, hide the truth about themselves. I arrange to visit him at his home. In the light of what James Hampton has told us and what I know about Doctor Buckley's personal life, I'm curious to hear what he has to say.

As I drive towards the village, the countryside bears long-awaited signs that winter is ending. Grass verges show new signs of growth and tree branches bear the faintest tinge of green. After the wettest few months I can remember, they're signs of hope that the worst is over, that spring isn't far away.

In the Buckleys' garden, the shelter afforded by the tall stone walls that surround it mean that the seasons have already moved on. Trees bear pale pink blossoms and clumps of primroses and bluebells are interspersed with verdant shoots of what's to follow. I linger, taking it in, unaware of Andrew Buckley watching me until I glance towards the house and see his face at a window. When I reach the door, he opens it before I knock.

'Come in, Detective Sergeant. I'm afraid my wife's at work. I hope that isn't going to inconvenience you?' His manner is smooth, with an authority he obviously doesn't expect to be questioned.

I can't help but wonder if it's by accident or design that he's arranged to meet me when he's alone here. 'Not at all. I just have a few questions for you. It shouldn't take long.'

His face is impassive. 'Absolutely. Would you like to come through?'

Instead of the kitchen, where I've spoken to Elise and Niamh, he shows me through to a large sitting room, extravagantly furnished with tall sash windows looking out onto the garden.

He gestures towards one of the large sofas. 'Do have a seat.'

Getting an impression of how it is to be one of his patients, I sit down, glancing around the room. It's deliberately imposing rather than comfortable, with a couple of large modern prints on one of the walls and an enormous elaborate mirror resting on the mantelpiece.

He waits a few seconds before sitting opposite me. 'So, how can I help?'

His deliberate affability isn't lost on me. Starting up my notebook, I take a deep breath. 'You're aware we're holding James Hampton?'

He nods, his face sober. 'I had heard. May I ask why?'

'Do you know a Philip Mason, Doctor Buckley?' Ignoring

210

his question, I study his face for a tell-tale giveaway sign as I mention Mason's name, but there's nothing.

'I have a drink with him now and then. He lives in the village but he's away a lot on business.'

'I understand from James Hampton that you know him quite well. You spoke to him at Hollie's funeral, didn't you?'

'Did I?' As he frowns, I can't work out whether his look of blankness is contrived before it clears. 'Of course. I remember talking to him about how terrible it was that Hollie had died.'

He's saying all the right things, but my instincts are on high alert. I change tack. 'I understand you and Stephanie Hampton had an involvement.'

His eyes narrow. 'Who told you that?'

'There were messages on Mrs Hampton's phone that make it very clear what was going on between you.' As I speak, the tightening of his jaw gives him away.

Slowly arranging his hands in his lap, he considers his response. 'Stephanie and I were intimate.' He looks at me. 'Plenty of people have affairs, Detective Sergeant.' There's the faintest hint of warning in his voice as he goes on. 'Can I ask you what relevance this has to Hollie's murder?'

I hold his gaze. 'Doctor Buckley, I'm sure you're able to understand that after a murder followed by another death – potentially a suicide – we need as much information as possible about the deceased.' When he doesn't say anything, I continue. 'Mr Hampton suggested that I ask you about someone called Dylan. He said that Hollie was in love with him, but he left her. He said it destroyed Hollie. Initially, he told me to talk to your wife, but then he backtracked and said the person I needed to talk to, was you.'

'Really.' There's a look of disdain on his face. 'Well, I'm afraid Hampton's got his facts wrong. But I'll tell you what I know,

211

for what it's worth. Dylan and Hollie were boyfriend and girl-friend – a teenage thing,' he adds dismissively. 'But it wasn't Dylan who left Hollie, Detective Sergeant.' Andrew Buckley shakes his head, taking his time. 'There are issues of doctor–patient confidentiality, obviously . . .' As I go to interrupt him, he raises a hand. 'It's well known that Hollie Hampton had problems, but they were worse than most people realised. I was going to refer her to a psychiatrist as I was increasingly convinced she was suffering from a personality disorder. But it's not straight-forward when you're dealing with a teenager as unstable as she was.'

I've heard various accounts of Hollie's free-spirited nature and her bunking off school, but no-one's even suggested anything like this. 'What makes you say that?'

'It's difficult to pinpoint – to the layman.' He looks at me briefly. 'But since you ask, there wasn't just one thing. As she and Niamh were friends, she spent quite a bit of time with us. Being a doctor, I'm obviously able to see traits that other people don't notice. She was unpredictable, exceptionally flighty, highly emotional and given to recklessness . . .'

'I assume this is documented in her medical notes?'

He shakes his head. 'It was a tricky situation.' He pauses. 'There was an incident at the surgery.' He goes on to tell me the same story I heard from Elise.

'I'm aware of the details.'

He frowns slightly. 'So you'll be aware Hollie claimed I assaulted her?'

'And you hadn't?'

'God, no.' Andrew Buckley looks horrified. 'Hollie wrote a letter of complaint and the practice manager got involved. I explained that Hollie had a crush, one that clearly I didn't reciprocate. That kind of thing is rare, but not unheard of. It's usually girls or young women seeking the attention of a father figure.'

I'm puzzled, because it doesn't add up. 'But that would hardly apply to Hollie. From what we know, she had a good relationship with her father.' I watch him more closely.

'I said usually. It isn't always the case.' But Andrew Buckley looks uncomfortable.

Alarm bells are ringing. If, as Andrew Buckley insists, nothing happened, Hollie must have had a reason for what she did. Staring at him, I trust my hunch. 'Doctor Buckley, could there have been any other reason why Hollie might have lodged a complaint against you?'

He shifts on the sofa. 'I'd rather this was kept quiet . . .' He pauses. 'If you must know, she'd found out about me and Stephanie.' He adjusts the lime-coloured cushions behind him.

'So you thought you could explain away Hollie's accusations as a teenage crush?' I stare at him, flabbergasted that he could do that.

'She made one hell of a fuss about what I'd allegedly done. I thought that she was young enough that explaining it away as a crush and referring her for psychiatric help was the most practical resolution.' He has the grace at least to look discomfited. 'I had the rest of my career to think about. I'm not proud of my actions, Detective Sergeant. But I did what I had to.'

His arrogance leaves me horrified. To think that he could lie about Hollie, just to save his own skin . . .

'Did you touch Hollie inappropriately, Doctor Buckley?'

He looks outraged. 'Whatever else I might have done, I could never have done that.' Buckley goes on. 'Detective Sergeant, none of this is ideal. I'm perfectly aware my marriage isn't what it should be, in spite of my best efforts. But none of us are saints.'

Brushing his infidelity under the carpet. Charming.

I wonder what Stephanie got out of their affair. From what I've seen, I'd challenge any woman to have a loving relationship with Andrew Buckley as my impressions are of a man who's cold, domineering, and unsympathetic.

He's also manoeuvred the conversation away from my initial question – deliberately, I wouldn't mind betting – and so I steer it back. 'Doctor Buckley, we were talking about Dylan. Where does he come into this?'

Andrew Buckley looks at me sharply. 'As I've explained, Hollie had a number of problems. I'm not sure he does come into it.'

Something flashes in his eyes. Too used to calling the shots, he doesn't like it when it's the other way around. 'That's not what James Hampton said.' Determined to keep him focused, I watch him closely. When he doesn't respond, I add, 'Don't worry. If there's nothing more you can tell me, I can talk to your wife.'

'There's no need.' His voice is calm, his words measured – and loaded with contempt. Knowing he's cornered, Andrew Buckley makes no attempt to hide his loathing. 'To be honest, it's quite surprising the police haven't found out before.' Despite his attempt to somehow turn this around and make it look as though it's the police who have done something wrong, it's obvious I've hit on something. 'Dylan and Hollie thought they were in love – as much as two teenagers can really be in love.' He speaks disparagingly. 'They went off the rails, as anyone you ask will tell you. They weren't good for each other. Hollie was difficult and when he met her, Dylan lost interest in everything else.'

I still don't understand the secrecy around Dylan. 'So what happened? All I know is he left. Do you know where he is?'

'Dylan died,' he says shortly. 'After he and Hollie split up, he took an overdose. It was a ludicrous waste of a life. He was sixteen years old. There's a lot about that girl people don't know. She really messed Dylan up when she left him. I probably shouldn't say this, but to be honest, I'm quite glad she's out of Niamh's life.'

He speaks cynically, bitterly, as though he blames Hollie for Dylan's death on some level. I'm astonished that in a small village, no-one else has thought to mention this. That sense of the villagers closing ranks I had before comes back to me. 'You knew his family?'

A shadow crosses his face as he speaks through gritted teeth. 'He was my son.'

I'm shocked. 'I had no idea.'

'Why would you?' His voice is accusing. 'It was two years ago, Detective Sergeant. Since then, it's been a difficult time for all of us. My daughter has lost her brother and my wife is emotionally fragile. She had a lot of problems after he died. She still isn't back to how she used to be.' His description of Elise bears no resemblance to the woman I've talked to. There's a vulnerability about her, but there's grit, too. The loss of her brother, however, may explain why Niamh finds it so hard to talk about Hollie's death, especially coming so soon after. He goes on. 'We're trying to get on with our lives. Dredging up the past is incredibly painful.'

I nod. 'I can imagine.'

'It probably explains why no-one's mentioned him to you.' His voice is calm again. 'James is just desperate to pin Hollie's death on someone – when people are at the end of their tether, they'll say anything to get what they want.' His eyes glint as though he knows something I don't. 'But wouldn't you say that's true of most of us?'

★

215

As I drive away, I replay what Andrew Buckley said about how most of us would say anything to get what we want. Maybe he would, but would other people? Then I think about another comment he made. *To be honest, I'm quite glad she's out of Niamh's life.* And suddenly I'm wondering just how much he wanted Hollie out of the way. Enough to kill her?

Dylan must be the secret I've sensed people in the village holding back from me. But his death was two years ago. It's more likely that Hollie's death is somehow related to the porn ring business.

On the face of it, Andrew Buckley appears to be a respected doctor. His marriage isn't happy, but that isn't necessarily damning. His daughter is self-contained, but given the obvious problems between her parents and the fact that she's lost her brother as well as her friend, it isn't surprising.

During our conversation, I saw many different sides of Doctor Buckley, ranging from professional and astute, to cutting and manipulative. Even when he speaks with compassion and understanding, it's cold, calculated, false, leaving me in no doubt that the only person Andrew Buckley cares about is himself. He displays all the characteristics of a psychopath.

Chapter Twenty-Eight

Elise

Days have passed during which the tension between myself and Andrew has silently escalated, and I know I have to try to find the courage to talk to him again. His car is in the drive that afternoon when I come back from shopping, and as I go into the kitchen, I hear the television on in the sitting room. After putting the shopping away, I glance upstairs. Seeing Niamh's door firmly closed, I hesitate outside the sitting room, taking a deep breath before walking in.

'We have to talk, Andrew.'

Engrossed in his phone, he doesn't even bother to look up. 'For Christ's sake, I've done enough talking today, to the police. Anyway, you and I have nothing to say to each other.'

'As a matter of fact, I do have things to say.' Speaking through gritted teeth, I step closer, suddenly furious at the way he treats me. 'Can't you put your fucking phone down even for a minute?'

On impulse, I reach to snatch it away from him. But as he holds it out of reach, I glimpse the screen. Taking in the image on it, I freeze with shock as it registers he's looking at an image of a young girl.

My stomach lurches, my heart racing out of control, thinking of what James is involved in. 'You disgust me,' I say with all the contempt I can muster. 'How can you?'

'It's not what you think, Elise.' He sounds furious. 'Someone sent me the picture. I'm hardly the kind of person who'd look at images of girls.'

'But that's exactly what you're doing, regardless of whoever's sent it to you.' Turning around, I walk back out to the kitchen, knowing I should tell someone what I've seen. But an abusive marriage creates debilitating self-doubt. *Who would listen? The police? His medical practice? Who's going to believe you over him?*

If the police were ever to question him, Andrew would know who'd told them. I can imagine what he'd do to me and the implications for Niamh.

But in the kitchen, I can't stop thinking about what I've seen. If James Hampton invested in porn, *could Andrew have invested, too?*

Something clicks into place inside my head. Andrew has always believed he holds the winning hand. And for today – maybe even tomorrow – he still does. But given what I know about James, the police need to know about my husband's nasty little secret. Even if the girl I saw on his phone isn't underage, it would embarrass him beyond belief. With his position and the trust and responsibility that comes with it, what I've seen could potentially bring him down.

Suddenly I realise I've reached a turning point, because up until now, fear has had me in its grip, fear of what he would do to me. But now I know how to ruin Andrew and that knowledge gives me iron strength, armour through which his cruelty can no longer pierce. For years, I've felt imprisoned by him, but Hollie's death is a reminder that life is too short to waste. Too much time has already passed. It's time for Andrew to get everything he deserves.

Chapter Twenty-Nine

Jo

Back at home in Chichester, I let myself in, closing the door and standing there briefly, taking a deep breath and letting the day's tension ebb away before going into the kitchen and putting the kettle on. The house is still too quiet, even though three months have passed since my marriage ended. Enough time for my wounds to start to heal, but only until I think about the end of my marriage again.

Making a cup of tea, I force myself to get my laptop. After taking it through to the small snug at the back of the house, I sink into one of the armchairs, sipping my tea while I wait for it to fire up before typing *'Dylan Buckley 2016'* into the search bar. A few rows down, there's a link to a press release. It's only three lines, stating that his death was due to the overdose of a prescription drug.

Searching further, I find the date of his funeral, which was in the village, at the same church where Hollie's was held. It occurs to me his grave must be there too — I make a mental note to search for it. Then I find an obituary page that's been closed.

Realising it's a long shot, I try Facebook, trawling through lists of people by the name of Dylan Buckley before I have a far better idea. There can't be many Niamh Buckleys in the world. Typing in her name, I find I'm right. There are only two results and I recognise her face instantly.

When I bring up her page, it's clear that Niamh keeps most of her posts private, but fortunately for me, not her friends list. I scroll down through them, and Hollie's avatar comes up; then, near the bottom, Dylan's. Clicking on it, I take a deep breath as I start reading. If Andrew Buckley knew what was here, I wouldn't mind betting he'd be furious.

*

'Sir, I had an interesting conversation with Andrew Buckley yesterday. It turns out that Hollie Hampton had a relationship with his son, Dylan.'

Even the DI looks taken aback. 'I didn't know there was a son. When was this?'

'Two years ago. Apparently he killed himself when Hollie ended things between them.'

The DI looks up. 'How come we didn't know about this?'

'It isn't the Buckleys we're investigating, right now,' I point out. 'According to Doctor Buckley, Hollie messed Dylan up. He told me he was glad Hollie was out of Niamh's life.'

The DI speaks sharply. 'He actually said that? Do you think he meant it?'

'Maybe. There's more. Hollie made an appointment to see him at the surgery.'

The DI frowns. 'When was this?'

'Last year. To start with, he said she had a crush on him. And that when he didn't reciprocate, Hollie allegedly accused him of touching her inappropriately. But then he

220

also admitted, very reluctantly, that Hollie had found out about him and Stephanie Hampton. I imagine that's the real reason she went to see him.' I pause, frowning. 'There's also something Elise Buckley said, about Andrew Buckley wanting people to believe Hollie had problems, though she had no idea why. By the way, he also made it clear that he doesn't want me talking to her about Dylan. Something about her being fragile, and how they're trying to get on with their lives.'

'If we have what we need, it sounds a reasonable enough request.'

I shake my head. 'If it was anyone else, you'd think he was protecting his wife. But not him. Both of them have alluded to the fact that their marriage isn't what it should be. The other thing is, Elise Buckley isn't fragile. She's calculating, but not in a self-interested way. I'd say she's protecting herself and her daughter − from him.'

'Where's this coming from?' He looks at me curiously.

I take a deep breath. 'Let's just say, when you've been there, you know the signs.' I pause. 'Andrew Buckley has all the trademark characteristics of a psychopath.'

'That doesn't make him a criminal. We all know the world is full of them, May.'

As I've found out, first-hand. 'About Dylan, sir . . . I've asked for his medical records and anything else we can find on him, and I looked at his Facebook page last night. There's a whole load of stuff on there that I'm sure Andrew Buckley doesn't know about.'

'Such as?'

'Messages from Hollie, telling him how much she loved him.' Heart-breaking messages that completely contradict what Andrew Buckley had told me about Hollie being the one who left Dylan. 'I'd say Doctor Buckley lied about what happened between them.'

The DI gets up. 'We need to look into it, May.' He pauses. 'Any luck locating Mason?'

'None, unfortunately, and there's no way of knowing when he'll be back.'

★

When I return to my office, there's an email with Dylan's death certificate and the coroner's report attached. The cause of death is cited as an overdose of antidepressants and I imagine Andrew Buckley did whatever it took to minimise the attention his son's death must have drawn to him. While I'm reading, my phone buzzes. It's Sergeant Collins.

'Sarah?'

'It's James Hampton, Jo. He wants to talk.'

Niamh

Before we were friends, I learned about Hollie by watching her hand entwined with Dylan's, her long hair tangled with his. Their world of sunshine and laughter that drew people to them, made you want to be like them – it was about much more than the two of them falling in love.

After he'd gone, Hollie had told me they were predestined. Like two blazing stars that collided, dazzling everyone they met. Dylan was a talented artist and Hollie wanted a stage career. With their shared unquenchable thirst for adventure, they had a brilliant future mapped out.

I couldn't imagine them not being together – and I didn't want to think about them leaving, how empty this house would be once they'd gone. Dylan and Hollie represented love, freedom, energy, hope. Once they'd left, there would be no light or laughter in this house. Instead it would be a cold, empty shell.

Chapter Thirty

Elise

On my first overnight stop since before Hollie went missing, I walk for hours through the streets of Marrakech, losing myself in new sights and sounds, stopping on an impulse at a market stall to pick out a beaded bracelet for Niamh, ridiculously touched when the old woman I buy it from presses a small stone into my hand. A gift.

On the flight home, I think about how long kindness has been missing in my life. It adds to my determination to break away from Andrew.

Back at home, as I look around the house, the familiar extravagantly furnished rooms suddenly feel like a prison. Needing to escape, I go upstairs and pull on running clothes. Within minutes, I'm outside.

The clouds that blocked out the sun when my flight landed this morning have burned off, leaving a clear azure sky. Reaching the main road, I break into a run, passing Ida Jones's house and waving as I see her across the garden, her small frame bent over, busy weeding. I run faster then, spurred on by a desire to set change in motion. In my head starting to work out a plan; knowing the first thing I need to do is find a house.

The status that comes with owning a large country house is what first brought us to Abingworth, but I no longer care whether I own a house or not. What matters is that Niamh and I have our own space, one that's free of Andrew. I imagine a small cottage, a little untidy, with second-hand furniture and maybe a cat – the opposite of our impressive, stark, toxic family home here.

As I take the path towards the church, I think of Hollie, and I'm struck by a pang of heartbreak that it's too late for her. Her life is over, but Niamh and I are still here. It cements what I'm thinking. I owe it to my daughter to live the kind of life I really want for her. Anything less would be a betrayal.

I still have to deal with Andrew – the impenetrable barrier between me and freedom – but I won't let him stop me. Too much time has already been wasted. I won't be blackmailed into staying with him any longer. Once I've found a cottage and moved out, he can carry out his threats. I may lose everything, but it's a risk I have to take. Otherwise nothing will change.

It will be OK, I tell myself. *You can do this. You have to do this.* The path beneath the trees is soft with layers of leaf mould that cushion my feet as I emerge from their shade to see someone standing across the churchyard.

It's DS May. When I notice where she's standing, my stomach turns over. Glancing over my shoulder, I think about turning around. I don't particularly want to talk to her, but then she looks straight at me. Raising a hand in greeting, I walk towards her.

In a denim jacket, her long hair loose and slightly windswept, she looks younger, softer than she usually does. 'Detective

Sergeant.' I can't keep my eyes from wandering towards the grave she's standing beside.

'Mrs Buckley.' She looks awkward all of a sudden. 'I spoke to your husband a couple of days ago.'

Suddenly I'm numb. I stare at my son's grave. 'He told you about Dylan.'

She hesitates. 'He did. It was actually James Hampton who told me first – about Dylan and Hollie.' She looks at me. 'I'm so sorry you lost your son.' There's compassion in her eyes. 'I suppose it explains why Hollie was in the graveyard so much. Look, I'm sure you've come here for some quiet. I'll leave you alone.'

As she walks away without saying anything else, a sense of powerlessness rises in me, followed by despair. Whatever Andrew's said to her, it'll be what he wants her to think about how Dylan died, rather than telling her the truth.

For a moment, I'm gripped by an impulse to run after her and tell her the whole desperate story. But there's nothing to be gained by that. Dylan's death can't be related to Hollie's. It was too long ago. Far more likely Hollie's murder is related to the porn ring her father got tied up with.

As I stand there, the sun's rays catching on Dylan's grave, a lump forms in my throat. The initial agony of loss has dulled into a raw ache that's become a part of who I am now. I will never get over losing him. His death was the consequence of events that should never have happened, which I should have been able to stop. But for him, just like for Hollie, it's too late.

★

When Niamh comes in, I give her the bracelet I bought her in Marrakech, suddenly realising it's of inordinate importance to me that she likes it as I watch her take it out of the small brown paper bag, then turn it in her hands. 'Do you like it?'

227

She nods. 'It's really pretty.'

After she goes upstairs, I turn on my laptop, then start to look at a local property rental website, grateful that I have a job and a reasonable income. I look at the details of a couple of small houses that are closer to Chichester than Abingworth, but still convenient for Niamh's school. One in particular catches my eye, not just because it's pretty, but because I could afford it easily on my airline salary. It's a terraced townhouse on a quiet road on the outskirts of Chichester. The photos show a flight of steps leading from the street up to a freshly painted front door, an interior that's light and spacious, and a garden at the back.

After filling out an online form to request a viewing, there's something else I have to do.

I glance towards the stairs, hearing the faint sound of Niamh's television coming from her room, then pick up my phone and find DS May's number. But when I call, it goes to voicemail.

'It's Elise Buckley. There's something I need to talk to you about.'

Chapter Thirty-One

Elise

I'm on edge waiting for DS May to call me back. I try her again, knowing I need to tell her about the image I've seen on Andrew's phone; my uneasiness growing when she still doesn't answer and Andrew's car pulls up in the drive. Not wanting to speak to her while he's around, I switch my phone off.

'Next time you talk to the police about Dylan, perhaps you could let me know.' The acid words trip off my tongue as Andrew walks into the kitchen.

'Why?' he demands. 'Are you worried, Elise? Frightened you'll say the wrong thing?'

'He was our son, Andrew.' My eyes fill with tears. 'How dare you use his death to manipulate me.'

His eyes narrow. 'There's no manipulation going on. The trouble with the truth is that sadly, for you, it hurts.'

I can't remember the last time we had a conversation that didn't disintegrate into a fight. He's goading me again, but I stand my ground. 'Let's talk to the police about what happened that day. Give them the facts.' I stare at him. Unable to tolerate more of Andrew's behaviour, the obvious solution is to lay my cards on the table and let someone else form a judgement.

'You're mad. You do know that, don't you?' His voice is scornful. 'Any psychiatrist worth his salt would have a field day with you.'

But again I don't respond. It's what he always says when he senses he's losing ground. 'We both know I'm not.' As our eyes meet, this time the shift between us is palpable. No longer can he cow me into acquiescence, just as he no longer has the moral high ground. I can tell from his hesitation that Andrew's not as sure as he usually is. 'If you pull that one, I'll get an independent assessment from someone out of the area. Don't fuck with me, Andrew. I've had enough.'

Without bothering to look at him to see the impact my words have had, I fetch my jacket and go outside, needing to remove myself from his toxic presence, to stand in fresh air and cleanse my lungs. Walking across the grass to a more hidden corner of the garden, I realise how desperate I am for a sense of calm in my world. In the dusk, a white clematis stands out. Just coming into flower, its delicate stems trail over the wall, its daisy-like flowers softening the stone. Further on, I see the first of the pale roses are blooming. For a transient moment, their fragrance reaches me, a scent that takes me back to my childhood, as a nostalgic desire for the past fills me – for days when life was simple.

Suddenly, I realise how few people there are in my life. But Andrew destroyed my relationships one by one in his escalating need for power over me. For years, I've hidden from everyone, cutting myself off because it's easier than justifying his behaviour, explaining why I stay with him. Without any allies to turn to and nowhere else to go, Andrew's control was absolute – and it's taken until now for me to see it.

Nostalgia hits me again. If only there was someone I could talk to who would understand what's going on. But this is how the abuser–victim relationship works; why Andrew holds the trump card. Because of him, I have no-one.

★

I don't have an appetite, but I cook a bowl of pasta, serving up plates for myself and Niamh, which we eat together at the kitchen table. Andrew has half a bottle of Scotch inside him when he comes into the kitchen.

'Fucking pathetic, Elise,' he snarls, with no thought for the fact that Niamh is sitting there, listening to his every word. 'Thinking you can exclude me.'

I glance at her, shaking my head slightly. 'I didn't want to interrupt you, Andrew. There's plenty in the pan.' I'd like to say more but I bite my tongue. If my plan works, evenings like this will soon be over.

Instead of going back to the sitting room, he comes and joins us at the table, even though Niamh and I have finished eating. Niamh's eyes scan mine, her face anxious.

We sit in silence for a few minutes, Andrew's foul mood like a stench pervading the room. In the end, it's too much for Niamh. She gets up and rushes out, then I hear her feet on the stairs. Glaring at Andrew, I get up to follow her.

'Stay here, Elise,' he growls. 'I want to talk to you.'

'There is nothing you can say that I want to hear,' I tell him before going upstairs and knocking gently on Niamh's door.

She's distraught. 'Why is he like this?' She sobs. 'He's so horrible to us. He's horrible to you. Why can't he be nice?'

Putting my arms around her, I hold her tightly. 'Listen,' I whisper fiercely. 'Your father can't go on doing this – to either of us. I won't let him. Hold on, just a little bit longer, Niamh. It isn't going to be forever.'

★

I sleep fitfully that night, inspired by the thought of freedom, but preoccupied by the reality of what's ahead. The next morning, I get dressed in my uniform and leave the house early, knowing exactly what I have to do. If the day goes the way I'm hoping it will, by the time Andrew gets home tonight, a very different future will lie ahead.

Chapter Thirty-Two

Jo

After picking up a voicemail from Elise Buckley, I call her back but she doesn't answer. Knowing she could be at work, I make a note to try her later on, before going to talk to James Hampton. When I reach the interview room, he and his lawyer are already seated.

'Mr Hampton.' I sit down. 'We won't keep you long. I'm just waiting for DI Saunders to join us.'

As I finish speaking, the door opens and he appears in the doorway. 'A moment, May?' He nods towards the corridor. I glance at James Hampton briefly as I stand.

Outside the room, the DI is jumpy as we move to a spot out of earshot of anyone else. 'Mason's passport's been picked up – not quickly enough unfortunately. Seems he got on a ferry – it docked in Portsmouth an hour ago and he got away before we could notify border police there. We've traced him back to Santander, where he was picked up on CCTV driving a black Audi. Fingers crossed, if he's headed for his house, we've got him.'

I frown. I can't believe that after avoiding us for so long, Mason's going to make it that easy. 'Why's he back?'

The DI shrugs. 'Maybe he's hoping to flog his investment opportunity to a few more idiots like Hampton. Maybe he needs the money.'

'We should get someone over to his house. Straight away.'

The DI nods. 'Ask Emerson. At this time of day, it'll take Mason at least an hour to get home, probably considerably longer.'

Glancing at my watch, I nod. 'Shall we go in, sir? Hampton's already been there a while.'

The DI is brusque. 'Don't go all sympathetic on him, May. He's a bloody criminal.'

He's right, Hampton is a criminal. But desperation and hopelessness lie at the root of so many crimes.

'Do we know why he wants to see us?'

The DI shakes his head. 'Haven't a bloody clue.'

James Hampton's lawyer looks impatient as we go back in. Once we're sitting down, he starts talking. 'My client's been thinking about your offer of reduced charges against him. He can't be certain, but he thinks he knows who else might be involved in the porn ring.'

Sitting back, the DI folds his arms. 'I thought your client had already told us everything he knows.' He addresses James Hampton. 'Have you thought how this is going to look in court?'

At the mention of court, James Hampton looks weary but as he glances at his lawyer, it's obvious it's a clumsy attempt to buy his way out of this.

'If I were you, I'd advise my client to tell us exactly what he knows, or on top of everything else, we'll add perverting the course of justice to the list of charges against him.' Finished addressing the lawyer, the DI turns to James Hampton. 'What is it that you'd like to say?'

'I want the charges reduced.' Hampton stares at the table. 'I didn't know the extent of what I was getting into. I was scammed.'

'We'll take your request into account once we've heard what you have to say.' The DI's voice is steely as he folds his arms.

Hampton's face is ashen. 'I think you should talk to Andrew Buckley.'

★

It wouldn't surprise me if Andrew Buckley was involved, but we need proof. The DI strides down the corridor, speaking over his shoulder and not letting me get a word in. 'Get Buckley in for questioning. Find out if he knows what Mason's involved in. We need his phone and his computer. And get over to Mason's. Is Collins going with you?'

I check to see if she's answered the text I sent earlier. 'Looks like she's nearly there. Sir, don't you think this sudden accusation against Andrew Buckley is simply Hampton grinding his axe? Buckley was having an affair with his wife, and Buckley's son was instrumental in Hollie going off the rails – at least, that's what Hampton would like us to believe. I think he's just attempting to buy his way out. Did you see his face when you mentioned court? I'm not sure I'd take him entirely seriously.'

The DI's face is impassive. 'We'll know more once we've spoken to Buckley.'

It's easy to imagine what Andrew Buckley's going to say when he's told the police want to question him again. I check my watch. 'I need to get over to Mason's.'

★

As I drive, I try to work out how long it would take Mason to drive from Portsmouth to his house in Abingworth, putting my foot down. If he's in some top-of-the-range Audi, he could have got here faster than the DI predicted.

As I approach Abingworth, the stone walls of the village houses suddenly seem sinister. It's like no other village I've ever been to, not just because there's so little interaction among the villagers. It's more that everything about this place is hidden – the people, their homes, their lives, their secrets. As I drive, the distant drone of a low-flying helicopter reaches my ears. Pulling over, I watch its outline rising above the trees.

It looks as though it's just taken off and, instinctively, I know where it's come from. Putting my foot down hard, I drive as fast as I dare to Mason's house, only slowing when I see Sarah's car in front of the locked gates.

Getting out, I look at her. 'That was him, wasn't it?'

She nods. 'I think so. The helicopter must have landed behind the house before we got here. I didn't see or hear it until it took off. I'd been here about ten minutes before it started up.'

Shaking my head, I imagine Mason in his house, laughing as he looked out of the window and saw her car, knowing how easily he could get away from us. Getting my phone out of my bag, I call the DI. 'Sir? Mason just left his house – by helicopter. He was airborne about two minutes ago.' I listen for a moment, then hang up and look at Sarah.

'He's going to try to track the helicopter. Chances are, it won't fly high enough to be picked up by radar.' I knew he wouldn't make it easy for us. Mason's too sharp to let himself get caught. 'Do you hear that?' I catch Sarah's eye just as a car comes into view. Reaching us, it pulls up and a young man in a suit gets out.

Imagining another of Mason's potential investors, I show him my badge. 'DS May. Chichester Police. Have you come to visit Philip Mason?'

The man looks uncertain. 'I have an appointment with him.' He looks at his watch. 'In ten minutes.'

So we *had* interrupted Mason's plans to stay around. 'May I ask if you've come here to discuss a business investment?'

He frowns at me, then glances at Sarah. 'I wouldn't call it that.' He pauses. 'I'm an estate agent. I've come to value his house.'

As Sarah's eyes meet mine, I ask quickly, 'You have a key?'

'As it happens, I do.' He looks at us suspiciously. 'Mr Mason did say that in the event that he got held up, I was to make a start with the house.'

'Can you give me a minute?' I nod towards Sarah, and pick up my phone again to call the DI back. The call goes straight through. 'Sir, Mason's arranged for an estate agent to let himself in to value the house. He has a key.'

'Stay where you are. I'll get an emergency search warrant organised. I'll call you back.'

Ending the call, I nod towards Sarah, then the estate agent. 'What's your name?'

'Adam Matterson.'

'Thank you, Adam. That was my boss I was speaking to. We're waiting for a search warrant, then he'd like us to go in with you.'

Adam looks taken aback. 'I'm afraid I can't let anyone else in with me. Mr Mason was most explicit when I spoke to him.'

'We'll just wait, shall we?'

★

It isn't long before the DI calls back. 'Get in there, May, and see what you can find.'

'Yes, sir.' I turn to the estate agent. 'OK. Shall we go in?'

He looks awkward. 'I'm not at all happy about this.'

'Mr Mason is wanted in connection with a serious criminal offence.' I pause, not taking my eyes off him. 'I'm afraid you don't have a choice.'

Reluctantly, he presses a combination of numbers into the keypad next to the gate. It opens, then closes behind us after we've driven in. The drive sweeps around in front of the house to what looks like a parking area, where I pull up beside Adam's car and get out.

'What's it worth?' I stare up at the impressive elevations. The house is old and gracious, too much so for someone like Mason. Its stone exterior has also been immaculately restored.

'It's hard to say until I've been inside.' Clearly not pleased that he's had to let us in, Matterson is brusque. 'I'd imagine somewhere between five and six million. Now, if you'll excuse me, I have to get on.'

Inside, the house is no less vast, its grandeur understated, its history evident in mullioned windows, arched doorways, stone floors worn smooth from age. While Adam walks from room to room recording measurements, Sarah and I start our own search.

As we walk into yet another beautiful room, she shakes her head. 'Some house, isn't it?'

I nod, not wanting to dwell on where Mason's money may have come from. I start carefully looking through a chest of drawers, finding nothing personal. We search more drawers and cupboards in each room but everywhere we look, it's the same. Everything is neat and orderly and sparse, as though Philip Mason always expected the police to come here.

When Sarah finds his office, my hopes rise that at last we'll discover something. 'What an office.'

A large desk is positioned by the window, with breath-taking views across the landscaped gardens towards the coast. There's a state-of-the-art screen and keyboard, a pair of speakers positioned discreetly and heavy curtains hanging in the windows, but that's all.

When a search of the desk reveals nothing, Sarah looks at me. 'Frustrating, isn't it? You'd have thought there'd be something.'

I shake my head. 'There wouldn't be, would there? Not if he was prepared to let an unescorted estate agent wander around. I wouldn't mind betting the whole house is completely clean. But we still need to look. Keep your eyes out for letters and photos. Anything that might tell us where he is.'

I'm hoping that we'll stumble upon wherever Mason's hidden his personal effects. When our search turns up nothing of interest, we wait in the kitchen while Adam finishes up measuring the outbuildings. When he comes back in, he looks perplexed.

'Is something wrong?'

He shakes his head. 'It's probably nothing. It's just that some of the measurements don't add up. I was redoing them to check I hadn't made a mistake.'

I'm suddenly very interested in seeing Adam's notes. 'Where is this?'

He's visibly less hostile than when we arrived. 'Outside. I'll show you.'

As we follow him across the garden to an L-shape of converted farm buildings, my eyes are drawn to the swathes of spring flowers breaking up the grass and the landscaped pond with its own jetty. Like everything about this house, it's impressive.

Beyond the garden is another large, open stretch of mown grass where I imagine the helicopter must have landed. The farm buildings themselves have been stylishly converted, the courtyard in front of them heavily gravelled. After unlocking a door, Adam leads us into a room towards the corner of the L. 'If you look here . . .' Showing us a floor plan, he indicates the space he's measured. 'You agree that fits with the plan?'

As far as I can see, it looks in order, but then he takes us outside, through the door in the other half of the L, into a similar-sized room. Along one wall, there's a trestle table and underneath it, several boxes. Opening them, I find unopened bottles of spirits, then in another, unwashed glasses. 'I'd say someone's been having a party.' I turn to Adam. 'You were saying?'

Showing us his floor plan again, he points to the wall. 'Even if you look outside, you can see there's quite a lot of space behind here that isn't accounted for.'

His words are confirmed by the measurements on the floor plan, but even without them, it's obvious that something is off. 'So how do we get in?'

Hurrying outside, I walk around the back of the building, following the narrow path that vanishes into overgrown rhododendron bushes growing up against the wall. Pushing my way through, I find a door into what could quite possibly be the area of space that's been bricked off, then notice the outline of a path leading off in another direction. My heart starts thumping. There's no question we've found something.

'This door isn't marked on the floor plan.' Adam's voice comes from behind me.

Mason surely couldn't have imagined an estate agent would miss this. But then I remember. His plan was to be here, until we interrupted him. Who knows what he was going to say to Adam? Standing back, I stare at what Adam's holding out to me: his bunch of keys.

I try each in turn, but none of them fit. Then I shove my shoulder against it, but it doesn't give even slightly. Handing the keys back to Adam, I get out my phone.

The DI answers immediately.

'Sir? We've found a locked room among some converted outbuildings at Mason's place. The estate agent doesn't have a key, nor does the space appear on his floor plan.'

'We need to see what's inside, May. Can you force it?'

'We've tried. It's pretty solid, sir.'

'Right. I'll get someone over to help. Stand by.'

I turn to Sarah. 'The DI wants us to check it out.' I glance at Adam. 'Could you give us the code for the gate? If you've finished what you're doing, you don't have to hang around. But if you could leave the keys with us, it might be useful. We'll make sure everything's locked and if you give me the address of your office, I'll drop them back to you later on. Meanwhile, if you hear from Mr Mason, I'd be grateful if you didn't tell him we've been here.'

It's clear from Adam's face that he's out of his depth. When he hands me a business card, I add, 'You might want to be careful. Mason's slippery. If he leaves you any contact details, call me.' I hand him a card.

After leaving us the code, he starts to walk back towards the house. I look at Sarah. 'The DI's sending someone over. It might be a good idea for you to wait on the drive.'

As she walks away, I cross the gravel onto the grass and gaze at the open space that stretches into the distance, wondering if Mason owns the woods beyond too. My blood chills at the thought that people can justify exploiting the vulnerable for their own gains, but it's something that happens all too often. There are too many powerful people driven by pure greed and self-interest. James Hampton is one, and it helped that he was weak so that Mason could take advantage of him when he was desperate. And then there's Andrew Buckley. From what I've seen, I have no shadow of a doubt that

Buckley is cold and calculating, capable of almost anything. But in spite of what James Hampton told us, there's still no proof that he's involved.

It isn't long before my thoughts are interrupted by the sound of voices coming closer. Turning around, I see Sarah with a couple of uniformed police officers making their way across the grass. They didn't waste any time. Then to my surprise, I see the DI behind them. By the time he reaches us, he's out of breath.

'Too much time behind a bloody desk,' he wheezes. 'Right, May. Let's not hang around. Where's this door?'

'This way, sir.' I lead them around the back of the L of buildings. 'This is it.'

Standing back, I watch him try the door, then shove his not inconsiderable bulk against it, but just as earlier when I tried, it doesn't budge. Nodding at the uniformed PCs, he stands to one side.

When two of them together fail to force it open, one of them opens the bag they've brought with them, then starts to work on the lock. It takes a few minutes, but finally the door opens silently, and one of them reaches for a torch. But when they shine the beam around the room, it's completely empty.

Chapter Thirty-Three

Jo

I follow the DI inside, disappointment washing over me as the beam of his torch illuminates empty space and dusty floorboards. My eyes scan the room before settling on the floor. 'Sir? That far corner . . .' The DI's beam flashes back to the spot I'm talking about. 'The floorboards are different.' As I look more closely, I see it isn't just the corner. There's a four-foot strip of floorboards along the length of that wall that are considerably narrower than all the others.

'Emerson? Prise those up, will you?'

In silence, we watch as the floorboards come up easily – too easily – revealing a narrow staircase. Stepping forward, the DI nods at Sarah. 'Collins? Stay here. Keep an eye out, will you? The rest of you . . .' He glances at me and the two policemen. 'With me, please. Let's check this out.'

At the bottom of the stairs, the DI shines the beam of his torch around, settling it on a switch. Then, as the lights come on, I gasp at the row of screens that have been illuminated. There must be half a dozen, each with a chair in front of it, while along one of the walls are shelves on which discs and folders are stacked. The DI goes further in and calls me. 'May?'

As I reach him, I see he's holding back a curtain, revealing an area just big enough to hold a large bed. It's covered in black sheets, and above it a number of cameras are mounted on the wall. I feel sick, imagining what goes on here.

'Looks like Mr Mason is exactly who Operation Rainbow have been looking for.' His voice is grim. 'Ask Collins to secure the scene. Then call forensics. I want them over here, right away.'

'Sir.' I head upstairs, then outside to where Sarah's standing. 'We were right,' I tell her. 'It looks like it's all there.' Moving my phone around, I manage to get a signal at last. 'He wants you to secure the scene. I'm calling forensics. This looks like the break we've been looking for.'

As I go back down to Mason's cellar, a horrifying thought occurs to me. What if Mason had groomed Hollie? What if she was one of his models? According to several of the villagers, she'd been noticeably more distressed shortly before she died.

The DI is still carefully looking around. 'They're on their way, sir.' Then I tell him what's just occurred to me.

He nods. 'You're right. We can't ignore the possibility. We'll get her photo over to forensics and ask them to check it against Mason's images. 'Meanwhile, see if you can find anything, May. Names of investors or any photographs of Hollie . . . Anything.'

In the dim light of Mason's cellar, even the air seems laden with darkness as I search for any evidence.

'Hard to believe that no-one would have known what was going on here. Look at these.' The DI passes me a handful of photos of naked and semi-naked girls.

It's a measure of how depraved so many people are that what might have shocked, even a few years ago, has become normalised, acceptable. But it's how the human brain works, and with mounting human desire for the ever more shocking, there is a growing market for acts of escalating obscenity. And for as long as there's a demand, there will always be Masons.

But to use children and young girls is to cross an unacceptable line. As I look at the photos of girls of a variety of ages and nationalities, I find their exposed bodies distressing enough, but far worse are the expressions in their eyes. Some are obviously drugged – oblivious – while others are simply terrified. Unable to take any more, I go outside.

Leaning against the wall, I glance at Sarah. 'Hampton deserves everything that's coming to him,' I tell her. 'As for Mason . . .' I shake my head, failing to find the right words.

'Even in our job,' she says slowly. 'You think you've seen it all, but there's always a lowlife who manages to surprise you. Doesn't say much for the human race, does it?'

I shake my head. There are many good people in the world, but at times like this, it's easy to believe that they are outweighed a thousandfold by the bad. 'We just have to make sure we get him.' Mason – and everyone else involved. To let them carry on with what they're doing is inconceivable.

Chapter Thirty-Four

Elise

After work, I see a missed call from DI May, but when I call her back it goes to voicemail yet again.

But I don't have time to worry about it. By the end of the day, having viewed a small cottage on the outskirts of Tangmere, I've managed to fast-track the usual rental process by paying a deposit and putting down three months' rent in advance. It feels like a momentous step, even though it's the easiest part of my plan. What will follow is going to be much harder.

By the time I get home, I've decided there's no time to waste; that the sooner I remove Niamh from Andrew's toxic influence, the better for both of us. And I don't want Andrew getting wind of our plans. It will take less than a day to pack what we need of our clothes and personal things – everything that used to be so important to me. But only one thing matters now, and that's freedom.

Already, I've mentally listed what I want to take – surplus china and cutlery in the kitchen that we've never used, spare bed linen, but most important are my photographs, books, and the old case I have that's filled with mementos of Niamh and Dylan growing up. As unwanted emotion wells up in me, I smother it before it takes a hold. This isn't the time. I have to stay strong.

When Niamh comes home, I wait for her to get herself a drink and go upstairs to change. When she comes back down, I seize the moment.

'Niamh? I need to talk to you about something.'

When she looks up, her eyes are troubled before the familiar guarded look masks them. 'Come and sit down.' I walk over to the sofa, sit, and wait for her to do the same. She seems reluctant as she perches next to me. I study her face. 'You know how, the other day, I told you I was going to do something to change things? Well, I've found a house, Niamh. For you and me.' I watch her blink several times. 'We don't have to stay with your father anymore, or put up with the way he treats us. I've let it go on too long. What he does isn't right – and it isn't how families are supposed to be. You do realise that, don't you?'

To my horror, she starts to cry. I try to reassure her. 'It will be OK, Niamh. I'll make it OK, I promise you . . .'

Just then, I hear Andrew's car, back two hours earlier than I expected him. Before I can say anything else, Niamh gets up and runs from the room. As he throws the back door open a few moments later, I can sense his mood even before I see his face.

Sudden, inexplicable fear strikes me, that Niamh will tell Andrew what I've done. After hurrying upstairs, I knock softly on her door, then push it open. Sprawled on her bed, Niamh is sobbing her heart out.

Pushing the door closed, I tiptoe over to her. 'Niamh,' I whisper. 'Honey . . .' The endearment is unfamiliar to both of us. 'What is it?'

My blood chills as I make out her words through her muffled sobs. 'I don't want to go.'

'*Niamh . . .*' Beside her, I'm frozen. I'd been so convinced I was doing what we both wanted. Now, I don't know what to say to her. 'We'll have a lovely home. It will be happy . . .' I'm so desperate for her to believe me.

She sobs harder. 'No . . .'

'I don't understand.' I'm utterly bewildered. 'He's hateful to you, Niamh. To both of us.' Or is it that she's used to it? It's what we're both used to, after all. She doesn't know any other way to be. The thought horrifies me, and I understand how blind I've been; how damaged she's become because of me and Andrew. I sit on the edge of my daughter's bed, thinking of what she's seen and heard, how she's lost her brother, and now Hollie, and in that moment, I recognise that she's more frightened of Andrew than I'd known.

Niamh

Sometimes it isn't possible not to hurt people. But life is a dilemma of impossible choices – between right and wrong, between what to tell and what must forever remain a secret.

Hollie knew that. Even when she wanted to put things right, she couldn't. Too much had happened. The damage ran too deep.

My dilemma is my parents. The light shining in my mother's eyes when she told me she'd found a cottage for us to move to. The happy life she imagines for the two of us, in which everything will change. Light that I know will be shattered by my father's cruelty, his darkness. My father will find a way to stop her. He won't let us leave. He'll do anything, including hurt her, if that's what it takes to make us stay.

There is no escape from my father. So, this is my dilemma. What matters most? Who is more important? Do I go with my mother, knowing my father will destroy her, or do I stay and let him destroy me instead?

I have to stop her. I have no choice, because otherwise he will kill her, just like he killed Dylan with the blunt words, the rejection, the hatred and the cruelty that leave no physical trace. Not that he'd admit it, instead blaming the pills my mother left out the morning Dylan took an overdose.

But she wasn't the one who left them out. It was my father. He doesn't care about lying, or who he hurts to get what he wants. He doesn't care if people die. My father is capable of anything.

Chapter Thirty-Five

Elise

Hearing Andrew moving around downstairs, I go to my bedroom, closing the door behind me before going over to the window. I'd thought Niamh would embrace the chance to get away from her father. I never imagined she'd want to stay. I feel the walls close in, knowing that if she refuses to leave, I have to stay, too.

The sense of freedom I felt earlier evaporates. Instead, the future feels like a jail sentence, the house a prison, to which Niamh holds a key she can't give me.

Knowing my only hope is to talk to her again, I get up. But as I reach her bedroom, I hear voices coming from downstairs. Crouching down at the top of the stairs, I try to make out what Andrew's saying. But instead it's Niamh's words that reach me, filling me with dread as suddenly I realise what she's doing.

My heart thumping, I tear down the stairs, almost tripping at the bottom, as Niamh rushes out of the kitchen and past me, her face ashen.

'Niamh . . .' But my cry is lost as she reaches her bedroom

and slams the door behind her. Swallowing, I walk into the kitchen, my uneasiness building, knowing I have to face Andrew.

Leaning against the worktop, Andrew is cool as a cucumber as he watches me. For a few seconds, relief floods through me. Niamh hasn't told him after all. He'd be ragingly angry if she had.

But if she hasn't told him, what had upset her?

'What did you say to Niamh?' I stare at him, guarded.

Shaking his head, he smirks. 'I simply told her that you and I were going to have a little chat.'

There's a pit of dread in my stomach and my eyes are riveted to his. 'What about, Andrew?'

His voice is deadly quiet. 'Your naïve little plan, Elise. What else?'

So Niamh had told him. I stare at him. 'You can't force me to do anything. Not anymore.'

'Can't I?' His upper lip curls into a snarl. 'I can do whatever I like.'

Trying to suppress the fear rising inside me, I swallow again. 'What do you want?'

'I want my wife to stop dreaming up ludicrous ideas and feeding them to our daughter,' he says lightly. 'I'm not letting you leave, Elise. And I'll do whatever it takes to stop you. You should know that.'

His threat isn't even thinly veiled. As he steps towards me, fear swirls around me, so dense that I can almost grasp it. But I have to stop giving in to him. Nothing will change if I don't stop this toxic cycle. 'This is no way to live, Andrew.' My voice is desperate. 'You'll have another affair – we both know that. It's over between us. It's been over for years. We don't love each other. There's no point.'

But as I look at him, I know our relationship was never about love. It's always been about control. As though reading my mind, he nods slowly, then his hand reaches out and he clasps my arm.

I try to shake free, but his grip is too tight, pinching my skin. 'Let go.' I say it as forcefully as I can. Then I feel the first of his blows across my face. It's swiftly followed by another, then another. His control gone, he unleashes the full force of his anger on me.

Chapter Thirty-Six

Jo

'This is Elise Buckley. Please leave a message.'

I'm uneasy. Given her multiple missed calls, it's clear that Mrs Buckley has something urgent to tell me. I think about going around there, then put it off. It's been a long enough day and if she wasn't able to speak to me, Elise may well have called the police station instead.

*

When I arrive at work the next morning, however, I realise I shouldn't have put off calling her.

It's Sarah Collins who tells me. 'Elise Buckley was admitted to hospital last night.'

Shock hits me. 'How did you find out?'

'The DI called Andrew Buckley to ask him to speak to us about Mason. Apparently he sounded flustered, then he told him he couldn't because his wife is in hospital and he needs to look after their daughter.'

I'm already shaking my head, alarm bells ringing loudly. 'What's happened to her?'

'He said something about her having a fall.'

It's a classic cover-up for domestic abuse. 'He may have said that, but believe me, Andrew Buckley wouldn't normally be taking time off to look after Niamh. Her mother is a flight attendant and he doesn't bother taking time out to care for his daughter when Elise is away working. Niamh's used to looking after herself.' My suspicions of Andrew Buckley are quickly building; I'm sure there's more to this. 'I'm going to the hospital. She's in St Richard's?'

When Sarah nods, I grab my keys.

★

As I drive, my doubts grow that Elise has fallen. She's almost certainly covering up an attack by her husband. Too much about Andrew Buckley reminds me of my ex-husband, just as Elise reminds me of how I used to be. I know first-hand how it feels to be caught in a psychopath's web, what it's like when they block your escape route. How, little by little, they diminish you until you feel worthless. I've seen it in Elise's eyes. She doesn't believe she deserves better.

I'm going on gut instinct, but if Andrew Buckley *has* beaten up his wife, it brings into question everything he's told us. But for now, my concern is for Elise.

Mercifully, the hospital car park is quiet, but it's too early for visiting hours. I stop in reception to find out which ward Elise is in and as I start walking in that direction, my phone buzzes. It's the DI. I know I should answer it, but I let it go to voicemail instead.

Elise is in a small room with two other women. Her back is to me as I walk towards her bed and I pause a few steps away. 'Elise?'

I watch her shoulders stiffen, and as she turns I see the full extent of her injuries. Her face is red, bruised, and bloody; one of her eyes swollen, half-closed.

'Oh, God . . .' I'm horrified. Going closer, I pull a chair up. 'What happened?'

'I fell.' She mutters the words and her eyes turn away from me.

It's impossible to believe that her injuries came from a fall. It looks as though she's been punched in the face, and definitely more than once. Wondering where else she's been hit, I don't say anything for a moment. 'Elise?' Leaning towards her, I speak gently. 'Did Andrew do this to you?'

I watch shock wash across her face as she looks at me, her eyes filled with fear. 'No. You mustn't say that. He'll kill me.'

As I look at her, memories are dredged up from a past I'd rather forget; memories of a time when I lived in fear, when I wanted to die rather than face another day with the man who abused me. 'I know,' I tell her softly. 'I know what it's like to be where you are. It happened to me, too. You can't stay, Elise. You have to leave him.'

As her eyes meet mine, they're filled with pain. Then, as her head rolls sideways, she utters one word. 'Niamh.'

In that instant, I understand what's happening. She believes she's protecting her daughter.

'You're frightened about what will happen to Niamh if you leave?' When she nods, I go on. 'We can find you somewhere safe, where Andrew won't be able to get to either of you. Think about it . . .' I pause. 'Was this why you tried to call me?' I ask. But as I speak, her eyes widen as they stare past me.

'Go,' she whispers, desperation written across her face. 'Please . . .'

Turning around, I see the cause of her fear.

'Good morning, Detective Sergeant. How unexpected.'

Standing just a few feet away, Andrew Buckley speaks with cold calm.

'I had to call in to see someone,' I lie. 'I was very sorry to hear that Elise had such a bad fall.' I glance at her then back at him. 'You need to do something about your stairs, Doctor Buckley.' His face is unreadable. 'I understand DI Saunders has been in touch?' I add, my eyes not leaving his. 'If you could come in at your earliest convenience, I know he's keen to talk to you.'

I don't want to leave her alone with him, but I have no choice. Surely he can't hurt her in hospital. On the way out, I pause at the nurses' station, just in case. 'Mrs Buckley's tired. She told me she didn't want any visitors. Can you check on her?' As I glance over my shoulder, I see Andrew Buckley is at the foot of his wife's bed, his arms folded.

★

On my way out to my car, I check my phone to find three missed calls from DI Saunders. When I call him back, he's less than pleased.

'Where the hell have you been, May?'

'To see Elise Buckley in hospital, sir. Her husband's been using her as a punch bag.'

'Dear God. Did she say as much?'

'Almost. But she didn't have to – the physical evidence is clear. There's no point in bringing him in though. She won't testify against him. She's terrified.' We see it far too often in abuse cases. 'What was it you needed, sir?'

'We've been questioning Hampton again. He's given us the name of someone else he says is involved in Mason's business dealings. Julian Calder. I'd like to you to talk to him. Don't give anything away. Start with a few questions about Hollie, gauge his response and go from there. I'll get someone to text you his address.'

By the time I've reached my car, my phone has already pinged with the address. But as I set off, I can't stop thinking about Elise Buckley. Knowing what she's gone through, I can't let this go. Domestic violence tends to escalate and if Buckley's done this to her now, God knows what he's capable of next time. I have to talk to her when her husband isn't around; try to persuade her that she needs to get away from him. Then help her find somewhere else to go.

*

Reaching Abingworth, I turn my attention to the Calders. They live in a large thatched cottage the far side of the village, set up a bank above the lane. I park at the roadside, pausing in the car to study the house.

Like most in this village, it's large – and of considerable value, I wouldn't mind betting. After getting out, I take the flight of stone steps leading to a heavy front door. When I ring the bell, a woman answers.

'DS May, Chichester Police.' I look at her, taking in obviously highlighted hair and a faded tan. 'I'd like to talk to Julian Calder. Is he home?'

'I'm his wife – Della.' An uncertain look crosses her face. 'Can I ask what this is about?'

'It's in relation to the investigation of Hollie Hampton's murder.' When she doesn't move, I add, 'Is your husband here?'

Della Calder nods. 'Come in.'

As I step into the large hallway, she closes the door behind me. Judging from the age of the house, the artwork and antique furniture, I'd say my hunch is right about the Calders being wealthy.

'He's through here.' I follow her along a panelled hallway, stopping outside a cracked-open door. Knocking quietly, she pushes the door open. 'Julian? The police are here.'

Inside, Julian Calder gets up from the chair at his desk. He's of medium height, overweight with thinning light brown hair.

'DS May, Chichester Police. I'd like to talk to you about Hollie Hampton, Mr Calder. May I come in?'

'By all means.' His manner is expansive, his charm excessive given the reason I'm here. He gestures towards an armchair opposite his desk. 'Do have a seat, Detective Sergeant. How can I help?'

'Thank you.' Sitting down, I take my notebook out of my pocket. 'Mr Calder, how well did you know Hollie?'

Sitting down again, he frowns slightly. 'Not that well. I know her father, but that's the only reason I had any contact with her.'

Nodding, I go on. 'You haven't seen anyone suspicious hanging around the village?'

Raising his eyebrows, he looks at me pointedly. 'I've answered these and more questions already, Detective Sergeant.'

He speaks with a level of arrogance that reminds me of Andrew Buckley. 'I'm sure you have.' I pause. 'But a teenage girl is dead, Mr Calder – quite probably murdered. I'm sure you can appreciate we're only being thorough. I won't keep you long.'

I watch his eyes shift, but this time, he doesn't say anything. 'How well do you know James Hampton?' I ask.

'Quite well.' He glances away. 'We drink at the same pub.'

'The one in the village?' When he nods, I ask him, 'Did Mr Hampton have any concerns that he mentioned to you in recent months? Or discuss his business interests?'

Calder's frown deepens. 'I'm not sure what you're getting at, Detective Sergeant. We talk about many different things – I couldn't possibly list all of them.'

I keep my face blank as I ask the next question. 'Did you – or he – ever talk about Philip Mason?'

The pause before he speaks gives him away. 'Can I ask what relevance this has to Hollie's death?'

'That's what we're trying to ascertain.' My eyes don't leave his. 'Could you answer the question, Mr Calder? Did you and James Hampton ever talk about Philip Mason?'

He blusters. 'Maybe. I've met Phil once or twice, of course – in the pub. It's a small village, Detective Sergeant.'

★

'His manner totally changed, sir,' I tell the DI. 'He made it clear he didn't want to talk to me. One minute he was polite, but the instant I asked about Mason, he changed. He knows him all right – he just didn't want to give me anything to pick up on.'

The DI frowns. 'Did he tell you anything about Hollie?'

I shake my head. 'It's the same with everyone we've talked to. We're still waiting for the tech team to get back to us. Hopefully then, we'll have the proof we need to put potential suspects like Mason and Andrew Buckley in the frame, but it's going to take time.'

'Forensics has been going over the photos. They've linked a few of them to cases of missing girls, but so far, that leaves most of them unaccounted for.' He pauses. 'They're cross-checking with cases around the country. Those girls – children – must have come from somewhere, May.'

I nod. We need to find out where.

'And we can't afford to wait.' He's silent for a moment. 'We must have missed something. Go over everything again, May. We need to find the needle in Abingworth's haystack.'

I nod. But I'm filled with a sinking feeling at the prospect of days at my desk, reading through everyone's notes. We're no closer to knowing if there's any connection between Hollie's death and Mason, or anyone connected to him. But there's still one person who might know something. 'Before I do, sir, there's someone I want to talk to again.'

★

I wait near the bus stop outside Niamh's school, searching the dozens of faces of students pouring out through the gates. She's alone when I see her, her expression shuttered, unreadable. As I walk towards her, she looks up.

'Hello, Niamh. Do you mind if we have a quick chat?'

She shakes her head. 'I'll miss my bus.'

I hesitate. 'If you like, I could give you a lift home?'

As she stands there, I wonder what's going through her head. I'm fully expecting that she'll insist on catching her bus, but then she nods. 'OK.'

'I saw your mum this morning,' I say as we walk towards my car, watching a startled look cross Niamh's face. 'I had to go to the hospital anyway,' I add. 'To see someone else. I'd heard she'd had a fall.'

Niamh looks anxious. 'Was she OK?'

I sigh. 'Not really. But she will be. Here. This is my car.' As I walk around to the driver's seat, Niamh gets in. After starting the engine and driving away, I go on. 'Is everything OK at home, Niamh?'

'Yes.' Her voice is small.

'What about with your dad?'

Niamh just shrugs.

I sigh. There's no easy way to do this. 'Last night . . . Did you see what happened to your mum?'

'No.' Her answer is too quick, too tight. 'I was in my room. She said it was an accident.'

'How well do you get on with your dad?'

I know I haven't imagined her sharp intake of breath. But again, all she says is, 'OK.'

In the end, I have to ask. 'Was it you who called me last night? After your mum fell? From her phone?' My voice is gentle; I want her to trust me.

She shakes her head. 'No.'

In the end, I have to give up. It's obvious Niamh doesn't yet trust me enough to tell me what really happened. As we reach Abingworth, she becomes increasingly agitated. 'Can I get out at the bus stop?'

'Of course.' Realising she's worried about her father seeing her in my car, I slow down, then pull over at the side of the road. As she opens the car door, I pass her my card. 'Niamh, if you're ever worried, or you want to talk about anything, you can always call me.'

Nodding briefly, she takes the card, then gets out and slams the door, leaving me with no choice but to watch uneasily as she walks away, her pale hair and slight shoulders making her look small as she crosses the road and disappears into the Buckleys' drive.

Chapter Thirty-Seven

Elise

The day my husband hits me puts my plans back, but the fact he now feels confident enough to beat me when Niamh is in the house makes me even more determined to get her away from him. *Just leave,* my heart tells me. *Get out while you can, before he does it again – or worse.* But there's another part of me, which has been subdued too long, that's growing louder all the time. A part that says, *Andrew deserves to pay.*

When DS May came to the hospital, I almost told her everything about my life – my husband's abuse, my son's death, my fears for Niamh. I would have told her about the image on Andrew's phone, too, but having experienced the force of his anger, I can't take the risk of him beating me again. Andrew needs to be seen for what he is – and he will be – I'll make sure of it. Until then, I have to let him believe he's won.

The medical staff don't seem convinced I've fallen. The psychologist who comes to the ward seems to be under the impression I have a drinking problem. I imagine the visit prompted by Andrew – another layer of his smokescreen, another seed of my intended destruction sown, while my husband waits to reap his rewards.

My body physically recoils at the sight of him when he arrives while DS May is visiting, bile rising in my throat, and it's all I can do to stop myself from throwing up.

'Say anything to the police, and I'll do worse next time,' he whispers after DS May leaves us together. 'You'll never walk again, Elise. Your legs . . .' He casts his eyes down my body. 'Do you know what it would take to damage ligaments, snap bones? How easy it would be to make it look like another accident?'

My fear knows a new level, but he doesn't have to tell me what he can do. Unable to move without pain shooting through my body, I already know.

Standing at the foot of my bed, he tells me, 'I've contacted the rental agency.'

I feel my eyes widen with shock.

'I told them you'd had a change of heart. Oh, and I said you felt bad about letting them down and not to worry about refunding your money.' He even fakes a chuckle. 'I explained that I was your husband, and that you'd had a repeat of a psychotic episode. To be honest, I think they were relieved I told them. They think I've saved them a whole load of problems.'

In his smug smile, I see what I haven't seen before. In Andrew's warped, twisted mind, any lies are facts if he wants them to be.

Once he's gone, I lie on my side, gazing out of the window over the rooftops, broken here and there by branches of trees clad in the pale green of spring. Before long, the first swallows will arrive, their dainty shapes carving graceful arcs across the sky. But right now, it's hard to find any beauty in my life. At this moment, I'd give away everything I have, trade our big country house for a two-bedroom semi on a crowded housing estate, if it meant leaving my marriage.

If it was just Andrew and me, I'd kill him. If I had to spend the rest of my life in prison, so be it. It couldn't be any worse than living with him.

Chapter Thirty-Eight

Jo

Back at my desk in the station the next day, I go through every-thing we have, the knot of unanswered questions growing ever more tangled. Trying to carefully unravel the case, I compile a list of the most credible suspects to discuss with the DI.

'The first is Andrew Buckley, sir. His cast-iron reputation as a GP has been shot to pieces now that we know what he's done to his wife. If he were pushed, it's easy to believe that he could kill.'

The DI frowns. 'We need a motive, May. Do you have one?'

'Hollie accused him of assaulting her, though he maintains it was revenge because she'd found out about him and Stephanie. And as you know, she was in love with his son, Dylan. Doctor Buckley claims it was Hollie ending their relationship that triggered Dylan to take his own life, but he's proven we can't trust him.'

'Go on.'

'Knowing the affair was still going on, maybe Hollie went to see him again. Maybe she challenged him. Maybe he lost his temper.'

'Too many maybes.' He shakes his head. 'Plus we only have Buckley's account of what happened and, as you said, we both know how reliable that is. We need something more concrete.'

'We have Elise's, too,' I remind him. 'Though she may only know what he's told her about it.' It feels like we're closing in, but proof remains frustratingly out of reach. 'There's also James Hampton, of course, though I'm not sure he could kill anyone, least of all his daughter. But you couldn't imagine him buying into child porn, either, and we know for a fact that he has. There's also the undeniable fact that all three of the important women in his life are now dead.'

The DI is silent for a moment. 'Anyone else?'

'Only two more credible suspects. The first is Phil Mason. What if Hollie realised he was blackmailing her father? She could have gone to see him and threatened to expose him to the police. Maybe he arranged to meet her in Park House so that the two of them could talk without being observed by any of the villagers. It backs onto his place and would be easy for him to get there without being seen. When she refused to keep quiet, maybe he killed her, then pushed her body into the pool, where it lay submerged under leaves until we found it.'

This time, the DI looks thoughtful. 'Without interviewing Mason, we can't know. You said you had one more?'

'Yes.' I watch him closely. 'Elise Buckley.'

The DI looks surprised. 'I wasn't expecting you to say that. Why?'

'She and Hollie were seen having a heated exchange by one of the villagers, shortly before Hollie disappeared. If Hollie knew something about Elise – or maybe her husband – which threatened her family, it would be motive enough. Elise is fiercely protective of her daughter.'

'You've only just got through telling me he abuses her.' The DI looks confused.

'I know. But that's the point, sir. Abusive relationships can't be understood the way most relationships can. I would imagine that, until now, Elise has normalised her abusive marriage. It's what happens . . .' I break off. 'Just before she ended up in hospital, I had some missed calls from her. When I went to see her, I was asking her about them when Buckley turned up. I still don't why she called; I need to go back and ask her. But regardless, she's kept his dirty little secret about what he does to her. Who knows what else she isn't saying?'

'That doesn't make sense,' he says firmly. 'And there's no motive.'

'Oh, but it does make sense.' I stare at him, then drop the pretence. 'People normalise the dysfunctional all the time. I was in an abusive relationship, sir. For ten years. My husband used to hit me when he was drunk or if something didn't go his way. I never told anyone. I had this misguided loyalty to him – I was scared of him hurting me, but I was also scared of being without him. That relationship came to define who I was. He completely suckered me in, then undermined me constantly, destroying my self-esteem until I didn't believe I was capable of surviving on my own.'

'I had no idea,' he says quietly.

'I became good at hiding it. And I don't particularly want people to know about it.' I give him a warning look. 'I'm only telling you because I understand how Elise Buckley may be thinking. Right now, after what he's just done to her, I don't suppose she can imagine a way out.'

'We still have no idea why she'd want to kill Hollie though. Are you planning to talk to her again?'

'Yes. I'm going to suggest she calls a domestic abuse hotline.

There are several and if she seriously wants help, they're good. But . . .' I hesitate. 'If Hollie knew something that threatened the Buckleys, I do wonder what Elise might have been capable of. Her husband's assessment of her is fragile and unstable. I don't think she's either of those things.' Watching him think, I give the DI a moment. 'And in all this, the missing piece is still Philip Mason.'

He nods. 'Tangled bloody web, isn't it?'

I nod.

'What about the connection between Hampton and Calder? Or Buckley?'

'Maybe forensics will come up with something from Mason's house. Shouldn't we have a report soon?'

He nods as he stands. 'I'll chase them up. In fact, I'll do that right now. I'll let you know what they say.'

★

Before I leave the office later that afternoon, I call the practice where Andrew Buckley works, asking to speak to him. When they tell me he's busy with patients until at least seven, I tell them I'll call back tomorrow. But knowing he's occupied for a couple of hours means I have a clear window to go and see Elise.

She's sitting up when I get to the hospital this time, and even though she's alone, she doesn't look pleased to see me. Pulling up a chair, I sit down near the end of her bed. 'How are you feeling today?'

'Sore.' Her words bear more of her usual no-nonsense manner. 'You shouldn't be here. If Andrew sees you, he'll be furious.'

'He's with patients until seven. I checked with his practice. Is that how he was yesterday when I left here? Furious?' When she nods, I add, 'I know how it feels.'

274

Her eyes glisten as she turns away. 'So you said.'

'Look . . .' I pause. 'I haven't come here on police business. I've come here as another woman who knows what it's like to be physically abused.' I watch her take in my words before asking quietly, 'How are you?'

Shaking her head, she sighs. 'Honestly? You have no idea. I'd found a house to move into. I paid the deposit and three months' rent out of my savings. When he found out, he went ballistic and I ended up in here. But it's nothing new. He constantly threatens me. He thinks he can bring me down, just like that.'

I frown. 'What do you mean – bring you down?'

'Oh,' she says softly. 'He thinks that, if he wants to, he can bring the mighty weight of the medical profession crashing down on me. He's told me he'll get me declared insane, an unfit mother. I'll lose my job, my daughter . . .' Her voice cracks as she says *daughter*.

'It's a bluff, Elise,' I tell her quietly. 'He'd never get away with it. The police know what he's capable of. I can't tell you much, but we're watching him.'

'Really?' There's a glimmer of hope in her eyes.

'How did he find out about your moving out?'

Her eyes are troubled. 'Niamh told him. I don't really under-stand why.'

I frown. 'I imagine she's as frightened of him as you are. She probably thought it would be worse if he found out later.'

'Maybe.' Elise nods. 'It's terrible that she knows what he's doing to me. I need to get both of us away. But I don't know how.'

Her distress is obvious. Getting out my phone, I bring up the number I found earlier. 'If I found you someone to talk to, would you call them?'

I wait for her to nod. 'I'll text the number to your mobile

– if that's safe?' When she nods again, I add, 'Why don't you call them before you leave here? They can help.'

'I doubt it.' She sounds defeated.

'Elise.' I wait for her to look at me. 'This, right now, is the low point. But however impossible it seems – and as I said, I know how that feels – there *is* a way out. For Niamh's sake – don't you think you have to try?'

Our conversation ends prematurely when my phone buzzes. As I walk back to my car, I have a flashback to when I reached my own rock bottom. My husband's abuse had been daily and at that point, I had no contact with my family as he'd destroyed the remaining links I had with them. The future had seemed utterly bleak, and without hope, just as it must for Elise right now. I can remember it like it was yesterday, and I know that it wouldn't have taken much more to push me over the edge.

Chapter Thirty-Nine

Elise

I call a taxi from the hospital and hide my swollen face from gawping eyes behind dark glasses and a large scarf, as I clutch a bag of newly prescribed painkillers. It's midday by the time I get home and the first thing I do is pour myself a large vodka, taking it upstairs with me. Back in my own bedroom, I examine my face in the large mirror in daylight. The bruising looks uglier than ever. Taking a mouthful of vodka, I start applying my heaviest makeup to hide the worst of it.

Even when it's done, there's a bluish pallor through the thick layer of foundation, but it's enough for now, and there are other matters to attend to. Firstly, the rent Andrew told the estate agent that they could keep, which I need back. They're reticent when I call them, until I remind them that it was my signature on the rental agreement and that they had no authority to act on what anyone else told them. I kick up a fuss, threatening them with legal action until eventually they refund it all and ask me not to contact them again. After calling them fascist bigots, I hang up.

Composing myself, my next call is to my airline, to whom

Andrew has also spoken. Deliberately and patiently, they tell me that my doctor has suggested a referral for mental health problems and that I've been suspended from flying duties. Managing to keep my calm, I tell them that my doctor is my abusive husband, who has an axe to grind as I'm about to leave him, and that I'll contact them as soon as I have a second opinion. After hanging up, I drink the rest of the vodka before hurling my glass at the wall.

There's only one person who understands what I'm going through – DS May. My fingers hesitate on my phone as I think about calling her, but then I remember the number she sent me. It's a lifeline I need, rather than a helpline, but I call the number anyway, the knot in my stomach tightening as I wait for someone to answer.

'Hello?' The warm voice on the other end of the line reminds me of the woman in the market in Marrakech, and of the stone she gave me. Kindness, again. It astonishes me how much can be conveyed in a single word.

It triggers a release, my tears erupting and flowing down my face, making it impossible to speak. Eventually they slow enough for me to mumble. *'Please. Help me.'*

*

An hour later, after the call is over, I understand the difference it makes to know that there's someone else who understands. Drained of emotion, I'm calmer. When I get up to look in the mirror, I gently feel my face where my tears have carved their way through my makeup, exposing a lattice of bruising underneath. Upstairs, I remove the rest of my makeup, flinching as the bruising comes into full view once again. I'd wanted to protect Niamh from it, but in order for her to understand, I need her to see what Andrew's done to me.

Then I do what the woman on the helpline number told me to do. I call the police – more specifically, DS May.

'It's Elise Buckley. I want to report an instance of domestic abuse.' My voice is shaky and I can't stop it, but it isn't because I'm having second thoughts. I've never been more sure about anything.

'OK. Have you spoken to the helpline number I gave you?'

'Yes.'

'Good. So they've run through what you can expect.'

My voice is a whisper. 'If he knows I've spoken to you, he'll be so angry.'

'Elise. Try not to worry,' DS May tries to reassure me. 'You've done the right thing. We'll be bringing him in as soon as we've taken a statement from you. I'm going to ask Sergeant Collins to come over right away. She'll have someone with her. They'll take you through what happens from here.' She pauses. 'It isn't going to be easy, but this is important. You've taken the first step, now. Keep strong.'

Nothing can take away my fear right now, but as with the woman on the helpline, I'm aware of the kindness in her voice, kindness that all of a sudden makes it impossible to bear the pain. I manage to say, 'Thank you,' before hanging up and doubling over, trying to stifle my sobs.

★

While I wait for Sergeant Collins, I make a mug of tea I don't drink, then pace around the kitchen. Eventually, her car pulls up outside and two uniformed figures make their way towards the door.

Without waiting for a knock, I open it. If Sergeant Collins is shocked by my appearance, she doesn't show it. 'Mrs Buckley? May we come in?'

'Of course. Please.' Leaving the door open, I hear one of them close it as I go into the kitchen. When I turn around to look at them, I lose my voice as the reality of what I'm about to do hits me full on.

Sergeant Collins nods towards the man with her. 'This is Constable Emerson.' Vaguely recognising him, I nod, and she goes on. 'Would you mind if we make us all a pot of tea?'

Realising she's trying to inject normalcy into a situation that's anything but, I start towards the sink. 'I'll put the kettle on.'

'If you show him where the teabags are, Emerson will do it.' She hesitates. 'Let's sit down.'

Nodding, I follow her to the kitchen table, pulling out a chair. She sits opposite me, waiting a moment before she says, 'I understand your husband has assaulted you.'

Years of habit kick in as I bite back the excuses I want to make. *I fell down the stairs. We had a row and he lost his temper. It was just one of those things.* But thinking of Niamh, I know I can't do that anymore. 'Yes.'

'When did this assault take place?' Her voice is gentle, but there's steeliness behind it.

My body is rigid as I sit there. 'Three days ago. I came back from hospital today.'

'Apart from the obvious bruises on your face, did he hurt you anywhere else?'

'He punched me in the stomach.' The words sound light, belying the force he hit me with.

As Emerson joins us, carrying mugs of tea, Collins puts down her pen, her face sympathetic as she looks at me. 'I hate to ask you this, but we need you to tell us what happened, including what was said leading up to his assault or what may have caused it.'

Knowing this was coming, I nod. 'I had found a cottage for Niamh and me to move to.' Seeing Sergeant Collins lift her hand slightly towards her pen, I pause.

'Niamh is your daughter, isn't she? How old is she?'

'She's fourteen. Andrew's behaviour has become worse lately.' I sigh, knowing I need to tell them everything, wondering how far back I should go.

'It's OK. We're not in a hurry. Take your time.'

But I shake my head, because there is a hurry. What if Andrew comes back? 'It's complicated.' My voice is unsteady, my thoughts all over the place as I look at them both. 'You already know, of course, that my husband was having an affair with Stephanie Hampton. Before her, he had other affairs. Anyway, since she died, he's been at home much more and his behaviour's been getting increasingly aggressive. He uses foul language and thinks nothing of letting Niamh see the full force of his temper. She's frightened of him.' My voice cracks slightly, and my hands are shaking as I take a sip of my tea. 'I knew things couldn't go on as they were so I found a cottage for me and Niamh, and paid three months' rent up front. When Niamh got home from school, I told her. I thought she'd be pleased.' I still don't fully understand why she reacted the way she did. 'But she ran upstairs and I found her sobbing on her bed. Then she told me she didn't want to go.'

Sergeant Collins is frowning. 'Did she say why?'

I shake my head. 'I know she's frightened of him. I don't know if there are other reasons for her reaction though. Then, when Andrew came in from work, she told him. I was upstairs . . .' The same despair I'd felt when I realised what was happening comes back. 'He said he'd told Niamh that he was going to have a chat with me about my *"naïve little plan"*, as he put it. I told him he couldn't force me to do anything, but he said he'd do whatever he liked. He wanted me to stop dreaming up ludicrous ideas because he wouldn't let me leave. In fact, he said he'd do anything to stop me.' I pause. 'I think it was at that point I knew I was in danger. But I'd gone so far, I couldn't back down and let him believe he'd won – again. I reminded him about his affairs. Said that we didn't love each other so there was no point continuing this charade.'

'What did he say to that?'

I shrug. 'He didn't contradict me. But you understand, don't you, that none of this is about love. It's about Andrew's need for control. When I didn't say what he wanted me to say, he started to hit me.'

'I know it's hard . . .' Sergeant Collins's eyes don't leave my face. 'But we need an account of his assault. Where did it happen?'

'In here. Over there . . .' I point towards the worktop beside the oven. 'He grabbed my arm and slapped me across the face. Then he pushed me into the corner and slapped me again. I think he must have punched me here.' I point to the swelling below my left eye. 'I remember his hands around my throat. I felt a blow to my stomach. After that, all I remember is arriving in hospital. Andrew was with me. He told the nurses that I'd had too much to drink and fallen down the stairs. He also told them he had concerns about my mental state – that he had for some time.' I shake my head, unable to keep the bitterness out of my voice. 'While I was in hospital, he called the estate agent I'd used to rent the cottage. He told them I wouldn't be taking it and that they could keep the rent I'd paid in advance. Told them to keep *my* money . . . Then he called the airline I work for and told them what he'd told the hospital staff. I'm suspended from flying duties. Basically, my employers now think I'm mentally unstable.'

'He's assaulted you before?'

I nod. 'A number of times. If you're looking for a pattern, I think it's to do with when he's under pressure of some kind. But there's an underlying current of emotional abuse that never stops.'

'Have you ever told anyone about what he does to you?'

This is the hardest part to explain. 'Until now, no. You see, Andrew holds the winning hand. He's always said he can prove that I'm unreliable and unstable. He can bring me down.' I stare at Sergeant Collins.

'Isn't that exactly what he's doing now?' Her voice is insistent. 'With the estate agent and your employer? How much worse can it get?'

Swallowing, I remember what he said in the hospital. 'He came to see me . . .' My voice is husky. 'In the hospital. He threatened me again. He said he'd see to it that I'd never walk again . . .'

A look of shock crosses Sergeant Collins's face, as I go on. 'You don't know my husband. If you spoke to him about what's happened, he'd convince you that my injuries are self-inflicted. That I make his life a misery, that I'm damaging Niamh. He'll even tell you . . .' I break off.

'What were you about to say?' Sergeant Collins looks at me.

I sigh shakily. 'He'll tell you it was my fault our son died.' A tear rolls down my cheek. 'And the trouble is . . . in many ways, he's right.'

Chapter Forty

Jo

'There's no question her husband abuses her,' Sarah Collins tells me. 'He's completely undermined her in every respect. He's also threatened her if she tries to leave him again. And it's all made much worse because he's a GP and everyone who knows him thinks he's God.'

'Not around here, they don't.' Getting up, I walk over to the window, shaking my head. Abuse cases are always complicated. 'We're bringing him in – he should be here shortly.'

'Good. We've given Elise the name of a bed and breakfast a few miles from here. She's packing a few things while she waits for Niamh to get back from school.'

'Is anyone with her?'

Sarah shakes her head. 'With us picking up Buckley, there didn't seem any point.'

I nod. 'Fair enough. He isn't likely to be leaving here any time soon. As well as arresting him on suspicion of abuse, he's potentially a suspect in Hollie's murder.'

Sarah stares at me. 'You couldn't make it up. And all in such a small village.' Her phone buzzes. 'Collins.' Holding her hand over the mouthpiece, she mouths *Elise Buckley* at me. Then she frowns. 'Look, just stay put. We're on our way.'

Ending the call, she's already walking towards the door. 'We need to get over there. It seems Andrew Buckley must have left the surgery before we got there. He obviously got wind we were on our way and came home early. Elise sounds terrified.'

Instantly on my feet, I pull on my jacket as we walk. 'I'll drive. Call Emerson and get him to join us. Tell him to bring someone with him.' Outside, I break into a run. If Andrew knows Elise has talked to us, she's in more danger than ever before.

*

I drive as fast as I dare, while Sarah goes on talking. 'Elise did warn us that he'll be utterly convincing about how unstable she is. She said he'll tell us she has mental health problems and that she was drunk when she fell down the stairs. He'll make it sound like it's completely her fault that it happened. She also said that he'll tell us it was her fault their son died.'

'What?' It's the first I've heard of that. 'He can't put that one on her. Their son took an overdose.'

'I'm just telling you what Elise said earlier.'

As we turn into the village, I slow down but only slightly. When we turn into the Buckleys' drive, I see both cars parked side by side. From the outside, it's the picture of a normal, well-to-do family home. But as we reach the back door, it's anything but. The sound of loud voices comes to me as I turn to Sarah. 'Check that Emerson's on his way.' Then I knock. 'Doctor Buckley? Mrs Buckley? It's DS May.'

The shouting instantly subsides. Andrew Buckley opens the door about half a minute later, his features arranged into an air of artificial calm, but his eyes are filled with anger. 'What is it, Detective Sergeant?'

'We'd like to come in. If you wouldn't mind . . .' I take a step forward, but he blocks the doorway.

'As a matter of fact, I do mind.' His eyes glint dangerously. 'My wife isn't at all well. I'm trying my best to help her, but you lot turning up makes it all far worse.'

From behind him, Elise's thin, desperate voice reaches me. 'It's OK, Andrew. I can talk to them.'

He briefly turns to glance at her. 'There is no need.'

Just then, Emerson's car turns up. I wait for him and another uniformed officer to join us at the door. 'We'd like to talk to you, Doctor Buckley – at the station.' Emerson holds his gaze.

He glares at Emerson, then turns to me, suddenly flinging the door open in a dramatic gesture and standing back. As I pass him, he mutters, 'You have no idea what's going on here.'

Ignoring him, I go through to the kitchen, aware of the others behind me. Elise looks terrified and her bruising has taken on a purple hue. I try to make eye contact, but she turns away.

'Now, what's all this about?' Trying to sound vaguely amiable, Andrew Buckley attempts to bluff his way out.

'We have concerns about your wife's safety, Doctor Buckley,' Sergeant Collins says calmly.

'There's absolutely no need. There's been a misunderstanding, hasn't there, Elise? My wife has difficulty distinguishing between fantasy and reality, ladies.' His patronising tone makes my spine prickle. 'Her problems started when our son died.' He lowers his voice. 'We're doing our best to overcome them, but as I said, this constant police questioning really doesn't help.'

'That isn't true.' As Elise speaks up, I recognise the courage it has taken to do this. 'There is no misunderstanding, Andrew. You did this.' As she points to her face, the blood drains from his.

His eyes narrow. 'That is nonsense and you know it,' he snarls, his rage getting the better of him as he starts launching accusations. 'You're deluded, Elise. I've tried to protect you, but you've forced me into this. I can't hide it anymore. We both know that it was you who killed Dylan.'

I watch shock register on Elise's face. Then she glances at me, even more terrified than before. But I've seen enough. I step forward. 'Andrew Buckley, I am arresting you on suspicion of violently attacking your wife.'

But he interrupts me. 'You can't arrest me. You don't have any proof I've done anything.'

Raising my voice, I talk over him. 'You do not have to say anything but it may harm your defence if you do not mention when questioned something you later rely on in court. Anything you do say may be given in evidence.' I nod towards Emerson, who comes forward and leads Buckley away.

I look at Sarah. 'You'd better go with them.' Then I notice Elise is trembling and add, 'I'll stay here. I'll let the DI know you're on your way.'

As the other officers go outside, I walk over to where Elise is sitting. 'I know it doesn't feel like it, but it's going to be OK.'

But she looks distraught. 'You don't know Andrew. He'll get me for this.'

'Elise, he can't. At the very least, there are legal measures we can take to keep him away from you.' I pause. 'Can I make you a cup of tea?'

She shakes her head.

'Is Niamh here?'

'She's upstairs.' A look of horror washes over her face. 'I have to protect her from this, but don't you see? Everything I do makes it worse.'

'Your husband will be kept in overnight,' I tell her. 'And I'm sure the hospital staff will confirm that your injuries were not the result of a fall. They see this too often, Elise.' I watch her. 'So do we. Meanwhile, you and Niamh should carry on packing. The sooner you're away from here, the better.'

★

As I walk out to the car, I call the DI. 'Sir, Collins and Emerson are bringing Andrew Buckley in. We've arrested him on suspicion of assaulting his wife. He denies it, of course, but he's guilty as hell.'

'Right. I'll address it when I talk to him about Mason.'

'I thought you might. I'll see you shortly, sir.'

As I glance back at the house, seeing Elise's battered face at the window is like looking at a mirror image of my past self. But it reconfirms my belief that if Andrew Buckley is capable of doing that to his wife, he could have done far worse to Hollie.

Chapter Forty-One

Jo

When I get to the police station, Andrew Buckley is still in reception with Emerson, loudly demanding to make a call to his lawyer.

'As soon as we've completed this paperwork, you can use the phone.' Looking up, Emerson catches my eye.

'Everything all right?' I say breezily.

When Andrew Buckley spins around, there's a look of rage on his face. 'No, Detective Sergeant. Everything is not all right. You've forced me to leave my unstable wife alone with my daughter. You have no idea what you're doing.'

'Your wife and daughter manage perfectly well when you're working.' I stare at him. 'Sign the forms, and then you can call your lawyer.' As I walk away, I hear him swear under his breath.

★

'He's digging himself a hole, sir,' I say to the DI. 'His behaviour is classic of his type. He's all about control. Now that he doesn't have any, we're seeing the real Andrew Buckley and he's a nasty

291

piece of work. But the problem is Elise. She's terrified of what he'll do when he gets out.'

'We need to find out where he fits into this case. That's if he does . . .' The DI frowns. 'I think we should catch him on the hop. Tell him about Mason and Operation Rainbow. Watch his reaction.'

'We already know Hollie had something against him – we need to find out what it was. He's calling his lawyer, by the way. I'll let you know when they've arrived.'

As I walk back to reception to check how Emerson is faring, my phone buzzes. It's Elise Buckley. My first thought is that she needs to hear a familiar voice.

'How are you, Elise?'

'Niamh's just told me something. I don't know if it's relevant, but I thought I should tell you anyway.' Elise sounds jittery.

My ears prick up. 'What did she say?'

'You know how Hollie used to wander wherever she pleased and that Niamh was with her sometimes? She said that Hollie recently climbed into Phil Mason's property. At the time, Niamh didn't realise whose house it was and she said she tried to stop Hollie . . . I just thought you ought to know.'

This confirms my suspicions that Hollie was on to Mason and my thoughts start to race. 'Yes. Thank you very much.'

She pauses briefly. 'I have to go.'

After she hangs up, something about what she said niggles at me. But then Emerson calls me. 'Buckley's lawyer is here. They're in the interview room. I said we'd give them ten minutes.'

'OK.' I hesitate. 'Do me a favour. Elise Buckley – do you have time to go back over there?'

He looks unsure. 'I have a stack of paperwork to write up. Is it important?'

'It's a hunch,' I tell him. 'Something's wrong . . .'

'Give me half an hour?' When I nod, he goes on. 'I'll shoot over there then.'

'Thanks. Just check she's OK. Reassure her that we're keeping her husband in tonight.'

Out of the corner of my eye, I see the DI coming down the corridor towards me. 'Right. Let's do this. Are they in there?'

I nod. 'I've just had a call from Elise Buckley. Hollie did take Niamh into the grounds of Mason's house. She must have known he was up to something.'

'If Buckley's involved, we need to nail him now.' His face is grim. 'From everything you've said, he's hiding something. I want to know what it is.'

★

Andrew Buckley's lawyer is tall with short black hair. He stands when we walk in. 'I'm Hamish McClure. On behalf of my client, I'd like to stress he strongly objects to being brought here.'

'Believe me, we have several very good reasons for keeping you here, Doctor Buckley.' The DI speaks abruptly. 'We will be recording this interview.' He glances at McClure but speaks to me. 'Start the tape, May.'

While the DI gives the normal preamble for the tape, I watch the look of disdain on Buckley's face, knowing he believes himself to be above the law. That's how people like him operate.

'Doctor Buckley, did you or did you not hit your wife three days ago?'

He folds his arms. 'As I've stated before, my wife had too much to drink and fell as she was coming down the stairs.'

'We've spoken to the hospital staff who looked after her.

General consensus is that she was the subject of a vicious assault. We also have photos.'

Reaching into a brown envelope, I pull out the photos the hospital sent over.

Andrew Buckley looks furious. 'Who took those? I didn't give them permission.'

'Your permission wasn't required. We had your wife's.' I pause as McClure glances at them. 'According to the doctor who admitted her, you tried to play down what were clearly significant injuries. But you must have been worried enough to take her in. Did you realise you'd gone too far? Or did you think everyone would believe your story?' When he doesn't answer, I go on. 'There was another injury to Mrs Buckley's stomach. She was in considerable pain.'

'She fell awkwardly. That isn't proof of anything.' Andrew Buckley glares at me.

'No. But a fist-sized bruise is, Doctor Buckley.' I pause. 'She also told us that you cancelled a rental agreement she'd recently signed. It was one you had no right to interfere with. You told the estate agent they could keep the rent she'd paid up front, then you called her employer and told them her mental state was questionable. Did you discuss any of this with your wife first?'

'Of course I didn't,' he says dismissively. 'She was in no fit state to make any decisions. It would have been highly irresponsible of me not to tell her employer. I've talked to her about this in the past, but she continues to hide it from them.'

I glance sideways at the DI, wondering if he realises how typical this behaviour is of an abuser. 'Hide what, exactly?'

'Her mental health problems.' He almost sneers as he speaks. 'She's very adept at pretending nothing's wrong, but you have to admit, she's all over the place. I've tried my hardest to take care of her, for all our sakes, but she makes it impossible.'

My voice is no-nonsense. 'And what about what's best for Niamh?'

'She would be far better off with me if my wife left, which I've no doubt is what she's said she wants.'

I'm speechless for a moment at his arrogant assumption that a court will give him custody of Niamh. 'You're assuming the court will agree with you.'

He opens his mouth to say something, then changes his mind.

The DI takes over. 'Doctor Buckley, is it true you weren't happy about your daughter's friendship with Hollie Hampton?'

McClure butts in. 'What does this have to do with Mrs Buckley?'

'We'll get to that if you'll let me go on.' The DI shows exemplary patience. 'Answer the question,' he says to Buckley.

'Hollie was unstable,' he says brusquely. 'She wasn't a good influence on Niamh.'

'She went out with your son, didn't she? By all accounts, they were in love.'

'Now look here,' Andrew Buckley starts to bluster. 'My son is dead. Leave him out of this.'

But the DI frowns. 'You told us that Hollie made an appointment to see you, with the express intention of causing you trouble. Is that correct?'

When Andrew Buckley nods, the DI says, 'Would you like to tell us what happened?'

'She asked me to examine a lump in one of her breasts. She refused a chaperone, then after taking off her top, she started screaming. She accused me of touching her inappropriately.'

'No-one witnessed this?'

'No.' There's a frown on Andrew Buckley's face.

'So it was your word against hers?' When Buckley nods, the DI says, 'And no-one doubted you.'

'It was obvious she was lying.' Andrew Buckley looks angry again.

'To you, maybe.' The DI pauses. 'But there's the possibility, isn't there, that you did touch her? Or frighten her? No-one can prove otherwise.' As Andrew Buckley opens his mouth, the DI shoots him a warning look. 'I understand you put the incident down to her having discovered that you were having an affair with her stepmother, Stephanie Hampton. Is that correct?'

'Absolutely. She told me to stay away from her stepmother.' He pauses. 'It wasn't enough for her though. Someone slashed my car tyres a little while ago. It doesn't take much to work out who.'

'You think Hollie did that?' The DI's eyes don't leave Buckley's face.

'For goodness' sake, there's hardly anyone else around here who would have.'

'Do you have proof?'

'I don't need proof, Detective Inspector.'

The DI leans forward. 'Did you report it at the time?'

'No, but . . .'

The DI interrupts. 'Apart from your affair with Mrs Hampton, was there any other reason she might have wanted to hurt you?'

'This has no bearing whatsoever on why my client is here.' This time McClure is more forceful.

'I think it does.' The DI keeps his calm. 'From what Doctor Buckley's just told us, it's clear he believes himself a more credible source than anyone else.' He corrects himself. 'No, infallible, I think the word is. I suggest that the same applies to everything he's said about Mrs Buckley, though his account is no less subjective and no more credible than hers. As I was asking . . .' He pauses. 'Is there any other reason, Doctor Buckley, why Hollie Hampton might have wanted to cause you trouble?'

'Not that I'm aware of.' His face gives nothing away.

'You've told us you don't think Hollie was a good influence on Niamh . . . Did you feel the same way about her relationship with your son?'

'My son is dead.' Andrew Buckley's whisper is menacing. 'Life was very different before he died – for all of us. Including Hollie.'

As I watch him, Andrew Buckley swallows. Then he turns and mutters something to his lawyer. As McClure clears his throat, I can guess what's coming.

'My client is exhausted. He's been under immense strain dealing with his wife's problems. I suggest we continue this conversation another time.'

The DI nods. 'Very well.'

'Thank God.' As Andrew Buckley stands up to leave, the DI interjects.

'Sit down, Doctor Buckley. I'd like to remind you that you're under arrest. You're not going anywhere.'

Niamh

I watch from upstairs as my father is taken off in the police car, and I run to the bathroom just in time before I'm sick. The police aren't going to make anything better. They didn't when Dylan died.

Whenever he speaks, my father undoes everything my mother says before adding his lies. 'Elise is unstable . . . She doesn't know what she's doing . . . I try to look after her . . . I don't know what else to do for her . . .' Then, when he thinks no-one's watching, he hits her.

My mother's shaky after the police leave, and when she looks at me, I see she's as frightened as I am. We both know he'll come back. He always does. Each time angrier than the last.

'I don't understand, Niamh. Why wouldn't you leave here with me?'

Shaking my head, I say nothing. I can't tell her that as long as he's alive, we'll never be free of him. It doesn't matter where we live. He'll find us. Nowhere is safe.

There is only one way for everything to be OK and that's to do what my father wants.

And he knows that.

Chapter Forty-Two

Jo

Something's niggling at me the next morning, just before we're scheduled to continue questioning Andrew Buckley.

'Sir, do we know how long Andrew Buckley's affair with Stephanie Hampton went on?'

He frowns. 'I don't know. Why d'you ask?'

'It may be nothing. But I want to check something out. I need to talk to James Hampton again.'

*

In the interview room, James Hampton wears the resigned expression of a condemned man.

'I need to ask you about your wife's affair with Andrew Buckley, Mr Hampton.' I watch as his face clouds over. 'Do you know when it started?'

'Not for sure, but something changed last summer. She was suddenly out much more. I knew she was busy at work so I put it down to that. She also seemed brighter than she had in a long time. I put that down to her work, too. She loved what she did. Now, I realise she was with him.'

'Can you narrow it down to a month?' I watch him closely, knowing that if he says what I think he's going to say, there are huge implications for Andrew Buckley.

He tries to work it out. 'My birthday's the first week in August. Everything was fine, then. The Buckleys even came to my party. I remember catching Stephanie talking to *him*.' He says it venomously. 'It seemed harmless enough at the time and I didn't think anything more of it. But after that she was different somehow.'

'Do you have anything more to back up your assumption that the affair started then?'

He nods. Then he frowns. 'A week later, I was at the pub having a drink with a couple of people. Buckley was one of them. Just before he left, he bought me a pint . . .' His laugh is hollow. 'Then, when I got home, I saw his car was pulling out of our drive. When I went in, Stephanie said he'd called in to drop off some blood test results. I had no reason not to believe her and I had other things on my mind by then . . .' His voice trails off as he stares blankly at the table.

★

After leaving Hampton, I make the phone call that will tell me everything I need to know.

★

In contrast to James Hampton, Andrew Buckley's demeanour is one of outrage when I see him later. When I walk in with the DI, he immediately gets up and starts speaking angrily. 'As soon as I'm out of here, I will be reporting this – and all of you – for the appalling way I've been treated.'

The DI stands there, an imposing figure as he stares across the table at Buckley. 'Sit down, Doctor Buckley. Before you go anywhere, we have more questions we need you to answer.'

'I'm not saying a word until McClure gets here.'

The DI folds his arms. 'Fair enough. In that case, we'll wait.'

An hour passes in which I watch as Andrew Buckley starts to behave like a caged animal. Experience tells me he's close to cracking.

As the time approaches eleven fifteen, he gets up. 'This is ridiculous,' he snaps, just as the door opens and McClure comes in.

'Apologies for keeping you.' Meeting Buckley's eye, he takes off his jacket and sits down.

The DI shuffles the papers in front of him. 'Right. Shall we get on with this? A question for you, Doctor Buckley. When did your affair with Stephanie Hampton begin?'

'I can't remember exactly.'

'Well, give me a month – or a season, even. Spring? Summer?'

I wouldn't mind betting Buckley knows the exact date.

'September.'

As the DI glances at me, I catch his eye. 'So Hollie must have made the appointment with you sometime after that, the one where she caused such a song and dance?'

'It must have been.' His eyes swivel between me and the DI.

'I called your practice this morning, Doctor Buckley. According to their records, the incident with Hollie took place on the thirtieth of May.'

When he doesn't respond, the DI leans forward. 'I don't think there's any doubt that Hollie had an axe to grind, but it wasn't about your affair with Stephanie Hampton. So my question is, what *was* it about? And was that the reason you killed her?'

Rigid, Andrew Buckley leans back in his chair, his arms still folded. 'I'd like a moment with my lawyer.'

★

Outside the interview room, the DI congratulates me. 'Nice work, May.'

'Thank you, sir, but we still don't know what Hollie had against him. It could be connected to Mason . . . There's definitely something he's not telling us.'

Back in the interview room, the DI gets straight to the point. 'Doctor Buckley, I understand you often drink in the village pub with one or two other villagers. Anyone in particular?'

At this new line of questioning, Andrew Buckley appears to relax slightly. 'Not really. There are a number of locals who I regularly see in there; James Hampton being one, as you already know.'

'What about Julian Calder?' The DI's face is implacable. 'And Philip Mason?'

As Andrew Buckley nods, his eyes narrow very slightly. 'As I told you, Detective Inspector, there are a number of regulars.'

The DI pauses, but only briefly. 'Did you know that James Hampton was investing in a business that belongs to Philip Mason?' As he speaks, he scrutinises Andrew Buckley's face.

'I'd heard some vague mention of it, yes.'

'What exactly did you hear?'

He shrugs. 'It wasn't specific. Mason makes a lot of money – I don't know exactly how – and he was trying to give Hampton a helping hand. It's obvious the man struggles.' His brusque, patronising manner does him no favours.

The DI frowns. 'What did you know about the Hamptons' finances?'

'Nothing.' He stares straight at us. 'Stephanie didn't mention anything, if that's what you're asking, Detective Inspector.'

And so it goes on. An hour later, we're none the wiser. On the subject of his relationship with Mason, Andrew Buckley refuses to be drawn, insisting on his story that they see each other only occasionally in the pub. When it comes to Hollie, other than declaring her emotionally unstable, he can supply no reasonable explanation for her behaviour in the surgery.

'Where were you the day Hollie died, Doctor Buckley?'

There's a split-second delay before he answers. 'I took the day off.'

The DI glances at me. 'What did you do?'

'I was at home. Catching up on this and that.'

'I assume your wife or daughter will confirm this?'

Buckley looks uncomfortable. 'There's no need for you to speak to them.' He hesitates. 'If you must know, I spent the afternoon with Stephanie.'

'Where, Doctor Buckley?'

'At her salon. Not that it makes any difference.'

'Can anyone verify that?'

He visibly tenses, then mutters the words quietly. 'Not now.'

★

I drive over to see Elise Buckley that afternoon and when she opens the door, she looks as though she hasn't slept.

'I really wish I hadn't started this.' Overnight, her bruised face has taken on a gaunt look, making her eyes seem even bigger and more desperate. 'I've made everything so much worse.'

'You haven't,' I tell her, knowing her guilt stems from years of brainwashing by her husband. 'And you haven't done anything wrong. This is all about your husband. You need to remember that.'

But my words seem to go over her head. 'Niamh's beside herself. She went to school, but she's worried that when she comes out, Andrew will be waiting for her.'

'Andrew won't be going anywhere fast,' I tell her. 'We're still interviewing him.' I pause, watching as she fiddles with her

305

hands. 'Listen. You have to take action. If you don't, what are you saying to Niamh? That it's OK to be bullied and beaten by your husband? That you're supposed to stay put instead of leaving him?' Pausing, I look at her sympathetically. 'Imagine Niamh's relationships in the future. You and Andrew are her blueprint. Yes, it will be difficult, but if you act, you will be empowering her. You have the chance to show her you're strong and that it's OK for her to be, too.' Pausing again, I watch the faintest flicker of hope in Elise's eyes. 'No-one's going to believe Andrew when he claims you're unstable. More and more people are seeing through him. And you're not going to lose your job.'

'But you know what he's like. We won't be safe.' There's desperation in her voice.

'He knows we're on to him. And you're not going to be doing this alone,' I say gently. 'You need a good lawyer who understands coercive control and domestic abuse, so that you can get things set in motion as soon as possible.' I pause. 'I was hoping to talk to Niamh. Has she said anything else about when Hollie took her to Mason's property?'

As Elise shakes her head, our conversation is interrupted by my phone buzzing with an unfamiliar number. 'Excuse me a moment.'

I turn away from Elise. 'May.'

After listening with interest, I end the call. 'I'm sorry. I have to make another call. I won't be a minute.' Going outside, I put a call through to the DI.

'Sir? I've just heard from the estate agent who measured up Mason's house. Mason's been in touch – apparently he's asked the agent to meet him there later today.'

Chapter Forty-Three

Elise

Just as there are two hundred and fifty-six shades of the colour grey, there are as many permutations of our ideas about what's right. But most of us know what's wrong.

The thought reminds me of the magazine headline once again. *Only Ten Per Cent of People are Good.* Out of the ninety per cent that aren't, I imagine most of them are ignorant rather than bad. But that's not the same as the percentage who know something's wrong and do it anyway, calculatedly and coldly, the way Andrew does.

But if I maintain a status quo where my daughter sees her mother verbally abused and periodically beaten by her father, it's the category where I belong, too. DS May was right. Andrew and I are Niamh's blueprint – it's a thought that fills me with shame. Most women would think me weak for staying this long. For them, the decision would be easy. They wouldn't understand that, in so many ways, it's easier to stay. They haven't lived for years with someone who's controlled their every move, crushed their self-esteem, made them believe they're worthless. It's why I love my job. Away

307

from here, behind my uniform and mask of makeup, the Elise who's married to Andrew disappears for a while.

While Niamh is at school, I finish packing our bags. I begin with my clothes, packing what I need, then carrying the cases downstairs before going to Niamh's room. The bracelet I brought back from Morocco, as yet unworn, lies in front of a photo on her dressing table. Picking up the photo, I study it. It's a picture of Niamh, Hollie and Dylan from two or three years ago.

Looking at it brings me up short. I don't even know if Niamh is still grieving; whether she still misses her brother. I didn't support her properly when he died. I was too lost in my own pain.

As I pack some of her things, I suddenly work out why she refused to leave with me; why she told Andrew I'd rented the cottage. Maybe having heard him say it so many times, she believes his lies. Maybe Niamh thinks it *was* me who killed Dylan.

*

After I confirm the address of the B and B where Niamh and I are booked in to stay for a while, the rest of the day seems interminable. Knowing we're leaving, I have no interest in anything here. In the end, I wander outside, but even the appearance of more roses and the wisteria's lilac hues hold no interest for me anymore. All I can do is wait on tenterhooks for Niamh to come home, terrified that Andrew could turn up at any minute.

Several times, I try to call DS May, needing to hear a reassuring voice, but it goes to voicemail. Finally, I hear the school bus slow to a stop then pull away, relief washing over me as Niamh's slender figure walks up the drive. By the time she reaches the door, I have a lump in my throat.

As she walks in, I swallow. 'Hi.'

Her eyes briefly flicker to me as she continues towards the stairs.

'Niamh? I need to talk to you.' My hands are shaking as I take one of hers and lead her over to the table, feeling sick, even though I haven't been able to eat all day. Pulling out a chair for her to sit on, I perch on another. 'We can't stay here, Niamh. The police have found us somewhere to stay for a while. It may only be for a few days, but your father and I can't be together. What he's done to me – to both of us – is a criminal offence. It's why the police have taken him in.'

'If he's being kept there, why do we have to leave?' Her face is suddenly pinched.

'The police say we have to. We'll come back, I promise you. But I don't know how long they're going to hold your father. We'll go somewhere safe until I've talked to a lawyer.' I pause. 'I've packed some of your things. Why don't you check that I have everything?'

She doesn't say anything.

'Niamh? It will be OK. The police know what he's been doing. If he does it again, they'll arrest him again.' I pause. 'He can't come after us – you do see that, don't you?'

But as she looks at me, I know it doesn't matter what I say.

Niamh

My mother thinks we can run away from him. She thinks she's worked it all out, imagining us in a small cottage with pretty curtains and a front door my father doesn't have a key to. But he doesn't need one. If he wants to break in, a lock won't stop him. Nothing will.

I imagine my mother's picture of sunlight and peacefulness ripped down the middle by my father's cruel hands before he tosses the pieces aside.

'We'll go somewhere safe until I've talked to a lawyer.'

But there aren't any lawyers he will listen to, just as there isn't anywhere that's safe. However long the police keep him – however many weeks, months, years – when he gets out, he'll find us. And this time, he'll hurt her far worse than he has before. She doesn't realise how bad it's become, she doesn't have to watch, like I do, as he hits her harder, as the attacks go on for longer. This time, she was unconscious when he'd finished. Next time, or the time after that, he'll kill her.

Chapter Forty-Four

Jo

As police from the surrounding area conceal themselves among the trees and shrubs along Mason's driveway, and wait in the woods behind to cover the area where his helicopter lands, I wonder if he's already inside watching us. The time he arranged with Adam is less than an hour away.

'I hope the bastard hasn't got wind of us,' the DI mutters grimly. 'We can't afford not to get him. Not now.'

'No. Sir, there's a car coming.'

He freezes briefly as he listens, then mutters into his radio. As we wait, the noise gets louder and then a black BMW estate comes into sight, speeding up the drive and stopping sharply at the gate. Immediately, twenty or so police surround it. Through the tinted glass, I see the driver's head turning frantically, clearly thinking about reversing before realising the futility of even trying.

The DI pushes through the officers surrounding the car, then knocks on the driver's window. After a pause, it's lowered.

'Philip Mason? Detective Inspector Saunders, Chichester Police. I am arresting you on suspicion of the possession and distribution of pornographic images. You do not have to say anything but it may harm your defence if you do not mention when questioned something you later rely on in court. Anything you do say may be given in evidence.'

Mason's mocking laugh reaches my ears. 'Porn isn't a crime, Detective Inspector. Now let me get on, please.'

'You're right, Mr Mason. But possession of pornographic images of children is. Out of the car.'

Behind Mason's BMW, a police car pulls up.

Maintaining his dignity, Mason gets out and stands in front of the DI. There's no struggle and his face gives away nothing. A minute later, the police car drives him away.

'Check Mason's car, will you, May? Then we'd better get back to the station.'

There's a briefcase in Mason's car and a few CDs in the glove compartment, all of which I remove. When I catch up to the DI, he's talking on his phone. After he's finished, he glances at what I'm holding.

'Check the discs as soon as we get back. They might be innocent but I'll bet they're not.'

★

As we drive back to the station, something is puzzling me. 'He was taking quite a risk, wasn't he – coming back to the house, when he knows we're on to him?'

The DI stares ahead. 'I imagine he had to get the cellar cleared out at some point. He wouldn't necessarily have known we've already done it for him. He may have sensed he was running out of time and it was a risk he had to take.' His face is grim. 'We're still no closer to knowing where those children came from. Maybe he can help us with that, too.'

★

Two hours later, after Mason's lawyer arrives, I join the DI in the interview room.

'Right. Let's get this started. I'm Detective Inspector Saunders. This is Detective Sergeant May. We'd like to question you about the contents of a cellar on your property, Mr Mason.'

Mason is cool as he looks at us. 'I'm afraid I'm not sure what you're getting at, Detective Inspector. What contents of which cellar?'

'The cellar in the converted farm buildings just in front of where you land your helicopter.' As I speak, something flickers across his face.

'I know the buildings.' His voice is calm, but he frowns. 'But I don't keep anything in there. I was going to do them up as holiday rentals. But as you obviously know, I've decided to sell.'

'As you're aware,' I go on, 'walls have been built leaving a space that's unaccounted for on the floor plan. The door is around the back. We found it.' I pause, watching Mason closely. 'The key wasn't among those you left with the estate agent, so we broke in. It was obvious from the floorboards that some had recently been replaced. When we lifted them, we found a staircase.'

There's a look of incredulity on Mason's face. 'This is news to me, Detective Sergeant. Did you find anything?'

'Enough of this charade.' The DI's voice is full of contempt. 'You know full well what was down there. We have witnesses, Mr Mason, who will testify about the business you encourage people to invest in, before blackmailing them when they find out children are involved and they want their money back. James Hampton, for one.'

As Mason visibly pales, the DI goes on. 'We're currently matching your fingerprints with those we've found on various items of computer hardware found in your cellar. I'd say it's a matter of mere minutes before we have proof.' Still studying Mason, the DI gets up. 'We'll take a short break now, and carry on once we have those fingerprints confirmed.'

★

When we reconvene outside the door of the interview room ten minutes later, the DI says, 'Mason's fingerprints are on everything. Let's break the news.' He holds open the door for me.

'Right.' He sits down. 'As we expected, your fingerprints were everywhere in that cellar, Mason. You may as well tell us what went on and who else was involved.'

Folding his arms, Mason sits back. 'I have nothing to say.'

The DI doesn't falter. 'I think we should talk about Hollie Hampton.'

Mason looks visibly shocked, but the DI goes on. 'Did you pay her? Or did she try to buy you off?'

As Mason frowns, the DI goes on. 'She came to you, didn't she? She'd found out what her father had got involved in and she knew you were blackmailing him. Maybe she offered you photographs in exchange for releasing him. But you wanted it all, didn't you? Killing Hollie allowed you to keep her photos and also continue to blackmail her father.'

'That's ludicrous.' But after his earlier performance, it's impossible to know if Mason's look of shock is genuine.

'Is it? We know you persuaded people like James Hampton to invest in your porn business. We also know that if they decide they want out – maybe because child pornography is a step too far for most people – you refuse to return their investment and then you blackmail them.'

I study Mason's face. 'James Hampton asked to meet you, didn't he? In private.' I'm thinking of what Elise saw in the

316

woods. 'He begged you to give him his money back. But you refused, didn't you?'

Mason looks shifty. 'Is that what he told you?'

'You were seen, Mr Mason. By one of the villagers, who said the exchange between you looked as though it got quite heated before you drove away. Or do you have a different version of events?'

After glancing sideways at his lawyer, Mason starts speaking. 'I did meet Hampton – it's hardly a crime. And I admit to some of the photographs – all of consenting adults. But I can't claim to know what goes on when I'm not there.'

'They're on your premises, on your machines.' The DI's voice is sharp. 'And we're talking about more than distributing. Evidence suggests they were taken there. Where did the children come from, Mr Mason?'

Mason folds his arms. 'I've never handled child pornography.' He pauses. 'That's all I can tell you.'

'I see.' The DI sounds sceptical. 'So, if it wasn't you, perhaps you can tell me who is responsible.'

Mason stays silent.

'For God's sake, Mason.' The DI looks disgusted. 'You're doing yourself no favours here. You're already facing charges of possession and distribution of pornographic images of children. Then there's deception, blackmail . . . It's already quite a list.'

But Mason says nothing further.

Chapter Forty-Five

Elise

Niamh grabs my arm, tears streaming down her face. '*You can't do this.* He's going to kill you.'

I stare at her, suddenly realising I've completely misunderstood the way she's been thinking. She hasn't been frightened for herself, she's terrified for me. As it sinks in that she believes her father is capable of killing me, I know a new level of despair. No child should have to carry a weight like that.

'Niamh . . . he won't, he can't . . .'

'He will!' She sobs. 'You know what he's like. He doesn't care what he does to you.'

I've never seen her so emotional. It's as though everything she's bottled up inside for too long is erupting from her. I try to grab her hands. 'Niamh. Stop. This isn't helping.'

'Neither will leaving,' she cries. 'It will make everything worse. You know it will. We have to stay.'

As I stare at my daughter, I know she believes what she's saying, but I have no idea how to respond. 'It may seem like that now, but it won't always feel like this. The last few days have been horrible – I know that. But the police are behind us and once we're away from here, you'll feel different. Everything passes, Niamh. Everything.'

As she calms slightly, I take a deep breath. 'Whatever your father told you and everyone else, I had nothing to do with what happened to Dylan.'

I hear her sharp intake of breath as her eyes look up at mine. 'I know he took my pills. But I kept them hidden in the bedroom. I honestly don't recall leaving them out.' It's true. I don't. But I'm not absolving myself of responsibility. I can't.

Another sob escapes her. 'It was an accident,' I tell her gently. 'One that should never have happened.'

Niamh stares at me. 'You don't know, do you?'

I frown at her. 'What are you talking about?'

She looks stricken. 'About what he told Dylan. It wasn't an accident – not the way everyone thinks.' Words tumble out of her, more words than she's spoken in weeks, and my blood runs cold as Niamh tells me what she heard Andrew talking to Dylan about shortly before he killed himself.

How he told Dylan he was ashamed of him; that he would never be anyone Andrew could feel proud of. That it would be better for everyone if Dylan was dead.

My hatred of Andrew reaches new levels, my heart breaking all over again as I think about what Dylan must have gone through. Then I think of what Andrew has put Niamh through, what she's kept silently, painfully, to herself since before Dylan died. 'You should have told me this a long time ago.' Suddenly I pull off my wedding ring. 'The police need to know everything.'

'No.' The fear is back in Niamh's eyes.

'Niamh. He pushed Dylan over the edge. It's the same emotional abuse he inflicts on us. It's why Dylan took an overdose. This is really important.'

'The police can't know.' Niamh's eyes are like a rabbit's caught in the headlights of a car. 'Not ever.'

'Why not?' I study her face, puzzled. 'What haven't you told me?'

'Nothing.' She shakes her head, the shutters coming down. I know she's lying.

Giving Niamh some space, I put the kettle on and make two mugs of tea, taking them over to her when they're ready.

'Here.' Passing her one, I sit down next to her. 'Niamh, what you've just told me strengthens the case against your father, making it easier for the police to charge him.'

She shakes her head. 'I won't talk to them.'

'I understand,' I say softly. 'But if you agree to let me, *I'll* talk to DS May. I'll tell her some of what you've said, but I'll also tell her how frightened of him you are. You've been through so much, Niamh. She'll understand.' I pause. 'It might even mean we can stay here.'

As we sit there a little longer, I pray to God that Andrew doesn't get out, because Niamh's right. There's no question that if Andrew comes after me now, it will be far worse than the last time. But I can't let my fear stop me. The time to do this is now, while the police are still holding him. Eventually she nods, and I get my phone.

*

DS May arrives an hour later. As she comes into the kitchen, I notice her long hair isn't as tidy as usual and that there are dark circles under her eyes. From what she's said, I know this case reminds her of what's happened in her own life. It's taking its toll on all of us.

'Can I make you a cup of tea?'

She nods. 'I'd love one. How are you both?'

'We're OK.' I glance at Niamh, then back to DS May. 'We've packed. But there's something I have to tell you. It's a conversation Niamh overheard between Andrew and Dylan, just before he died.'

DS May frowns. 'Niamh? Can you tell me what he said?'

'She'd rather I tell you,' I say, then repeat what Niamh told me earlier.

There's an expression of revulsion on DS May's face as she makes notes. 'I take it your father had no idea you overheard?'

Niamh shakes her head, an anxious look on her face.

DS May hesitates. 'Did Hollie know about what he said to Dylan?'

Niamh looks away without speaking.

'Niamh? It's OK to tell me. Did Hollie know?'

Slowly Niamh nods, then a single tear rolls down her cheek. 'We were talking about Dylan and I didn't mean to, but I told her.'

'So Hollie knew what your father said to Dylan?' When Niamh nods again, DS May asks, 'Do you remember when you told her?'

'Last year.' Niamh sounds so very young.

DS May's gaze doesn't waver. 'This may sound trivial, but do you remember when exactly?'

Niamh shrugs. 'It was the 10th of May – Dylan's birthday. We were remembering him.'

'Thank you. You mustn't worry about your father harming either of you.' She turns from Niamh's pinched face to look at me. 'We have evidence from the hospital, statements from both of you – and now, this. We'll be holding him overnight again and almost certainly will be charging him.'

Thinking of Andrew's fury at being held by the police, I feel myself shiver. 'What happens then?'

322

'Most likely he'll be remanded in custody.'

'Does that mean he won't be coming back?' I try to take in what she's saying. 'So can't we stay here?'

'I'll keep you in the picture, but I think it would be wise to go away, just for a few days, until formal charges are brought against him. And I need to know the number of work days you've missed, as well as other occasions when he's assaulted you in the past. I'm guessing he's kept your medical records clean to cover himself, but the airline you work for will have logged it. Do you have a phone number of anyone I can speak to there?'

Nodding, I get my phone, bringing up the number of my fleet manager. 'She'll have a record of all my sick days.' I pause. 'Can we stay here tonight, at least? I think Niamh needs a little more time before we leave.'

She hesitates. 'You'll be fine if you want to stay until the morning – but I'd still recommend you move out first thing – and if I were you, I'd make an appointment to see a lawyer.'

Chapter Forty-Six

Jo

Even with mounting evidence against Andrew Buckley, I worry for Elise and Niamh. There is still an outside chance his lawyer could get him out.

When I tell the DI what Niamh said, he shakes his head in disbelief. 'We're holding him tonight, on suspicion that he's connected to Mason's business. But regardless, he'll be charged with assault.'

'I advised Elise Buckley that she was OK to stay in the house tonight.'

'Fine. But we need them out first thing. We may need to begin searching the house.'

I nod. 'They have somewhere to go. She knows we're holding him but she's still terrified he'll come after her.'

'He won't be going anywhere.' The DI frowns. 'We need to talk to him again. Press Buckley on what Hollie Hampton had against him. We have to get it out of him. Between him and Mason . . . One of them must have killed her.'

'About the abuse charge . . . Niamh Buckley just told me something. She said that just before Dylan died, she overheard their father talking to him. Basically, he told Dylan he was a worthless human being and that they'd all be better off if he was dead.'

'Jesus.' The DI looks appalled.

'I know. Hollie didn't know about this, according to Niamh, until what would have been his last birthday. They were *"remembering him"*, as she worded it, when Niamh told Hollie what her father had said. Dylan's birthday was the 10th of May. It fits with Hollie going to the surgery later that same month and causing trouble for Buckley – and it's more than enough to give her a motive.' I pause. 'Incredible, isn't it, that someone would speak like that to their own son.'

'Sadly, it's all too believable.' The DI's voice is quiet. 'We see too many people like Andrew Buckley who are capable of anything.'

'We should talk to James Hampton again, sir. Hollie may have told him something.'

'He hasn't been exactly forthcoming so far.' The DI scratches his head. 'Go and see him. Then when you come back, we'll talk to Buckley together.'

*

As I drive to the custody centre where James Hampton is being held, the sun breaks through the clouds. By the time I arrive, it's hot outside. In the distance, the sea is a pale shimmer, just about visible before it merges with the sky. Then I glance at the building, thinking of James Hampton waiting in one of its soulless rooms for the next stage of his life to be decided for him – a life inside. One he's brought upon himself thanks to his own weaknesses and his association with Mason.

When I reach the room we've been assigned, he's already waiting. When he sees me, there's a flicker of hope, as if somewhere he entertains the fantasy that this is all a mistake, that I've come to get him out of here. Pulling out a chair, I sit opposite him. 'We've been talking to Andrew Buckley.' A shadow crosses Hampton's face. 'You must be aware of the incident when Hollie accused him of inappropriately touching her?'

When he nods, I go on. 'He's adamant he didn't. I'm not sure we'll ever know whether he did or not. But . . .' I pause for a moment. 'He said Hollie did it for revenge, because she found out about his affair with Stephanie. It seemed a perfectly reasonable explanation for her behaviour – until we found out the affair hadn't started at that point. It appears the real reason she wanted to cause him trouble was she'd found out what he said to Dylan just before he died.' I frown. 'What did Hollie say to you about Dylan?'

'Not much.' He looks wretched.

'They were really in love, weren't they?'

He looks surprised. 'I suppose they were.'

I try to push him. 'So what went wrong between them? I know Hollie broke it off with him, and he was heartbroken . . .'

But James Hampton interrupts. 'That's not right. That isn't what happened. It was Dylan who broke it off. I didn't know what to do with Hollie, after, and when he died, she went to pieces. I was really worried about her. For a while, I thought she was going to do what he'd done.'

I stare at him, speechless. 'Andrew Buckley told me Hollie ended it. Can you think of any reason why he might have lied?'

'Buckley.' As he says the word, hatred fills his eyes. 'You can't believe anything that man says. But if he lied, you can bet there was a reason for it.'

'But you don't know what that is?'

He shakes his head, the rage in his eyes now gone. His

327

daughter is dead. So is his wife. It's as though James Hampton has decided his life is over, too.

*

'Buckley told me Hollie screwed up his son, Dylan, when she ended their relationship. But according to James Hampton, it was Dylan who called it off,' I tell the DI. 'Buckley definitely lied.'

The DI looks at me sharply. 'You don't think it's Hampton who's lying?'

'I don't think he is. And his version would explain what Hollie wrote on Dylan's Facebook page – all the love messages she sent him – she poured her heart out.'

He's silent for a moment. 'Buckley's in the interview room with his lawyer. He's raging to get out of here today, so we need to break the news he won't be leaving. Are you ready?'

*

After being held overnight, Andrew Buckley isn't his usual immaculately groomed self. When he sees us, he immediately stands. 'This better not have cost me my job,' he says menacingly.

'Sit down, Doctor Buckley.' The DI pulls out a chair. 'Mr McClure, I suggest you inform your client that the fastest way through this is for him to quickly and accurately answer our questions. Right. Shall we begin?' He glances at me.

I wait until there's quiet before addressing Andrew Buckley. 'We have a witness who overheard a conversation you had with your son—'

His eyes glint at me as he interrupts. 'My son's dead, Detective Sergeant. There's no mileage in this.'

'Doctor Buckley, let me finish. You were overheard using

abusive language. You told him you were ashamed of him and it would be better for everyone if he was dead. It wasn't long after that, that he killed himself.' He opens his mouth to speak, but before he can get a word in, I ask, 'Why did you lie to us about Hollie ending the relationship with your son? It was Dylan who broke it off, wasn't it?'

'Look, this has absolutely no relevance to what's happening now.'

'I beg to differ,' the DI butts in. 'What we're hearing is proof of a longstanding pattern of your emotional abuse of your family, not to mention your own unreliability. Go on, May.'

I continue. 'You've already told us that it was Hollie who messed Dylan up. However, I have it from a reliable source that after Dylan broke it off with her, Hollie was devastated.'

'Then your source is incorrect,' he says coldly.

'Just as your medical practice had incorrect records of the date Hollie came to see you? And your wife incorrectly remembers how she got all those bruises?' I say pointedly. 'Isn't that rather a lot of other people getting it wrong?'

For once, he's silent. The DI takes over. 'Tell us about Mason, Doctor Buckley. We know he and James Hampton are involved in a business investment. Did either of them ever approach you about it?'

'I've told you before, I have no idea what you're talking about.' His voice is icy.

The DI gets straight to the point. 'We're talking about porn, Doctor Buckley, including pornographic images of children.'

'Do you honestly think I'd get involved in something like that?' His voice is full of contempt.

'Seeing as we have your phone, and forensics is taking a look, we'll soon find out. We've also seized Mason's computers. If

329

your name appears anywhere, it's only a matter of time before we find it.'

When he doesn't speak, I go on. 'Meanwhile, your wife and daughter are staying somewhere else for a while. So far, Doctor Buckley, we will be charging you with controlling and coercive behaviour, as well as assault. Potentially we're looking at adding possession of child porn and perverting the course of justice, so if you know anything about Mason's business, now would be your time to tell us.'

A light glints in Buckley's eye as he struggles to rein his anger in. 'I have not assaulted anyone. Nor am I in possession of pornographic images. This isn't the end of this, Detective Inspector. I have a busy surgery and patients to see. This is insanity.'

The DI gets up. 'I'm afraid your patients are going to have to manage without you.'

*

Outside the interview room, the DI looks irritated. 'He's a tricky bastard. He could well be connected with Mason, probably using a false name. And if he is, we'll find it. It's just a question of how long it takes to dig through tech forensics.'

'I'll call Elise Buckley and let her know what's happening.'

'Impress on her that even though we're holding him, she can't stay at their home. She needs to be somewhere safe, just in case Buckley's lawyer pulls some stunt.' He starts walking towards his office. 'There must be someone in that village who knows something.'

'Someone who knew Hollie, who watches what goes—' Then it occurs to me. 'Actually, there is someone, sir . . .'

*

'I appreciate your seeing me at short notice,' I say to Ida Jones as she shows me into her sitting room. 'I couldn't think of anyone else to ask.'

'I'm not sure I can help. I told you before what I know.' Her face softens. 'So what is it?'

'Do you know Philip Mason, Mrs Jones?'

She nods. 'I do. Can't say I think much of him. He's too charming. People like that are never what they seem.'

'Like Doctor Buckley.' His name slips out before I can stop it.

She frowns. 'I wouldn't say he was charming. That man's a common bully. He thinks the world of himself, doesn't he? I feel sorry for her, though – Elise. She's a nice woman, but he rules that house. And that poor girl . . .'

'Niamh?'

Ida Jones nods. 'Best thing for her was when young Hollie was her friend. Gave her a bit of normality in her life. Didn't last though, did it? That father of hers saw to that.'

'What do you mean?'

Her face is sharp as she looks at me. 'Didn't like her, did he? Or has he lied and told you he thought she was wonderful? She *was* wonderful, you know, just like her mother. Hollie should have been a film star.'

I level with her. 'Mrs Jones, I'm not sure how much I really know about anyone in this village. It's as though there's an unspoken secret they're all keeping.'

'And you think I might know what it is.'

I nod. 'Did you know Dylan?'

'Yes,' she says softly. 'Him and Hollie . . . they were a real love story, those two. I was very sad after everything that happened.'

'Can you tell me what you remember about that time?'

Her face is sombre. 'I used to see them all over the place – walking along the road, up at the churchyard. They never argued. All you saw was his arm around her shoulders, his head leaning down towards hers . . . They had the same dark hair.' She pauses, remembering. 'That's how it was whenever I saw them. At my time of life, it was a blessing to be reminded of how true love felt . . . they seemed to be everything love should be.'

I feel myself frown as I listen to her. 'So what went wrong?'

Her face clouds over. 'I never really understood. But after they broke up, and before he died, I remember I kept seeing Hollie on her own, running along the road, all times of the day and night. She looked desperate . . .'

'Do you remember seeing Dylan after they broke up?'

'Once.' She sighs. 'He was standing in the churchyard and he looked as if his heart had been broken. I didn't talk to him. You can tell, can't you, when someone doesn't want to talk? Of course, after he was gone, I wished I had. But I left him alone that day, thinking he and Hollie must have had a big bust-up. I remember thinking it was odd that he was staring at the graves.' Her forehead wrinkles into a frown. 'Then, just a week later, they were digging his.' Ida's eyes fill with tears. 'After seeing him so full of life, it was tragic. I suppose the village did close ranks, as you put it. I think they were protecting the memory of that beautiful couple rather than anything else. And you know what Doctor Buckley's like.'

Rather than respond, I let her go on talking.

'I've never understood that household. Elise is a smart woman. She knows what he's up to and she seems to turn a blind eye. I know it's what women used to do, back in my day, but not now, Detective Sergeant. Modern women don't have to let men treat them so shabbily.'

'I know what you mean.' My eyes meet hers. 'It might seem unbelievable, but it does happen. I know that for a fact.' As she looks at me, taking in what I'm telling her without saying the words outright, she's silent for a moment.

'Did you know Hollie's mother well?'

'Quite well. I met her years ago, when she first moved here with James. Never really grew up, that one. Beautiful, free-spirited girl, she was. No wonder James fell in love with her.'

'They were happy together?'

'Yes.' She hesitates. 'You have to understand, Kathryn was driven. James, bless him, never was.'

Her words surprise me. 'He wrote a book and got it published. That hardly happens easily.'

She gives me a knowing look. 'That's right. But his agent was a friend of Kathryn's. That's how he got his first break. After that, when Kathryn died, it didn't go so well for him.'

I hadn't realised. 'When you say she was driven . . .' I hesitate for a moment. 'Did that cause problems between them?'

'Oh, I'll say. It was terrible for a while and I'm not sure there wasn't someone else on the scene. But they got over it. It was before Hollie, and after she was born, they seemed to sort themselves out.'

I pause. 'Kathryn killed herself, didn't she?'

'She took an overdose.' Ida Jones looks sad. 'She must have been in a terrible state to leave her daughter like that. But in many ways, Kathryn was too good for this world. There are people who take advantage of girls like that. And women were jealous of her looks. But she was kind, too. Wouldn't say a bad word about anyone.'

I imagine an older version of Hollie, struggling to find her place in the world. Another tortured soul. 'Was it the same for Hollie? Do you think people took advantage of her?'

Ida Jones shakes her head. 'I don't know. She was less tolerant than her mother. But I think the hurt of losing her mum, then Dylan, was too much for Hollie.' She pauses. The tick of the clock on the wall punctuates the silence. 'If you want to know what I think happened to Dylan and Hollie, I believe someone broke them up. It's only my opinion, but from the outside, it didn't seem to be what either of them wanted. And I never saw either of them with anyone else after that. I don't think there was anyone else for those two, to be honest. Anyway, maybe, now, wherever they are, they're together again.'

'Why would someone have broken them up?' But as I ask the question, I'm thinking of Niamh's account of the conversation she overheard between her father and Dylan; of Andrew Buckley's comment about how he was glad that Hollie wasn't in Niamh's life anymore. Had he felt that way about Dylan? Had he seen Hollie as a negative influence on his son and somehow forced them apart? But why would they have let one of their parents stop them from seeing each other? Shaking my head, I know I'm missing something.

'There's someone else who sees what goes on around here. More than you think she might.' Ida Jones looks at me. 'Young Niamh.'

Niamh

The police have charged him with assault, my mother tells me after talking to DS May, in a voice that is shocked, relieved, and terrified, too – both of us knowing that if or when he gets out, he'll come after us.

But we still have to leave. I lie awake that night, wondering if I'll ever sleep in this bed again, listening to the sounds of the night through my cracked-open window. The distant car driving through the village, the hoot from a nearby owl, the sound of the breeze rustling the leaves.

Even though the police are holding my father, I'm still waiting for the sound of his car on the drive, then his key in the door, his heavy footsteps as he comes upstairs, his angry voice. I imagine him breaking in, slapping my mother's face – which still hasn't healed from the last time – shouting foul words at her and glancing past me as though I don't exist. And if we're gone when he comes here, he'll search the countryside until he finds us.

My father didn't like Hollie coming here; her way of questioning what my parents said, never accepting what everyone told her, digging deeper until she found what she was looking for. Hollie's independent streak, her free-spiritedness, threatened his hold over me.

I remember her coming over to my house that evening. Fragile in her silver dress, her hair tangled. When she told me what she'd found, I didn't believe her. I remember her hands shaking as she pulled it from her pocket, handed it to me. A piece of paper that changed her world – and mine – forever.

All this time I've kept Hollie's secret, but when I think of what my father's done, I know I have to tell my mother, even if it means breaking my promise to Hollie. But Hollie isn't here anymore, and my mother should know why Dylan died. Then, when she does, she'll be able to understand why Hollie died, too.

Chapter Forty-Seven

Jo

As I drive to work the next morning, I call Elise Buckley and discover that she and Niamh are already on their way to the B and B. Then I find myself thinking about what Ida Jones said, about someone forcing Dylan and Hollie to break up. As I pull into the car park, I already know what I want to do.

Inside, I head straight for the DI's office. When I knock on his door, I find he's talking on his phone, but he beckons me in and gestures for me to wait while he finishes the call.

'Sorry about that, May. That was Forensics. They're sending over a list of names in connection with Operation Rainbow.'

'Have they found any images of Hollie?'

'Nothing so far, but they're going through everything more thoroughly now. Ah, here it is.'

While the DI prints off the email that's just arrived, I tell him what I've been thinking. 'Sir, I want to speak to Niamh Buckley again.'

He looks up from the printer. 'Why?'

'It was something Ida Jones said to me. She's convinced someone must have forced Hollie and Dylan to break up, though she doesn't seem to have any idea why. She also said that there was one person who may well know more than she's said so far – Niamh.'

The DI looks thoughtful. 'That girl drip-feeds information, doesn't she?'

I nod. 'She's painfully shy – and damaged by her father. You know . . .' I break off, thinking. 'There are a lot of people who are all too keen to hint at what other people know. James Hampton said I should talk to Andrew Buckley. Buckley doesn't give anything away and when he does speak, you can't believe a single word. Ida Jones hints that various things have happened – like James Hampton and his first wife went through a rocky patch – but Hampton hasn't mentioned it to me, and until now, Ida Jones hadn't, either. Then there's this whole story around Hollie and Dylan, neither of whom are still alive to tell us what really happened.'

The DI frowns. 'Very well. Go and talk to her again.'

I nod. 'They're on their way to the B and B. I'll check to see if they've arrived.'

*

I drive along the narrow road that carves its way through miles of downland pasture, the landscape painted in hues of verdant green as I pass a flock of sheep and newborn lambs, suddenly hankering after a much simpler life, like the one I imagine Chris Nelson has. He's the retired detective superintendent who runs Mitchelgrove Farm, where Elise and Niamh are staying.

The small cottage Chris lets out from time to time stands in its own garden, away from his farmhouse, a dense beech hedge affording its occupants privacy. And his background presence is a safety net. After a career of policing, Chris misses nothing.

When I pull up outside his house, he wanders outside holding a mug of tea.

'Jo . . . They arrived about an hour ago.' As he nods towards the cottage, I make out Elise's car parked in front of it.

'Thanks for having them here. You look well, Chris.'

'You're welcome. Always happy to help in the war against the underworld. I don't suppose it changes much.' His face lightly tanned, he has the ease of a man who's comfortable in his own skin. 'I've left them some supplies and I'll take them bread and milk tomorrow. They'll be fine for a few days.'

'Her husband is a piece of work. He's hiding something – I'm sure of it. Everyone in this case seems to be hiding something.' I look at him. 'I bet you don't miss any of this.'

He's relaxed as he nods. 'Not really. There's the odd occasion, but I could never give this up.' I follow his eyes across the patchwork of fields – some of them dotted with grazing animals – and the motley assembly of barns. 'One of those cases, is it?' His voice is more serious.

'You could say that. One of those villages where everyone has a secret. I'd better go and talk to them.'

'I heard,' he says suddenly, just as I turn to walk away. 'About your marriage. I'm so sorry, Jo. You deserve better.'

I feel myself start. It isn't just his words that are unexpected. It's the sentiment. When you work long hours and live alone, you get used to there being no-one who cares. 'Thank you.' My voice is husky and I clear my throat. 'I'll see you in a bit.'

★

As I walk across the yard, I'm conscious of the depth of the silence here. Untouched by even the most distant sound of traffic, the air has a purity, the colours around me a softness. Niamh's face appears fleetingly in one of the cottage windows

339

before disappearing. I imagine that even here, she'll be constantly on edge, thinking it's only a matter of time before her father finds them.

Closing the garden gate behind me, I find the grass neatly mown, the flowerbeds carefully tended. When my knock on the door isn't answered, I push it open.

'Hello? Anyone home?'

Elise's face appears in a doorway, her anxious look quickly fading when she sees it's me. Her bruising is still an ugly purple red, her eyes haunted.

'I'm sorry, I didn't mean to startle you. Is everything OK?'

'As OK as it can be, in the circumstances.' Like Niamh, she's clearly on edge, her voice sharp. 'I'll make us a cup of tea – if I can find anything.'

I know from the bitterness in her voice, from the way she opens cupboards, then closes them loudly as she looks for what she needs, that she's uneasy. Eventually finding some mugs, she fills the kettle. 'How long do we have to stay here?'

I'm evasive. At the moment, there are too many unknowns to give her a straight answer. 'Probably a few days.'

Her shoulders stiffen. 'And Andrew's definitely being held?'

I nod. 'He's been charged, as I told you, and we're remanding him in custody for further questioning.' I pause, knowing that whatever he's done, Andrew Buckley will continue to deny everything for as long as he thinks he can get away with it. 'How's Niamh bearing up? I saw her face just now, in one of the windows.'

'She's frightened. We both are. I know you're holding him, but we both know what he's capable of.' She pauses. 'Neither of us feels safe – and neither of us really wanted to come here.' Elise's voice is tight. 'I know it doesn't make sense – but I don't expect you to understand.'

340

Given the memories their house holds for both of them, I'm surprised. 'I know this is a difficult time for you, but I thought you were all set to move. You'd even found somewhere, hadn't you?'

'That was different. It would have been our choice – and our new home. This isn't. And all the time, I'm waiting . . .' Her voice falls to a whisper. 'When he gets out, he will be so angry. You have no idea what he's capable of . . .' With shaking hands, she pours boiling water onto teabags, swearing as she spills some before putting down the kettle and mopping up the water. Fetching milk, she hunts around for the sugar. 'It doesn't look like there's any sugar,' she says tearfully.

I want to reassure her that she's safe, that there's no way her husband will be able to get to her, but until he's sentenced, nothing is certain. 'I don't take sugar.' Accepting the mug she passes me, I watch her nervous movement. 'Shall we sit down?'

I follow her across to a small kitchen table made of antique pine on ornately turned legs. Chris has furnished the cottage simply, creating an air of calm that Elise clearly needs.

'You can still look for a new home,' I say gently. 'Do you have enough money to tide you over?' I imagine Andrew Buckley using whatever he can as a means of manipulation, including money. I've seen it happen many times.

She nods. 'I stopped at the bank on the way here in case he managed to empty the joint account. I transferred what I could into mine.'

'Good.' I pause, relieved that at least she has her own account; many women in marriages like hers don't. 'Have you thought any more about talking to a lawyer?'

She sips her tea. 'I'll have to find one. The only one I know of is Andrew's. That's hardly going to work.' She raises her eyes to meet mine. 'Is that something you can help me with?'

'Of course. I'll get some numbers for you.' My voice is quiet. 'You really should see someone as soon as—'

'You've already told me,' she interrupts, her voice shrill as she talks over me, symptomatic of the strain she's under as she rests her face in her hands. 'I'm so sorry.'

'You don't have to apologise.' Reaching across the table, I touch her arm, a gesture of human comfort. 'I know this is unsettling.' I pause for a moment. 'And I know you have a lot on your mind right now, but there are a few things I wanted to ask you about.'

Looking up, she nods briefly as I go on.

'I had a conversation with Ida Jones. She was telling me about Hollie and Dylan, about how in love they were. She couldn't understand why they broke up. She said it was as though they'd been somehow forced apart, but she had no idea why.'

'I don't know what went wrong between them. Dylan told me it was over, but he didn't tell me the reason.' Elise's face is blank. 'I assumed their relationship had run its course. They were young. It seemed inevitable at that age.'

I think back to what Ida Jones said, about how they had had something rare, that she felt blessed to witness it. 'Your husband said that Hollie ended it, but James Hampton said it was Dylan. Do you know what happened?'

Her voice is cold. 'I know that Dylan wouldn't have confided anything in Andrew. Niamh told you what she heard her father saying to him before he died. It was Andrew who tipped him over the edge. It wasn't Hollie.'

I'm silent. So why has Buckley told us these lies? There's the sound of quiet footsteps coming downstairs, and when I look up, I see Niamh standing in the doorway.

Chapter Forty-Eight

Jo

For a moment Niamh doesn't move. 'There was a letter.' Her voice is thin, clear.

'What letter?' Elise's voice is sharp.

'Dylan wrote a letter to Hollie. I found it after he died.'

'Did you give it to her?' My voice is gentle. When Niamh nods, I ask, 'When?'

'A few weeks ago.'

'Did you read it?'

Niamh nods again.

'Why did you wait until then to give it to her?'

'I shouldn't have kept it.' Niamh speaks quietly. 'Dylan wrote it for her.'

'What did the letter say?' Elise speaks harshly, but everything about her is brittle right now, as though she'll snap. 'Why didn't you tell me?'

Then I get it. She's frightened about how much Niamh knows. As I study Niamh, suddenly I know the answer. She hasn't told us until now because she's been protecting her mother from something – drip-feeding information to us, as the DI said, on what she judges to be a need-to-know basis. Suddenly I know, with certainty, there's more.

Niamh goes on. 'In the letter, Dylan told Hollie he loved her – more than this world. He said she should never forget that.' Her voice is surprisingly unemotional, but this isn't new to her. She's been sitting on it since her brother died. 'But he said that if they were together, his father had told him he would cause Hollie a whole lot of trouble. The only way to save her was to give her up.'

'What did he mean by that?'

Niamh's eyes flicker over me. 'Before she was with Dylan, Hollie had problems. She was bulimic – and she self-harmed. Dylan helped her stop, but my father was her doctor. He knew because he was treating her.' Her face is expressionless. 'He would have told everyone – her school, her parents. Everyone.'

I stare at her, frowning. It's easy to imagine Andrew Buckley threatening them, but if Hollie and Dylan were in love, this was hardly enough to stop them 'And you're sure Dylan wrote that just before he died?'

Niamh nods. 'It was the day before. He left the letter in his room. I went in there before the police got there and took it. He wouldn't have wanted anyone else to read it. Just Hollie. But if she had . . .' She tails off.

'You thought she'd be angry with your father, so you didn't give it to her – until recently,' I say quietly, remembering how the tyres on Andrew Buckley's car were slashed. It's why you became friends, isn't it?' My heart twists as I look at her. 'You were each other's links to Dylan. No-one else could understand.' I wonder how Hollie could have tolerated seeing Andrew Buckley, knowing what he'd said to Dylan – unless she'd been waiting while she planned a way of getting back at him. Except she ran out of time.

'What happened that day Hollie took you to Phil Mason's house?'

'We went in the back way. She checked no-one was in, then she showed me this building that wasn't part of the house. There was a window . . .'

'What did you see?'

'Photos.' Niamh's voice is soft. 'Of girls.'

Glancing at Elise, there's a look of horror on her face.

'Niamh? We know about the photos.' Trying to reassure her, I wonder how much she could have made out through the window. 'And we're holding Phil Mason.'

'And my father?' The words, reed-like, chill me. Did Niamh know about Andrew's involvement?

'What did Hollie know about your father?'

'She said he knew Phil Mason – very well.'

'Is there anything else we should know, Niamh?' But as she shakes her head, I know that even if there's more, she's told me all she's prepared to at this stage.

I turn to Elise again. 'I have to get back to the office.'

Getting up, she walks with me to the door. 'There's something else.' Her voice is low, her eyes not quite meeting mine. 'Something I saw on Andrew's phone.'

My heart starts to race. 'Go on.'

'I should have told you, but I was terrified – you've seen what he can do – and if you questioned him, he would have known it was me who told you.' Desperation flickers in her eyes before she glances away to make sure Niamh can't hear. 'But he had a photo on his phone – an indecent photo of a young girl. I challenged him and he made it sound like it was nothing.'

'How young?' My voice is sharp.

Elise shakes her head. 'It's hard to know. She could have been

345

fifteen or sixteen, but she could have been younger.' Her voice is low, her eyes imploring me to understand. 'I'm so sorry.'

I'm silent. 'You should have told us.' In the circumstances, I can see why she didn't, but this is the evidence we've needed. 'I'll send you over some phone numbers of lawyers – or if you see Chris, you could ask him. You can trust him,' I emphasise, looking past her at Niamh, still in the kitchen. 'If you're worried about Niamh, or if you think she needs to talk to a professional, we can put you in touch with someone who can help.'

*

'Sir, when Hollie took Niamh to Mason's property, she saw some photos through a window – of girls. She also told Niamh that our doctor and Mason know each other *very well*, as she put it. But there's more. A couple of weeks ago, Elise Buckley caught her husband looking at an image of a young girl on his phone. The girl looked fifteen or sixteen, but could have been younger.'

'Why hasn't she told us this before?' the DI demands.

'She said he'd know it was her who'd told us and she was frightened of what he'd do to her. I suppose it's only knowing we're holding him that's given her the courage to talk.'

The DI looks at me. 'We need to get over and search the Buckleys' house, pick up his computer – see what else we can find. I'm going to step up the investigation into his finances, too. If he's involved with Operation Rainbow, the chances are he'll have a tidy sum stashed away somewhere. Buckley clearly knows more than he's saying. I wouldn't be surprised if his daughter does, too. But we'll start with him.'

'There's more, sir. Apparently, Andrew Buckley had found out that Hollie was bulimic and used to self-harm. He overheard her talking with his son. He threatened to tell her parents and school if Dylan didn't break things off with her.'

'Who told you this?'

'Niamh. After her brother died, she found a letter he'd left for Hollie.'

'Did she say where the letter is now?'

'She gave it to Hollie.' I hesitate. 'I can believe Andrew Buckley would have threatened them, and that it could have caused Hollie a great deal of embarrassment, but they were in love. Surely they wouldn't have let that break them up?'

'It does seem unlikely – unless there's something else we don't know.' The DI pauses. 'And it surely wouldn't be a reason for Buckley to kill her, either.' As we reach the door of the interview room, he stops outside. 'Let's see what he says.'

★

The interview room reeks of the thinly veiled threat of Andrew Buckley's anger. I pull out a chair and sit opposite him, as the DI settles next to me. 'I'd like to talk to you about your son, Doctor Buckley.'

He folds his arms. 'Is there any point? I've told you all there is to know about my son. His death has nothing to do with Hollie's.'

'You told us that it was Hollie who left Dylan.'

He frowns irritably. 'What's your point?'

'James Hampton told us that *Dylan* broke it off with Hollie.'

'He'll say anything. You do realise that, don't you? Hampton isn't reliable. He never has been.' Andrew Buckley speaks quickly.

I ignore him. 'Your wife said Dylan wouldn't have confided in you. So my question is, how are you so sure that's what happened?'

'You had to be there.' He's bluffing. 'It was obvious. Elise will say anything. She's—'

I interrupt. 'Unreliable, Doctor Buckley? Like James Hampton and everyone else who doesn't agree with you?' As I watch him, he looks less sure of himself. 'There's also the letter.'

'What letter?' he snaps.

'The letter Dylan wrote to Hollie, the day before he killed himself. Apparently, he told her she meant the world to him, but you told Dylan that unless they broke up, you planned to cause Hollie a lot of trouble.'

His face pales. 'That's ludicrous. Who told you this?'

'It's irrelevant where the letter came from. You'd found out about Hollie's problems, Doctor Buckley, and used them to threaten her and Dylan. That's correct, isn't it? Or was there some other reason?'

His manner subtly changes. 'I meant no harm. I was doing what I thought was for the best – for my family. Hollie wasn't good for Dylan.'

'So you keep saying. It would almost be believable that you cared if you hadn't been overheard shouting at your son.'

His eyes narrow. 'If you want to find out what really happened with Hollie, you're talking to the wrong person, Detective Sergeant. I suggest you talk to my wife – I'm assuming you know where she is?'

He looks at me, as if expecting me to take him seriously, as the DI leans forward. 'Let's switch gears and talk about Mason's business. As we speak, a search of your house is under way – which includes seizing your computer and anything else we deem necessary.'

Buckley's eyes flash with fury. 'You can't do that. You have no grounds.'

'I think the image of the young girl your wife saw on your phone is reason enough.' The DI speaks through gritted teeth just as there's a knock on the door of the interview room. 'One moment.' After a brief exchange at the door, he comes back.

'We'll break for now. Ten minutes. May.' Nodding to me, he walks out.

As soon as we're away from the interview room, the DI starts talking. 'We've found enough to implicate him in Operation Rainbow. He and Mason were in cahoots. Calder's involved too.'

'You're sure, sir?'

'A tidy sum in a bank account set up under a false name that's been found among Mason's records – and that he's accessed from his laptop. He and Mason corresponded by email – Mason used a false name too. It very much looks as though they were partners.'

After all of his lies and inconsistencies, an odd sense of relief fills me that this evil man will be removed from circulation for a long time.. Then I think of Elise, at last free to begin her new life without him.

*

When we return ten minutes later, the DI is icily calm and the friction in the interview room is palpable. 'Doctor Buckley, I'm asking you for the last time if you know anything about Mason's business.'

Sitting back and folding his arms, Buckley doesn't miss a beat. 'I've told you more than once, you're barking up the wrong tree.'

Knowing what we now know, I realise we truly are looking at a psychopath.

The DI is silent for a while. 'We have incontrovertible proof to the contrary, Doctor Buckley, and I am arresting you on suspicion of the production and distribution of pornographic images of children, as well as perverting the course of justice.'

'You're making a mistake.' The look he gives me before he turns to his lawyer makes my blood run cold, and I'm reminded of what Elise has lived with. 'Do something about this.'

'There is nothing to do, Doctor Buckley.' The DI stands up.

'You've committed a crime – several, in fact. You couldn't honestly have believed you'd get away with it?'

*

As we walk back to the DI's office, there's something on my mind. 'There was something he said just now, sir. He said we were talking to the wrong person – that we needed to talk to his wife.'

'You have – several times.' The DI sounds impatient. 'Don't get drawn in by anything he says. We know he lies. In any case, we've ruled her out as a suspect.'

'I don't know, sir, but her behaviour is erratic. That could be put down to the stress of her marriage, but she isn't the most stable of people.' I pause. 'Think about it for a moment. Elise has an unpredictable working pattern and her family takes for granted that she is where she says she is. She could put on that uniform and go anywhere, for all we know. She might go somewhere else, even meet someone, especially given her husband's series of affairs. Or she could just be hiding from her miserable marriage. We've never actually checked out her job.'

'Then do it,' the DI says quietly. 'The next time her slippery husband tries to distract us, we'll know exactly where we stand.'

*

When I check my notes, I find that according to Elise, the day Hollie died, she flew to Athens and back. I call her airline, waiting five minutes to get through to her manager and explain the reason for my call.

There's a brief pause. 'That's right. She was rostered on an Athens flight that day. But hold on a moment . . . I need to check something.' The phone goes quiet for a moment. 'She was definitely rostered to go to Athens that day, but on that morning, she didn't turn up.'

350

Chapter Forty-Nine

Elise

In the farm cottage, Niamh and I are still in limbo, waiting for one of the lawyers to get back to me, when my mobile buzzes.

'Elise? It's DS May. I thought you'd want to know that your husband has been charged and remanded in custody. I'll let you know more in due course, but I wanted you to be the first to hear.'

My heart lifts. 'Does this mean we can go home?'

'I'm afraid not.' DS May hesitates. 'We're searching your house as part of our investigation. I'm sorry about all this.' She pauses again. 'I'll stop over later on and fill you in on everything.'

As the call ends, I stare in disbelief at my phone, then turn to Niamh. 'That was DS May. The police have arrested your father.'

'So we can go home?' Niamh looks hopeful.

'Not yet.' I look at her. 'The police have to search the house, apparently. She'll come by later to let us know what's happening.'

The colour drains from Niamh's face.

'What's wrong, Niamh?'

She shakes her head. 'Nothing.'

'Are you sure?'

She's silent. Then she says, 'I have some of Dylan's stuff, that's all. They won't take it, will they?'

I frown at her, wondering how I hadn't come across it. 'What kind of stuff?'

'Just things he wrote. Some of his drawings. Photos.'

'It's your father's stuff they'll go through. I can't imagine the police will want to look through your things.' I look at Niamh more closely, taking in her anxious look. 'Are you all right?'

She nods, but before I can ask her more, my phone buzzes again with an unfamiliar number. 'I need to get this. It could be one of the lawyers.' I answer the call, frowning as I watch Niamh slip upstairs.

★

An hour on the phone to Alison Wantley, the lawyer, to start divorce proceedings leaves me fortified. That I have an idea of where I stand and what to expect going forward gives me new strength. But also, now that Andrew's being held by the police, there is no need for me and Niamh to stay in hiding.

'You could go back to school tomorrow,' I say to Niamh. 'I have an appointment to see a lawyer in the morning to sign the paperwork. It won't be long before things can get back to normal.' I'm trying to reassure her, but both of us know that normal doesn't exist anymore; that more time is needed to undo the years of damage inflicted by Andrew.

She nods, then suddenly remembers something. 'I haven't got any of my school stuff.'

'I didn't even think about that.' I hadn't packed her uniform or any of her books. 'I'll call DS May. Hopefully, they'll let us collect it.'

★

352

Later that afternoon, the farmer, Chris, raises a hand in greeting as we get in the car. As we drive home to Abingworth, I realise the weight of what's been hanging over me. For a brief moment, I can almost pretend nothing's happened, but the feeling doesn't last. When we turn into the drive, several police cars are parked there, including a white van. When we walk in, a man carrying Andrew's computer passes us on his way out.

Niamh turns to me in horror. 'They won't want mine, will they?'

'I don't know. I shouldn't think so. Your father never used it, did he?' I notice Sergeant Collins coming towards us. 'Mrs Buckley? Niamh? The DS said you needed to pick up your school uniform. I'm really sorry about all this.' She glances back towards the house. 'Niamh? I'm afraid I need to go with you. Is that OK?' She speaks as if we have a choice, but I know we don't.

Coming here has brought back too many unpleasant memories. 'I'll stay here,' I say.

As I watch them disappear inside, it's as if I'm standing outside someone else's house. Several policemen go to and fro carrying what I imagine to be the contents of Andrew's desk. Then a light goes on upstairs, in our bedroom, where no doubt the police will be going through mine and Andrew's clothes.

A few minutes later, Niamh comes back – carrying an armful of clothes and her school bag – with Sergeant Collins. Without speaking, she climbs into the car.

'Let's go.' Putting the car into reverse, I turn it around, not wanting to linger a moment longer than necessary. In the short time we've been away, an invisible line has been drawn between the past and the future, and we've crossed it. Now, the only way is forward. I can no more imagine living here than I can imagine being with Andrew. As we drive away, leaving

Abingworth behind us, the realisation hits me. I've no desire to ever come back.

★

The next morning I drive Niamh to school, then go to my meeting with Alison Wantley. In the safety of her office, with a view onto a quiet street in the heart of Chichester, I start to tell her everything about my marriage. It's painful. It's also cathartic.

I walk around the town centre after, doing a bit of shopping and looking in the windows of estate agents before I drive back to the farm. For the first time in years, I feel a tentative sense of hope. I'd never loved living in Abingworth. I miss nothing about village life, nor have any desire to bump into familiar faces. None of those people really care. Even Della has made no attempt to contact me. All these years of living there and no-one will miss me, even slightly.

When I get back to the cottage, I start to tidy away the breakfast things, then go upstairs, throwing open windows, picking up Niamh's discarded clothes on the floor of her bedroom. Underneath them, I find an envelope.

Niamh

When Dylan and Hollie fell in love, my father always knew he'd have to stop them. But he let it go on, until their hearts grew closer, their love deeper – to the point where they couldn't live without each other. Then he went to Dylan's room and told him. My father likes to watch people suffer.

I heard my father shout, Dylan's cries of pain. Later, when I found out what he'd done, I knew he might as well have given Dylan a loaded gun and told him to point it at his head.

Dylan was expected to be the brilliant academic who'd have the same high-flying medical career as his father. Anything else – being the talented artist and musician he was – that was a failure in my father's eyes. But it was never about what Dylan wanted. My father only cared about my father.

The sun was shining the day he told Dylan the truth. A day he destroyed his son's dreams, tearing Dylan from Hollie. Then my father took it further, told him he wasn't good enough to be his son, dismantling Dylan's future piece by piece, with layer upon layer of his cruelty. Dylan didn't kill himself; my father destroyed him.

Chapter Fifty

Jo

Noticing a missed call from Elise Buckley, I call her back. 'Elise, it's DS May. Sorry I missed you earlier. Is everything OK?'

She sounds jittery. 'I found something. I think you should see it.'

*

As I drive over to the farm, the toxic effect of being in close proximity to Andrew Buckley seems to hang over me, and I think about what I have to ask his wife. I thought I'd got the measure of Elise Buckley, but now I'm less sure.

When Elise opens the door, she looks flustered. 'Come in. I'll get Niamh.'

'In a moment.' I wait until we go through to the kitchen. 'I need to ask you something. It's probably nothing, but when we were asking your husband about Hollie, he said we were talking to the wrong person – that we needed to talk to you. Do you have any idea why he might have said that?'

I watch her tense.

'No.'

'There's no easy way to say this, so I'm just going to come out with it. You told us you were on a flight to Athens the day Hollie died. I checked with the airline, Elise. They said you didn't show.'

I've never imagined Elise could have killed Hollie, but when her face turns white, suddenly I confront the fact that I've let my own experiences influence my perception of her. Maybe I've read her terribly wrong.

'It isn't what you're thinking,' she says at last. 'If you must know, I had a hospital appointment. I found a lump. You've no idea how difficult it's been taking phone calls without anyone knowing. I couldn't let Andrew find out. He'd use it to wear me down. Another addition to his list of reasons why I'm an unsuitable mother . . . I've been back several times – scans, a biopsy. It's malignant, but they think they've caught it early enough. I'm waiting for a date for surgery.'

It's a lot to deal with, on top of everything else, as well as keeping it from her family. 'I wish I'd known.' Then I frown. 'But he couldn't use your illness to discredit you.'

'You think Andrew wouldn't do that? You really don't know my husband. He'd say I couldn't possibly look after Niamh if I'm about to have surgery and all the follow-up treatment – on top of everything else.' She sighs. 'It's true I went to pieces after Dylan died. Andrew has kept it out of my medical records, so far . . . but he said that if he wanted to, he could tell the airline enough that I'd lose my job.' For the first time, she looks directly at me. 'Basically, my husband's been blackmailing me.' She pauses, swallowing. 'And I've let him.'

It might sound implausible to anyone who didn't know them, but I can all too easily imagine Andrew Buckley's exaggerated account of the problems his wife has, no doubt most of them caused by years of his abuse. Shaking her head, Elise changes the subject. 'This is what I wanted to show you.' She passes me an envelope.

Inside there's a single piece of paper. Taking it out, I unfold it, feeling a sense of shock as I read it, the missing pieces falling into place at last, as I discover the reason behind Dylan's death and Hollie's behaviour, why Andrew Buckley had to force Hollie and Dylan apart.

It was nothing to do with Hollie's problems. It's to do with an affair Andrew Buckley had, years ago. With Hollie's mother, Kathryn.

Hollie Hampton was Andrew Buckley's daughter.

I look at Elise in disbelief. 'You didn't know?'

She shakes her head. 'I had no idea. But I'd no idea the bastard was shagging Stephanie, either. It's ironic, because we moved here to make a fresh start after Andrew had been having an affair – it must have been soon after that he met Kathryn.'

'Where did you find this?'

'Niamh had it. She has a collection of things that were Dylan's. It was among them.'

'She knows you're showing me this?'

A new calm seems to have come over Elise. As she nods, I ask, 'Is she here?'

Elise glances towards the door. 'She's upstairs. I'll call her.'

She goes to the stairs to call her daughter and I think of Niamh, keeping her secret all this time, determined to protect her mother. When Elise comes back to the kitchen, she looks exhausted. 'Niamh was worried what it would do to you if you found out.'

'Yes.'

As Niamh comes in, her expression is wary as she looks at me. 'I should have shown you before.' She glances anxiously at Elise.

'It would have been helpful – but I understand why you didn't. You were trying to protect your mother, weren't you? She knows everything now, Niamh.' I pause, thinking not just of Niamh's secrets, but the way Elise kept her potential cancer diagnosis hidden. 'It isn't always easy, but sometimes it's better for everyone to be honest.'

'Did he kill Hollie?' Her voice is quiet.

'We're still not sure. Tell me . . .' I pause. 'Where did you get this?'

'Hollie gave it to me.' Her eyes don't leave mine.

'When?'

'A week before she died. She'd only just found out. She asked me to look after it for her.'

'Did she say where she'd found it?'

'Her mum had this little case of letters and stuff. Hollie had read some of them, but always felt guilty about it. But then she found this one.'

I shake my head slowly. 'For the first time, she understood why Dylan ended their relationship. She must have been beside herself.' As I pause, I figure it out. 'But you already knew. Before Hollie did.'

Her calm is eerie as she nods. 'Dylan told me. He didn't want Hollie to know that James wasn't her father. He said she didn't need to.'

'But Hollie found out anyway.' Poor Hollie. Surrounded by lies and tragedy – no wonder Stephanie described her as a tortured soul. Frowning, I go on. 'Did she talk to your father?'

Niamh shrugs. 'She said she was going to. She said she wanted to hurt him really badly, like he'd hurt Dylan, then she wanted to kill him, not just because of Dylan but because he'd had an affair with her mother. She never believed her mother killed herself.'

'Did she tell you what she thought happened to her mother?'

Niamh's narrow shoulders shrug. 'She said she took some pills.' She pauses. 'Hollie thought . . .'

'Oh, Niamh . . .' Realising the magnitude of what she's carried, my heart goes out to her. 'Did Hollie think your father gave the pills to her mother?'

'She said he was her doctor.' As Niamh says it, I feel sickened. Andrew Buckley could have prescribed the pills, then left it to Kathryn whether she took them or not – not caring either way, because that's the kind of man he is. 'Do you know if Hollie told her father – James, I mean – about the letter?'

Niamh's face is blank. 'She was upset with him about something. But I don't think so. Hollie couldn't bear to see him upset.' In the same way Niamh couldn't bear to see her mother upset.

'But she didn't say what she was angry about?' Had she found out about James's involvement in the porn ring?

'No.'

So, Hollie had kept the truth from her father because James Hampton had been hurt too many times, through circumstances beyond his control. Andrew Buckley had had affairs with both his first and second wives. For the first time I understand just how much James must hate him. But, at last, Buckley's time is running out.

Niamh

After our father told Dylan that Hollie was our half-sister, Dylan told me, 'He's evil, Niamh. He doesn't care about any of us. His whole life is a lie. Get away from him as soon as you can.'

Over the days that followed, I saw how Dylan suffered. Our father had watched him fall in love with our half-sister, taunting him with cruel words, dragging him lower, twisting Dylan's life in his bare hands until the morning it snapped.

The night before, there was a dullness in Dylan's eyes. 'There is no point anymore,' he told me. 'I love Hollie and I can't be with her.'

'You'll love someone else,' I tried to tell him. 'There'll be another girl, Dylan.'

But the light was dimming in his eyes, his life force ebbing away even as I watched, shame taking its place, guilt that he hadn't known and it was wrong. He already knew there wouldn't be anyone else. There wasn't anyone like Hollie.

I remember the quiet in the kitchen the next morning. The sense of emptiness, as if the house already knew Dylan had gone. It was an hour later that my mother tried to wake him, calling up the stairs, 'Dylan, it's late. You need to get up.'

He didn't reply. But time didn't matter where Dylan had gone. I sat listening as she opened his door; when she cried out, I knew. There was no-one to keep him here. When the greatest love is warped into something twisted, there is nothing left.

Chapter Fifty-One

Jo

When I get back to the office, the DI wants to see me.

'Border Police at Newhaven have arrested two men for trafficking migrants. Children.' The DI looks grave. 'They said they were on their way to a house in Sussex. Near Chichester. They haven't said much more than that but they're being interviewed as we speak.'

'You think they were headed for Mason's place?'

'We'll find out in due course. But if they were, it would explain where Mason's images came from. Poor little souls – after everything they've been through, to end up in the hands of men like this.'

'Niamh Buckley finally gave us what we need, sir. Turns out Andrew Buckley was Hollie's father. Even now, I'm not sure that Hampton knows as Hollie only found out a week before she died. It's hardly surprising so many people described her as being agitated. But it doesn't explain why she went to the surgery that day and accused him of assaulting her. The chances are she'd found out about James's – and obviously

Buckley's — involvement in the porn ring. Don't forget, she took Niamh to Mason's place.'

The DI frowns. 'We don't have proof of that.'

'Not yet. But the evidence is stacking up against our doctor.' I pause. 'Poor Hollie . . . You can imagine how she must have felt when she discovered James wasn't her father at all — and that Andrew Buckley was, which meant Dylan was her half-brother . . .'

The amount of damage one man's selfish actions can cause is utterly devastating.

Chapter Fifty-Two

Elise

Over the days that follow, I discover the extent of what Niamh's kept from me. Putting it together with what she still keeps to herself, I edge closer to the truth. Whether Andrew will ever admit to killing Hollie is another matter, but the weight of evidence against him, his proven violent behaviour and aggression, his treatment of Dylan, his possible involvement in both Kathryn and Stephanie's deaths, and not least his determination to keep Hollie's relationship to him a secret, all paint a clear picture.

Andrew's arrest offers me a chance to reset my life. When Forensics finish in our house, Niamh and I go back to sort through what we're taking with us, putting the rest in storage for Andrew until he's released. Pitched from limbo into a process of rapid adjustment, I gradually come to terms with a failed marriage and a husband who's a criminal.

But though there is evil in this world, there is also good. In an uncertain life, Chris Nelson is an unlikely guardian angel, offering us his farm cottage for as long as we want it and giving Niamh a place to stay while I have my surgery. It's a breathing space, a gesture of kindness that I accept gratefully. In our own time, we'll work out how to move on.

When Andrew is charged for his part in Phil Mason's porn business, he's jailed. But as far as Hollie's death is concerned, the evidence is circumstantial and the investigation into her murder remains unsolved. When my divorce comes through, I'll be leaving Andrew in the past, and by the time he gets out of prison, Niamh will be an adult and able to make her own decision as to whether she wants him in her life. But his part in mine is over.

So that's what it's about now. Leaving the past behind; moving forward. We're all human, with short lives and instincts we have limited control over, and in an ever-changing world, all any of us can do is keep moving forward.

Niamh

No ending is ever perfect. But just occasionally, there is closure.

For a while I thought my mother was having an affair. It was those mysterious phone calls, the shadows under her eyes, her secrecy. But it was the cancer – and everyone in my family has a secret, just as everyone makes mistakes.

'I'll fucking kill him, Niamh,' Hollie had sobbed the night she showed me the letter my father had written to her mother. 'I hate him. He killed Dylan . . .' Her voice grew more high-pitched with every word, until she fled, distraught, into the darkness. Running from pain there was no escape from, towards a future that, like Dylan, she didn't want.

Everyone noticed Hollie was at breaking point, but only I was the holder of her secret, the one who had the power to ruin lives.

'There's no point, Hollie,' I'd tried to convince her. 'You don't know what he's like. He'll hurt you. He hurts everyone. Don't tell him. Believe me, you don't want him in your life.'

★

She persuaded me, against my will, to go with her that day, climbing over the fence into the gardens of Park House. 'Can't we go somewhere else?' I asked.

But she ignored me. 'Come on! I want to show you something!' She started marching towards a gap in the hedge. Reluctantly, I followed her through into a rectangular area away from the house, surrounded by tall hedges and carpeted in fallen leaves. Bending down to pick something up, Hollie grabbed my arm. 'Listen.'

She threw something into the middle of the leaves. After a couple of seconds, there was a loud splash as it hit water. 'The pool.'

I shrank back against the hedge. With all the leaves, it was impossible to tell where the ground ended and the water started.

Around us, the wind was picking up, the sky a shade of yellow under clouds that had blotted out the last of the sun. 'I want him to suffer.' Her voice was murderous. Then, stretching out her arms, she spun around in circles. 'I want everyone to know what he's done. My dad, first . . . Then your mum.'

'No.' My cry was drowned by the sound of the wind, as I felt anger rip through me. I'd kept everything to myself for so long, protecting my mother from what really happened. Growing up, I'd had to watch her suffer so many times at the hands of my father. And now Hollie had the power to make everything a million times worse. 'It'll destroy her.'

'What about me?' Her face was pale under a sliver of the new moon.

'You can't change the past, Hollie. It's happened. You have to move on,' I begged her.

But her eyes were wild, desperate, as she stared at me. 'He's evil, Niamh . . . Look what he did to Dylan. We can't let him get away with it. He has to pay.'

As she said that, I knew she was right. My father deserved to atone for his sins, for the cruelty inflicted on all of us. But an image of my mother's face came to me. She'd suffered too much already. 'You can't hurt my mother,' I said softly.

'God, Niamh . . . this isn't about your mother.' Throwing her arms up in the air in an exaggerated show of frustration, Hollie turned her back on me and started walking away.

I felt rage explode in me then, that Hollie didn't care about my mother or about me; that she had the power to destroy what remained of my family. 'You don't understand,' I screamed, running at her, knocking her off her feet.

As she lurched sideways and fell, I heard her hit something. When she sat up, she rubbed her head. When she looked at her fingers, they were covered in blood. 'Shit, Niamh.' But her voice was subdued now. 'We'd better go back.'

We'd reached the hedge by the pool when her steps became uneven. Suddenly, she lurched closer to the edge, then started to lose her balance, reaching out for something to grasp on to. I heard the wind gusting through the trees, saw the wildness in her eyes as they met mine. I wanted to reach out and grab her hands, but something stopped me.

It happened in a split second. She didn't cry out as her head cracked against the side of the pool. Then her body hit the water beneath the leaves. In the dim light, I stood there as she floated for a moment, motionless. Around me, the wind was picking up force. Glancing up, I saw the clouds racing across the sky. When I looked back down towards the pool, the leaves had closed over the surface. Hollie had gone.

Acknowledgements

It's hard to believe that this is my sixth psychological thriller and my second to be published by the dedicated team at Avon. I've worked with two brilliant editors this time, Tilda McDonald and Phoebe Morgan – and I'm so grateful to both of you, as I am to Laura McCallen and Helena Newton for expertly scrutinising every last word of this manuscript! Huge thanks also go to Ellie Pilcher, Molly Walker-Sharp and to all of the Avon team for your hard work getting my books out there.

None of this would happen without my superstar agent, Juliet Mushens. And also Liza DeBlock. A heartfelt thank you for everything you do.

And the biggest thank you to you, my readers, for buying my books, sharing them with other people, blogging and writing reviews, because every single one makes a difference. I'm grateful to each and every one of you.

This isn't the first time I've written about abusive relationships and coercive control, and I hope I have done them justice. The consequences can be far-reaching and while the scars may be invisible, the damage is very real. If in any way this book helps highlight this, it can only be good.

Last, but by no means least, I want to say thank you to my wonderful family and my friends. To my sisters – Sarah, Anna and Freddie – to whom this book is dedicated. Thank you for being my first readers and supporters, and so much more – I know how lucky I am to have you. To Dad. And to Georgie and Tom: you ceaselessly inspire me. Thank you for being the centre of my universe.

Don't miss the #1 bestselling thriller

'A terrific new talent' PETER JAMES

TWO WEEKS UNTIL THE WEDDING.

THEN THE GROOM DISAPPEARS...

THE VOW

DEBBIE HOWELLS

'A sinister, twisty tale you won't want to put down'
Sam Carrington, author of
The Open House